Choice
of
Weapon

A Garrett Storm Novel

C. Marten-Zerf

Anglo American Press

LONDON, UNITED KINGDOM

Anglo American Press
London
England
United Kingdom

Book Layout © 2017 BookDesignTemplates.com

Choice of Weapon/ C. Marten-Zerf/Craig Zerf. -- 1st ed.
ISBN 978-0-0000000-0-0

Once again –

For my wife, Polly and my

son, Axel

Your light chases the

shadows from my soul.

Romans 13:4 - *For he is the minister of God to thee for good. But if thou do that which is evil, be afraid; for he beareth not the sword in vain: for he is the minister of God, a revenger to execute wrath upon him that doeth evil.*

This is a novel…that means I made it up, however…many of the people mentioned do actually exist. You all know who you are. Some of the scenes and places have been deliberately changed, this was done for two reasons, firstly to protect the identity of some involved and secondly as a narrative tool. If you would like to discuss the reality then please drop me an email at zuffs@sky.com

Garrett used the back of his glove to wipe the moisture from his face. It wasn't raining but the morning mist was thick in the air. Everything that it touched was jeweled with thousands of tiny droplets of water. Clumps of snow lay in piles as if a giant gardener had swept it up, ready to dispose of later. The smell of winter heather lay heavy in the cold air. Male musk with a top note of honeysuckle. Over it all the sharp iron tang of snow. The smell of the Highlands.

And Garrett breathed deep. Reveling in the crisp cleanness of the air. For years it had seemed that all he could smell was African dust, and cordite. Fear and flame. The rank odor of blood overlaid with the pungency of diesel fumes. The unmistakable perfume of war. But that was then.

The far away sound of the red grouse punctured the morning silence. A distinctive guttural bark ending in a warning trill. *Go-back-go-back-go-back.*

It was the end of November and the grouse-shooting season had been over for a few days now. Come April the birds would breed and their numbers would grow. And then come August, the glorious twelfth, the Laird would have his guests over and the cycle would start again. Rows of men in tweed, guns in hand. Ritual slaughter followed by Sloe gin and breakfast. The dead would be piled high, bright eyes turning dull. Feathers of burnished gold becoming leaves of unpolished copper. The polite pop of gentlemen's shotguns as opposed to the insane hammering of a 7.62mm machine gun. The trill of the grouse instead of the screams of agony and mortal terror.

As the estate gamekeeper, Garrett had been up since five twenty five that morning. A full two hours before sunrise. He traveled on foot, having nothing to do with the quad bikes that other gamekeepers in the area used. Sometimes he stayed out all night. Watching over the estate. Other estates in the area had been suffering from a massive increase in poaching that had arisen in the past couple of years. With red deer now fetching over fifteen Pounds sterling per pound weight, an average male could sell for as much as three thousand Pounds. Alladale estate next to his, had suffered the loss of over fifty deer so far this year. One hundred and fifty thousand Pounds Sterling. A staggering amount of money.

Garrett had lost one. He had caught the poachers. Two Eastern Europeans armed with single shot, 20-gauge H & R shotguns loaded with deer slugs. He had given them a stern warning. This had included confiscating their weapons, breaking both of their trigger fingers and spray-painting their faces with purple Etro-

Mark livestock branding paint – guaranteed not to wash off for six months. Word had spread. Garrett's deer were safe. Had it been another time, another place, the ground would have been stained with the scarlet of retribution. But that was no longer Garrett's way.

The gamekeeper walked down to the Loch's edge and looked into the clear water, catching his rough-shaven reflection as he did so and wondering, not for the first time of late, whether he was starting to get old. He stood at a little over six foot two and weighed in at two hundred and twenty pounds. No fat. His dark hair was devoid of gray and it tumbled in waves to his shoulders. This was not through any form of fashion consciousness or style. It was merely because he hadn't had a haircut for a while. His hands, large with long fine fingers, like a surgeon or musician, were thickly calloused from manual labor and his muscles strained the seams of his thin cotton shirt that he wore despite the low temperature.

It was immediately apparent when one looked at him that this was not a physique born in the sterile environment of the gymnasium or health club. It was a body forged through hard work and tempered by the outdoors. Muscles long and corded like plaited sisal, the skin of his face brown and windswept by countless sunrises and sunsets. Laughter lines etched deep into surprisingly smooth skin. And although his smile was ready and open, when you looked into his deep set dark green eyes you could plainly see a well of violence that stood ready to be drawn to the surface. He had learned, over time, to hood his eyes. To hide the violence deep within him. But sometimes, if he let his mind stray, it would crackle to the surface like sheet lightning.

He decided to patrol the East border of the estate. Check the fences. See if there was any sign of poachers. He snapped his shotgun shut, a 12 bore sidelock side-by-side, hand made by Boss and Company in 1930. One of a pair.

He skirted the loch at a run. Stride long and loping. A soldier's run that came without effort. Light footed. Mile-eating. He could run like that all day. Indeed he remembered many days that he had. Days when he and his men had ran in hot pursuit of an enemy that seemed to appear and disappear at will. Carrying only water and ammunition, nerves strung as tight as piano wire. Running towards death, towards victory. And sometimes defeat. But now he ran mainly for the simple joy of running, stopping every now and then over the next two hours to see that the fence was intact, or check for tracks, both animal and human.

As he crested a small brae his mobile phone rang. The strains of Debussy's Syrinx flowed from it, the haunting notes of the flute rising into the frigid air. It was unusual to get any signal in an area as remote as he was but the height of the hill must have brought him on line.

He stared at the unfamiliar number on the screen before flicking it open and answered.

'Talk to me.' White noise hissed in his ear. 'Hello, is anyone there?'

A female voice asked. 'Is that you?'

Garrett paused before he answered. 'Manon?'

The hiss of static.

'Garrett. I need you. Please, help me.'

'Where are you?'

'South Africa. Outside Johannesburg. I'm running an orphanage called "The Sunlight Childrens' Home."'

'I'm coming for you. I'll be there tomorrow.'

And behind him a deer broke cover, its hooves drumming on the earth. Like distant machine gun fire. And for a tiny moment the air smelt of dust, and something else. Something feral.

It took Garrett a little over forty-five minutes to run back to his croft. Legs pumping. Shotgun held at high port. He pulled his bed away from the wall and lifted one of the flagstones to expose a metal strongbox. He picked it up and opened the combination lock. Throwing back the lid to reveal shrink-wrapped bricks of USA Dollars. Hundred Dollar bills. Wrapped in blocks of one hundred. Ten thousand Dollars per brick. He grabbed four bricks. Shut the lid. Spun the lock. Replaced the box, the stone, the bed. He packed a small carry case. Two shirts, one pair of pants, socks, underwear, iPod. He wrote a quick note to the laird. Two lines. Fixed it to the front door with his hunting knife. Then he ran to Old Man Fergal's lodge. The old man lived on a grace and favor cottage on the laird's land.

Had done since time began. He was closer than the main house and he had a car. Garrett knew that he could rely on the old man to give him a lift to the village. From there he would get a taxi to the airport.

He arrived at Aberdeen airport at four forty that afternoon. The only flights still available to Johannesburg at such short notice were first class with South African airways. Garrett paid and went through to the first-class lounge. The price of the ticket didn't bother him. He wouldn't have been comfortable in a coach seat at any rate and money was merely a thing to exchange for commodities or services. He had long since learnt that cash had little to do with wealth. He used the facilities to have a long hot shower and, after he had dressed, he went back to the lounge and grabbed himself a complimentary platter of sandwiches and a bowl of cashew nuts. While he ate, he used one of the computers to look up the address for the Sunlight Children's Home. He did not avail himself of the free bar facilities. He hadn't had any alcohol for almost five years and he wasn't going to start now. Not just before he was strapped into a seat, in a steel box with four hundred strangers for over nine hours. He did, however, sit in the smoking room for a while where he puffed his way through a couple of free cigars. He didn't talk to anyone and, as is often the way in first class travel, no one attempted to strike up a conversation with him. False bonhomie and newfound companionship are traits usually limited to the close confines of cattle class. First class passengers pay for anonymity and privacy, something that Garrett was very comfortable with. He experienced the usual thrill of excitement as the massive liner powered free of the runway, its four Pratt & Whitney engines producing over a quarter of a million pounds of thrust in order to enable the nine hundred thousand pounds of steel to soar free of earths gravitational constraints.

He accepted a glass of fresh orange juice from the hostess and then took his iPod out of his top pocket, plugged the earphones into his ears and lay back to the sounds of Joachim Raff's Symphony No. 3. At the beginning of the second movement the hostess interrupted to offer him dinner. Garrett asked for one of everything. Three starters; venison ravioli in a red wine sauce, Parma ham with fresh figs and *foie gras* with an onion compote. Two fish courses consisting of poached salmon with stir fried vegetables and seared tuna with a green salad. He eschewed the vegetarian main course option and plumped for the grilled beef tenderloin with shrimp and the rack of lamb. Both came with generous helpings of potatoes and vegetables. Instead of pudding he went with the cheese board and finally coffee.

After brushing his teeth, he settled back into his bed, plugged his iPod back in, turned off his lights, relaxed and let his mind drift.

It had been over five years since had left Africa. Five years since he had been a soldier for other people's wars. He had sworn never to return. For it was there that the beast had first been unleashed. It was there that he had first smelt its fetid breath. Hot and damp on his cheek. Reveled in its power. Until, as it always does, the beast had overcome him. He and it became one. Eventually he had become known as such and the local tribes had called him *Popobawa* or The Beast. He had become the ultimate warrior. Unbeatable, implacable. Forged in the fires of mortal combat. Annealed in the heat of battle.

And later, as he realized what he had done, the unbelievable savagery and death he had dealt out, he came face to face with what he had become. And he could not live with it. So, he had fled. He had left the continent of Africa and come to Scotland. A country of savage beauty without a savage soul. People who were tough without being hard. He had fled from the horror. From the death. The destruction.

Mainly he had fled from the beast.

But you cannot escape from yourself.

So, over time, he had learnt to control it. To cage it. But still, in the dead of night, if he turned around really quickly. He would catch a glimpse of it. Huge. And dark. All-powerful.

Now she had called.

So he was traveling back to Africa. And the beast was coming with him.

He felt its breath on his cheek again. Hot and wet. Like blood.

***

It was five twenty-eight ante-meridiem and Sister Manon Dubois sat silently in her room. Although she had drawn the drapes the African sun treated them with scorn, blazing through and filling the room as if the thin cotton was not even there. Thus, she woke every morning with the sun. Her body clock a visceral thing, connected to the land like a peasant.

She was on edge. Worried. Even though she was sure that she had done the right thing. She had exhausted every other avenue. There was no other way to turn. She had prayed for guidance and was sure that she had done the correct thing when she had phoned Garrett and asked for his help. She, more than anyone, knew what his acceptance was going to cost him. But she needed him. The children needed him. For did not the Psalms say, 'The right hand of the Lord is exalted, and with it shall he give joy and salvation, and with his left hand He shall give damnation and eternal fire to the devil and his angels.'

So, she had called him. And he was coming. The left hand of the Lord.

But now was the time for more mundane things. Getting the children up and making sure that they made their beds and washed. Preparing breakfast. Getting them to the local school. Sister Manon dressed in her usual attire; severe khaki pants, a loose cotton shirt that she buttoned to the neck and a pair of ankle-high leather boots. And hanging outside the shirt, a silver crucifix. Her choice of clothing was a deliberate but unsuccessful attempt to de-feminize her body. The fullness of her breasts and hips made mockery of her attempts.

She did not wear a habit. In fact, very few sisters of the Benedictine order had worn the habit since the nineteen sixties. Although, when she had first met Garrett, she had been wearing one. She had been working in a Benedictine mission in Sierra Leone during the Revolutionary United Fronts last gasp. The ruling government had just begun running the slogan, 'The future is in your hands,' and, as a result, the RUF soldiers had taken to catching government sympathizers, particularly children, and cutting off their hands. The scale of the atrocities was horrendous and at times the small clinic in the mission had upwards of ten youths, some as young as seven, stoically waiting for treatment. Both hands brutally hacked off with machetes.

Garrett had been a captain in President Kabbah's army with a squad of twelve men under him. They were an elite force that called themselves 'The Warriors' and, initially, the president used them as a rapid response unit, however, as the war had continued, they had become more of a roving response unit. They were transported in a Jeep and a Land Rover series three 109. The troops were issued with the standard FNLA

Belgian assault rifles and there was a two-man machine gun team that sported the FN Mag. They worked autonomously of the chain of command. Re-supplying off enemy kills and living off the land and the people. He had arrived late that night with his detachment. They had heard the rumors of the RUF's retribution and had come to ascertain the truth. They also brought with them a small amount of medical supplies. Bandages and antibiotics. A pitiful amount compared to the physical abuse and damage that had taken place. He had taken the cache of supplies through to the clinic where he had met sister Manon. But when he had seen the extent of the savagery that had been inflicted, he gathered all his troops together and made them hand in all of their personal supplies of medicine, bandages, antibiotics and, most importantly, morphine.

And at that same time, knowing full well the futility of it, Garrett had fallen in love. From the moment that he had seen her, her heart shaped face drawn by exhaustion, framed by the black and white of her wimple and veil. Her eyes so deep blue as to be almost black. Her lips full, pale pink. An unblemished jewel in a cesspit of violence and corruption. And he knew, even then, that he was falling in love with a concept, a vision and a respite from the horror. As opposed to a flesh and blood woman.

He silently offered the medicines and she smiled. He laid them on the floor next to where she was seated and then looked around the room. Perhaps ten or so children lay on rush mats on the floor. Their foreshortened arms wrapped in bandages. Their faces gray with pain, as there were no painkillers. But no one cried or complained. And when his gaze swept over them, those with enough strength nodded a greeting. One young child, a girl of perhaps eight, even managed to smile. Teeth as white as innocence. And more than anything that he had ever wanted in his life, Garrett wanted to find the men that had done this. He wanted to track them down and exact retribution upon them. When he looked back at the nun she actually flinched from his expression and he was immediately contrite.

'I am sorry to barge in like this, Sister. These supplies are for you. I will send some of my men for more, whatever they can find they will bring back for you. Meanwhile, I must find the people that did this and prevent it from happening again.'

She nodded, hesitantly. 'I know how you feel. I used to cry. Every day I used to cry. But I no longer have any tears left. Now I pray instead.'

'Does prayer work, sister?'

She nodded. 'You are here.'

She took his hand and stared deeply into his eyes. And to him that small contact felt as though he had been branded by Aphrodite. In a world of harshness and misery her unblemished soul stood out like a beacon of light. A light to which Garrett felt irresistibly drawn.

'My name is Garrett.'

'Manon. Sister Manon Dubois.'

They sat together for a while. Not speaking, their hands clasped firmly together like shipwreck victims holding onto a lifeline.

Abruptly Garrett stood up. 'I swear to you, sister. I will find these men that did this to the children and I will punish them.'

She watched him walk away, his green eyes ablaze with purpose, beckoning to his troops as he did so. And she slowly let her breath out and wondered at the strength of her feeling. Her heart was racing, her legs felt weak and when she closed her eyes, she could still see him looking at her with his gaze of green fire.

Garrett left corporal Ron Taylor, an older ex-Rhodesian fireforce soldier, in charge of guarding the mission with four riflemen. He took with him two South African ex-parabats, huge solid men, both with well-balanced personalities in that they had an equally large chip on each shoulder. As well as them there was his sergeant, a solid noncom and a good friend who went by the name of 'The Dentist' due to the horrendous state of his teeth, courtesy of a lifetime of neglect and self-professed dental-cowardice. Three more riflemen made up the rest of the team.

It took Garrett just over two weeks to track down the perpetrators and exact what he considered to be appropriate retribution. And when Garrett and his men arrived back at the mission their infamy had spread before them. People averted their eyes when the warriors walked past and fear hung around them like a miasma. Garrett was puzzled. Where he had expected thanks, he received apprehension. Instead of releasing the innocents from the dread of mutilation his actions had replaced it with something else entirely. He had replaced fear with dread. For now, instead of mere revolutionaries the villagers had *Popobawa*. The devil himself walked amongst them. The stealer of souls. The eater of dreams.

Only Manon seemed to understand why he had done it. Although she did not condone what he had done. He had spent an evening trying to justify himself to her. He had stopped the atrocities, he told her. But at what price, she had countered. It was worth it at any price, he said. Then she had asked him the one question that he had been avoiding. The one question that he refused to ask himself. She had asked him if he had enjoyed it.

And because he would not lie to her he told her the truth. When he answered she recoiled as if he had struck her.

He left the next morning. He took the Jeep to Freetown and resigned his commission. He had not worked out his contract so he received no bonus pay. Simply a one-way ticket to a country of his choice. He chose to return to Scotland, having lived there once before. He flew to Heathrow via Jan Smuts airport in Johannesburg, South Africa.

***

In the five years since Garrett had last been there, the airport had changed completely. Not only had it experienced a name change from Jan Smuts to Oliver Tambo it had also tripled in size. As he only had carryon luggage he was quickly through customs and he followed the signs to the Hertz counter. He waited in a short queue and then chose a Jeep Cherokee, figuring that it had enough grunt and could perform off road if it had to. Also, it was fitted with a satnav which he would need as it had been a very long time since he had last been in Johannesburg or Joburg, as the locals called it. There was a slight problem when it transpired that he didn't have a credit card and wanted to do the deal in cash. However, this minor issue went away after he pushed an extra handful of one hundred Rand notes across the counter. The extra Rands disappeared as if by magic to be replaced with a key and a smile. He got lost once on the way to the car pick up area because he had stopped at an MTM kiosk to rent a cell phone. After retracing his steps, he got back on track and found the Jeep soon after. He bleeped it open, threw his bag onto the back seat and slid in. The interior smelt overpoweringly of bubblegum and hot leather, so the first thing he did was turn on the power and roll the windows down. Secondly, he switched on the satnav and typed in the address that he had looked up at Heathrow, waited for the system to initialize and pulled out into the traffic.

As he drove from the airport, through Johannesburg he was amazed at how the city had fallen into ruin. Particularly Hillbrow, an inner-city area that was the place to be seen back in the late seventies. There used to be nightclubs, restaurants and five-star hotels. He cruised past the former five-star Chelsea Hotel. There were old mattresses on the pavement outside and long streaks of filth ran down each window opening.

Garrett wondered how the same government that could create something as amazing as the Oliver Tambo airport with its world-class subway system could also allow a ghetto like this to exist. And then he thought of cities like Detroit and New York and the devastation that still remained after hurricane Katrina and he wondered no more. He drove through the leafy suburbs of Houghton and marveled at the massive mansions there. He remembered 'The Dentist', his sergeant in Sierra Leone, had once told him that Joburg was the most treed city in the world and, driving through it, he could believe it. When you looked down from the highway across the burbs the trees were so thick as to mask the houses amongst them. Eventually the satnav guided him to his destination. The Sunlight Childrens' Home in the Honeydew area.

It wasn't at all what he expected. The home was in the middle of an industrial area and was converted from an old factory, as was evident by the square aluminum windows and sheet metal roofing. He pulled into one of the designated parking bays and climbed out, locking the Jeep behind him.

There was an armed guard lounging in a plastic chair outside the double door entrance to what was probably the lobby or reception area. He wore a faded green uniform and carried a Norinco Hawk, a badly made Chinese copy of the Remington 870 12-gauge pump action shotgun. The bluing was already worn and the barrel had a light patina of rust. Garrett would have bet all that he owned that the weapon had never been cleaned. But the guard himself was a pleasure. He jumped out of his seat and snapped to attention, giving Garrett a whippy, over the top salute accompanied with a wide grin. 'Welcome to the Sunlight Childrens' Home, sir. How may I help you?'

Garrett smiled back but abstained from saluting. 'Hello. I've come to see sister Manon.'

'Straight through both doors and up the stairs to your left, sir.'

Garrett nodded his thanks and followed the guard's instructions. The small entrance hall was furnished with a couple of cheap office chairs, one each side of a low fake-wood table. There was a small pile of old magazines on the table as well as a stack of brochures with the home's logo on them. The floor was bare polished concrete. He went through the area and up the stairs, pausing at the top to glance out of a window that looked down on what used to be the factory's main production space. It had been divided into a central corridor and two large dormitories. Because the factory roof was so high the dormitory walls served only as partitions and were not floor to ceiling structures. There was a fully covered area at the end of the corridor that he took to be the bathrooms. He glanced up at the un-insulated roof. It was obvious that the place would be freezing in winter and an oven in summer. But better an un-insulated roof than none at all, mused Garrett as he turned and entered the passage that led off the landing. He was faced with a long corridor with seven or so doors running down the one side and one at the end. Not knowing what else to do he decided to simply call.

'Manon!'

The door at the end of the corridor opened. She walked towards him, hesitantly at first and then, over the last few meters, at a sprint. She threw her arms around his neck and pulled herself hard up against him. Garrett had forgotten how tiny she was, at five foot two she was fully a foot shorter than him and she must have weighed in at much less than half his two hundred and twenty pounds. She smelled of soap and flowers and something else. And he breathed in as deeply as he dared, savoring her fragrance. Reveling in the feel of her.

'You came.' She whispered up at him.

He nodded. 'I am here for you.'

The marble table in the corner of the room served as a bar. Bottles of Armand de Brignac Champagne stood in silver ice buckets. The golden contents of the Glenmorangie Signet single malt refracted bullion bars of light across the room and the deep cut crystal glasses painted orgiastic rainbows of color onto the pale cream tabletop. There were no waiters. No wine stewards and no hostesses. Even the armed guards were stationed outside the room. The doors were locked.

A Cambridge audio system discreetly filled any potential uncomfortable pauses with Classical music and the air slowly took on a blue-gray tinge from the exhaled cigar smoke. There were seven males, all middle to later middle age. All seemingly cast from the same mold with small differences. Like cabbage patch dolls. Average height, running to fat, their pear-shaped bodies concealed well behind hand tailored English suits. A thickset Nigerian, wearing a traditional Agbada, stood out from the rest. The round pink faces contrasting with his burnished defined features, his arrogant walk. His power. All showed signs of manicures and facials.

As well as the Nigerian, another African man stood out in his difference. Tall and graceful. Dressed in a maroon velvet jacket. Obviously, the host. From their accents it was easy to tell that the Nigerian was the only foreigner. It was also fairly obvious that he was here as an observing guest. As opposed to a client. The rest spoke with the flat vowels and abrupt sentences of native South Africans. The host had purposely kept foreigners from the meetings. They were an unknown ingredient. He could exert little pressure on those who lived and traded outside of his borders. And he was a man who thrived on exerting pressure. The host had met all of them at least three times before and, although he knew every small detail of their lives from sexual proclivities to approximate bank balances, he referred to them by number only. Mr. Twelve, Thirteen, Fourteen, Fifteen, Sixteen, Seventeen and Eighteen. The pretense that they were dealing under the protection of anonymity made them feel more at ease. Like revelers at a masked ball. Clandestine, aloof. Above persecution. He allowed them their small fantasy.

The atmosphere was tense. But not in a negative way. Perhaps apprehensive would describe it better. The host clapped his hands and showed the guests to a row of leather wingbacks that faced the one wood paneled wall, standing back perhaps ten feet from the paneling. At the touch of a remote the music stopped, lights dimmed and a large screen descended silently from the ceiling. The room immediately turned into a private cinema. A frisson of excitement rippled through the guests. Race horses in the stalls. Sprinters at the blocks. Bulldogs and prime rib.

'Gentlemen,' greeted the host. 'The auction will take place as before. We have a total of thirteen *objects d'art* to bid on.' There was a titter of amusement at this small witticism. 'As always, we will show a minute long preview after which the bidding will start. Please remember, gentlemen, that you are bidding on the worldwide rights. All bids are final and binding and will be paid via bank transfer directly after the end of tonight's trading.' A finger pressed a remote-control button and the DVD projector whirred into life.

Bidding started at forty thousand dollars and ratcheted up in *tranches* of ten thousand until it finally stalled at eighty thousand. The next eleven bids reached similar prices, one as high as one hundred and ten, one as low as seventy. A total of a little over one million one hundred and twenty thousand dollars.

Before he started the thirteenth viewing the host busied himself refilling drinks and cutting fresh cigars. Once again lights were lowered. Silk clad rumps were sat upon leather. The host rubbed his hands together. 'Gentlemen. I have saved this one until last. I am sure that you will all agree, the wait will have been worth it. This, my friends, is truly a masterpiece,'

Lights. Sound….

The film lasted twenty-seven minutes and was shown in its entirety. And at the end the room stank of sweat and lust and something else. The stench of Gomorrah.

Bidding started at five hundred thousand and the competition lasted perhaps forty seconds before number Fourteen closed the bids, topping out at nine hundred and twenty thousand. The bidders clapped politely. Congratulations were given. Toasts were made.

And somewhere, not that far away, the Beast attacked the bars of its cage and howled to get out.

***

The host showed the last of his clients to the door, bar the Nigerian whom he asked to stay. A hand on his shoulder. He poured them each a generous measure of single malt, handed one over. A toast. Sip. Neither spoke for a while as they savored the smoke and peat and heather of the superb Scottish nectar.

The Nigerian, Valentine Tsogo, lived in Hillbrow. He owned the top three floors of a thirty-story apartment block; seven bedrooms, two kitchens, a servant's wing and a home cinema were merely some of the more notable aspects of the fantastically over-the-top residence. He also owned the rest of the block. The original service elevator had been converted into Valentine's private car and took him directly from the underground parking to his double-vaulted entrance hall.

Five years ago, Valentine had moved from Lagos with his entire extended family of around thirty people. He had arrived in the country with lots of capital in the form of gold and diamonds but he had very little in the way of local connections. The move had not been through choice but rather through his abortive attempt to oust one of the major crime families in Nigeria. His failure had cost him three family members and more than four million dollars in lost cash. It had also cost him the right to continue living in the country of his birth.

But since Valentine had arrived, he and his family had done very well. Within months they had set up an office specializing in emailing out millions of different versions of the Nigerian 419 scam letter. This gist of which went;

Dear Respected One,
GREETINGS,
Permit me to inform you of my desire of going into
business relationship with you. I got your contact
from the International web site directory. I prayed
over it and selected your name among other names
due to it's esteeming nature and the recommendations
given to me as a reputable and trust worthy person I
can do business with and by the recommendations I

must not hesitate to confide in you for this simple and sincere business.

I am Wumi Abdul; the only Daughter of late Mr and Mrs George Abdul. My father was a very wealthy cocoa merchant in Abidjan, the economic capital of Ivory Coast before he was poisoned to death by his business associates on one of their outing to discus on a business deal. When my mother died on the 21st October 1984, my father took me and my younger brother HASSAN special because we are motherless. Before the death of my father on 30th June 2002 in a private hospital here in Abidjan. He secretly called me on his bedside and told me that he has a sum of $12.500.000 (Twelve Million, five hundred thousand dollars) left in a suspense account in a local Bank here in Abidjan, that he used my name as his first Daughter for the next of kin in deposit of the fund.

He also explained to me that it was because of this wealth and some huge amount of money his business associates supposed to balance his from the deal they had that he was poisoned by his business associates, that I should seek for a God fearing foreign partner in a country of my choice where I will transfer this money and use it for investment purpose, (such as real estate management). Unfortunately we have come upon a dire problem. Due to the corruption currently being experienced in our country we need a small sum of money to bribe the bank official to release the money. This sum would be $20 000 which *must be transferred via Western Union to me. As well as this we would need the following.*

1) To provide a Bank account where the $12 500 000 would be transferred to.

2) To serve as the guardian of this since I am a girl of 17 years.

Moreover Sir, we are willing to offer you 15% of the sum as compensation for effort input after the successful transfer of this fund to your designate account overseas. please feel free to contact ,me via this email address xxxxxxxxxx@yahoo.com

Anticipating to hear from you soon.
Thanks and God Bless.
Miss Wumi Abdul

There were a few variations on the theme but the basic script was the same. The bad grammar and punctuation were deliberate; after all, Valentine had graduated with a second-class degree in philosophy from Oxford and spoke English better than most English people. But the clunky wording gave the recipient a feeling of superiority. And that, in turn, led the mark to believe that they were the sophisticated party in the transaction.

The actual mechanics of the scheme were very basic. Most people are not aware of the fact that for a mere five hundred US Dollars one can purchase a list of fifty million valid email addresses from an IT company based in Calcutta, India. Then one blasted off the emails via a Chinese based bullet-proof hosting center that stopped your ISP from knowing that you were sending out thousands of emails every few seconds.

It never ceased to amaze him how gullible people were. And how greedy. It was impossible to con a truly honest person but it seemed that there were enough dodgy characters out there to make the 419 scam a great business. Sometimes they hit two or three a month. People would literally send them thousands of dollars. But usually, one had to play the long con. Emails back and forth, personal details, even family photos. Lately, however, it was getting harder. It seemed that everyone in the world who had access to a computer had received a letter from Valentine or someone similar. In fact, there were now large numbers of people out there who practiced 419 baiting. They would enter into communications with Valentine's people and then string them along for as long as possible, wasting precious time and, quite frankly, eventually leaving you feeling like a bit of an asshole.

So, Valentine had decided to branch out. He had decided to expand his business. And this was why he had approached the man who now stood before him. Valentine was not taken in by the man's veneer of suave sophistication. He had met men like this before. Dangerous men. Their desire to control governed their lives. Power was their drug of choice and they would exercise it whenever possible. And they would do so in an utterly ruthless way. Adi Amin, Robert Mugabe, BJ

Vorster. Africa bred these sorts of men in abundance. They were men to be feared. But not necessarily respected. Except, perhaps, in the way that a rabid dog commands respect.

'So, Valentine, how is our mutual partner doing?'

'As well as can be expected, mister Zangwa.'

'Please, my friend, call me, Texas.'

Valentine nodded in acknowledgment. 'Thank you, Texas. As I said, slowly, slowly. He's not comfortable with the situation yet. Not actually sure that he ever will be but he keeps prying eyes away from the location. He gets rid of the evidence. Does what we need him to do, so as long as your boys keep bringing the stock, we'll keep supplying the product.'

'And in return? Are you taking care of him?'

'Yes. Our side of the transaction is very simple. Money.'

'Perhaps we could save some. Get him to carry out his side of the deal by simply…' Texas held his hand out in front of his face and formed a fist.

Valentine shook his head. 'If we threatened this man it could escalate. He has many guns working under him. Professionals. The last thing that we want is a war.'

'I am not afraid of war.'

'Of course not, Texas. I merely advise prudence. In the scheme of things, the payments are less costly than the alternatives.'

Texas nodded agreement and then started to walk towards the door. The meeting was obviously over. They shook hands and one of the guards showed the Nigerian out.

Texas sipped at the whisky. It had been yet another exceptional evening. A gross of two million and forty thousand Dollars. Capital outlay; eight thousand Dollars' worth of alcohol and tobacco. A net profit of two million and thirty-two thousand dollars. A fair cut had to go to the Nigerian and their new partner but he would still be left with an extortionate amount of cash. He had discovered the true wealth of Africa. Over the last six months he had made almost four million Dollars. More than many multinational companies make in a year. He shook his head to himself. Personally, he couldn't understand these soft white men and their strange obsessions. But he was merely a businessman. Not a connoisseur of the goods that were being purveyed.

He walked out through the open double doors onto the balcony that overlooked his park like grounds. The hedges and trees were artfully planted and pruned so as to hide all evidence of the high walls and electric fencing. The late-night air was crisp and dry and smelt of Jacaranda and Jasmine. Far in the distance he heard the crackle of small arms fire. Nine millimeters. And then police sirens. The sound of Johannesburg at play. He smiled broadly to himself, God how he loved this country.

He sensed more than heard his chief bodyguard walk into the room behind him. Silent on rubber soled shoes. A buffalo of a man that gave the impression of being almost as wide as he was tall. His dark suit was tailor made, as befit his position in the hierarchy, but his shoes were off-the-shelf. His weapon, however, was state of the art and customized to his exact requirements. A Desert Eagle .50 action express with a seven-round magazine, a compensator and molded Pachmayr grips. Eleven inches of firearm that weighed in at over two kilograms fully loaded. In his meaty hands the gargantuan pistol looked normal sized.

The bodyguard cleared his throat before he spoke. '*Ubawo*, my father,' he greeted respectfully. 'It grows late. Soon it will be morning. I have set the guards and the house is secure apart from this room. You have an early start tomorrow and perhaps it is time to seek sleep.'

The man in the velvet jacket smiled again. 'Thank you, Dubula,' he handed his almost empty glass to the huge man. 'Put some more in this. Help yourself to some as well. And a cigar.'

Dubula returned and handed back a half full glass of whisky. He did not partake of any himself, as the host had known he would not. He never drank. And, as far as he could tell, he never slept either. Or, at least, he had never seen him sleep. 'So, my friend, we did very well tonight. In one night, we make more than all of our other enterprises do for a whole month. What do you think of that?'

Dubula said nothing. His eyes flicked constantly over his master's shoulder to the garden. Scanning. Protecting.

'I wonder,' continued Dubula's master. 'Is it time to specialize? To hone our operations down. The robberies, the hijacking, the commerce. These are all very labor-intensive enterprises. How many guns do we have working for us at the moment?'

'It varies. Sixty-six, maybe sixty-seven.'

'A lot of men. An army, some would say.' He laughed again, loudly; his mood expansive. Ebullient. And why shouldn't it be…he was two million dollars richer than he had been a mere twelve hours earlier. 'A good day. A good, good day. Be well, my friend.'

As he walked from the room, he could feel Dubula's eyes on him. Hooded. Dark. And fanatically loyal.

***

Less than one-mile away Vusi spread his thin jacket over his sister's sleeping form. He was thankful that it wasn't raining. Even when the weather was warm, rain made life very unpleasant.

He was worried about his little sister, Thandi. She had been coughing now for over three weeks. Not violent wracking coughs, simply persistent. Particularly when it rained. Vusi had found a sheet of thick cardboard that afternoon and he had lashed one side of it to the front of their shack with assorted pieces of string. If one pushed very carefully it would open and close. Like a real door. Thandi had clapped when he had finished and that had made him very proud. Because he was the man and the man was meant to do things like provide shelter. And collect food. For the last six months since their mother had died Vusi had provided for his sister. And protected her. They continued to stay in the cardboard and plywood lean-to in the Alexandra Township that they called home. An eight-foot square plot of bare earth squeezed between two other slightly more substantial shacks. A cardboard back wall, plywood roof and cardboard door. It kept out the scorching sun and some of the wind but very little of the rain. In winter, if they lit a small fire, it stayed above freezing.

Vusi did not know it but today was actually his birthday. Today Vusi was eleven years old. His sister, Thandi, had been born two years after him. She was still a child. But Vusi was a man.

He dipped a tin mug into the water bucket that they kept in the corner of the lean-to. This mug, the plastic bucket, two tin plates, two spoons, a small aluminum cooking pot, an old paint tin fire bucket and the clothes that they wore were all that the two siblings owned. Apart from Vusi's most prized possession; a six-inch long screwdriver, the tip of which had been sharpened to a needle-sharp point. Self-protection. He had not used it yet but knew that, when the time came, he would do so without hesitation.

Vusi put a block of wood into the fire tin, more for its meager light source than for its warmth. The dull orange glow gave a feeling of safety, however transient. He slept fitfully. Waking at every small sound, his yellow and silver screwdriver tight in his hand. Guarding. Protecting. Keeping his little sister safe.

CHAPTER THREE

Only a few moments after Garrett and Manon had greeted each other the children all came back from school. A tidal wave of noise and youthful energy entered the building, sweeping all before it. There were twenty-six of them. By chance equally divided into male and female. All between nine and twelve years old. The majority were black Africans but there was a smattering of White and Indian children as well. They were introduced to Garrett *en masse*, greeting him together, their combined voices stretching his name so it came out as 'Gaaretteh' instead of the more abrupt original.

It was close to lunchtime so three of the oldest girls got to preparing food in the small kitchen upstairs. The rest of the children, obviously working to some sort of roster, did general cleaning. Sweeping and polishing and tidying. Garrett was impressed. The place was as squared away as an army barracks. But with incongruous touches. A bowl of flowers. A brightly colored child's drawing. A teddy bear.

There was no dining area so each child queued solemnly for their food and then sat on the edge of their bed. When all were seated sister Manon asked Garrett to say grace.

Without thinking he bowed his head and spoke. *'Benedic, Domine, nos et dona tua, quae de largitate tua sumus sumpturi,et concede, ut illis salubriter nutriti tibi debitum obsequium praestare valeamus,per Christum Dominum nostrum.'*

There was a pause while none of the children moved, unsure of whether the grace was over or not. Garrett scowled to himself in embarrassment and quickly carried on. 'For what we are about to receive may the Lord make us truly thankful. Amen.'

There was a chorus of Amen's and a rattling of cutlery as youthful hunger was assuaged as quickly as possible. The meal was a simple one. Stiff maize meal porridge served with a *sheshebo*, spicy onion and tomato gravy with small pieces of bacon chopped into it. Water to wash it down. Filling, nourishing. Cheap.

After the meal the children washed up and then sat cross-legged on their beds to do homework. Garrett and Manon went to her bedroom upstairs and, with the door open, she sat on her bed and he on the single wicker chair in the corner of the room. Garrett tapped two cigarettes out of his pack of Gauloise, lit both and handed one to Manon. She took it with a smile.

'How do you know that I still smoke?'

Garrett shrugged. 'You're French.'

'Belgian.'

'Same difference.'

She laughed. It was a private joke between them. Not funny, but personal.

Garrett pointed to a small tin ashtray on the windowsill. 'So, Manon, why am I here?'

She took a drag on the Gauloise before she answered. Her lips pink as they wrapped around the white, unfiltered cigarette. The color, virginal, intimate. And when she let the smoke trickle out of her open mouth Garrett had to look away. 'Children are going missing,' she said.

'Have you told the police?'

'Yes.'

'And?'

Another drag of hot smoke. Pout. Release.

'Orphans are so far down the list of priorities that they don't exist. They ran away. Decided that they didn't like it here anymore. Just left.'

'Could that be true?'

'Yes. Sometimes. But not often. Three have gone missing from here in the last two months. One, maybe two a year, acceptable. Not only that, there are four other Sunlight Children's homes. The same has happened to them. Almost twenty children in two months.'

'What about the Pope?'

Manon laughed. 'You mean the Cardinal.'

'Whatever. Chief holy dude. Have you spoken to him?'

'I am a nun, Garrett.'

'So?'

'When you were in the army, could a private have gotten permission to see a general to talk about some groundless suspicions?'

Garrett shook his head and lit another cigarette off the remains of the first. He didn't offer Manon a second. She never smoked two in a row.

'I'm not sure that I can help. I'm no detective. I'm a…was a soldier. Now I fix fences, carry things, look after game. Live.'

'I can help.'

'Sister Manon. Detective extraordinaire.'

'Be nice.'

'Sorry.'

'Anyway, I didn't mean me, personally. Do you remember Brain Davies?'

Garrett peered intently at the glowing tip of his cigarette. 'The Dentist, my sergeant in Sierra. Of course.'

'He lives here. In Johannesburg. He moved here after the war. About three years ago. Owns a big detective agency. Done very well for himself. I spoke to him and he told me to contact you.'

Garrett felt a twist of disappointment. The call had not been solely of Manon's doing. Would she have called at all if it hadn't been suggested? And what did it matter? She was a nun. Forbidden. Regardless of his irrepressible feelings for her.

'I would have called you anyway,' she continued. 'I truly believe that you are the only one who can help.'

Relief. A warm balm.

'So why did he say to call me?'

'Kindness, I think. He doesn't believe me. He grew up in an orphanage and said that he ran away all the time. Says I should spend my time helping the ones who stay. Forget the runaways.'

'He said that?'

'Sort of. A lot more swear words.'

Garrett laughed. 'He always had a foul mouth.'

'He said that I should call you. Said that he would help you look into it. But really, I think that he simply wanted someone else to tell me that I was wrong. Anyway, he never thought that you would actually come.'

'I need to see him.'

Manon pulled a slip of paper from her trouser pocket. 'Here. His office address. It's close. In Sandton City.'

Garrett stood up. 'As good a place to start.' He leant forward and kissed Manon on the cheek. 'Good to see you again, sister.'

Manon smiled. Garrett left the room, closing the door behind him and walking down the stairs. When he came out of the front door the guard was still there. Standing next to his chair, shotgun propped up against the wall. Garrett offered him a cigarette.

'*Siyabonga*, thank you.' He took the cigarette and placed it behind his ear for later. Garrett shook the packet at him and he removed another Gauloise and put it in between his lips. Garrett snapped open his Zippo and proffered a flame.

'*Wena amaZulu?*'

The guard smiled broadly. 'Yes, I am Zulu. How come you speak the language?'

Garrett shrugged. 'I don't. Not really. I worked once with a Zulu. Good soldier. Ex South African Defense Force. He taught me enough to get by.'

The guard drew mightily on his cigarette causing the tip to glow like a blast furnace. 'That is good. *Igama lami ngu* Petrus, *ngubani igama lakho?*'

Garrett held out his hand and the guard took it. They shook in the African way, reversing grip. 'Pleased to meet you, Petrus. My name is Garrett. Have you worked here long?'

'Yes, sir. Ever since *imbali encane* was here. I live in a room around the back.'

Garrett struggled with the translation. 'Little flower?'

Yes, sir. The small nun. Sister Manon. The people call her *imbali encane.*'

Garrett smiled. The name was perfect. 'So, tell me, Petrus, why do you keep your weapon in such a sorry state?'

Petrus literally took a step backward in shock. 'Sir, my weapon is in the best of condition.' He turned around, bent down and pulled a long blanket wrapped item out from under the chair. He stripped the blanket off to reveal a two-foot-long Zulu assegai. The blade of the weapon, fully one foot long and three inches wide at its widest point, shimmered in the sun due to the thin layer of protective oil. The edge's, razor sharp. The wooden handle was dark with the sweat from many thousands of hours of training. He flipped it in the air, catching it by the blade and offered it to Garrett, handle first. Garrett took it and swung it a few times experimentally to get its heft. And then he stabbed at an imaginary enemy, twirling and cutting. Blocking, moving, counter thrusting. The blade alive in his hands, whistling and fluting as it sliced through the air. He finished by jumping high in the air and slamming the broad blade down through his fantasy opponent's clavicle. Twisting the blade and then withdrawing. He handed the spear back to Petrus. 'Thank you. That is a man's weapon.'

The Zulu tilted his head in respect. 'I see you have fought with the blade before.'

Garrett nodded.

'But,' Petrus continued. 'A different blade. I think, perhaps, the machete.'

Garrett nodded again.

'So, you understand,' continued Petrus as he pointed at the sad Chinese shotgun. 'That is not my weapon. That is a rusting piece of shit.'

The men shook hands once more and Garrett climbed into his Jeep and programmed in the address that Manon had given him. As soon as the satnav found signal, he pulled off. He left the driver's side window open to provide cooling as opposed to using the aircon. He had nothing against air conditioners; they simply made him feel cut off from the outside, whereas now he could smell the dust of the Highveld. A crisp, flint like tang, carried on a hot breeze. The smell of Africa. He drove past what appeared to be some sort of up market golfing estate and then the satnav took him by twists and turns through Bryanston to Sandton City, a massive shopping mall situated in the suburb of Sandton. Garrett was sure that there was a much quicker way, but he let the satnav take control and allowed his mind to wander, keeping only a peripheral attention on his driving. He was excited to see Brian again. The last five years had been solitary. Not lonely, but alone. He had worked hard, listened to his music, talked as much as was necessary and kept his own company. He had walked next to the path; close enough to see it, following it but never on it. And the more that he was alone the quieter was the beast.

The satnav led him to a massive shopping mall that seemed to stretch for miles in every direction. A glass-topped tower that provided some frame of reference dominated the spreading pile. Garrett followed signs for parking and eventually found himself crawling up an endless spiral ramp while red digital arrows flashed Full at him and directed him onward and upward. Finally, a green arrow came into view and he grabbed the first empty space that he could. He memorized the color, row, number and floor and headed off to find the office tower that held Brian's establishment. Intrepid.

A fearless explorer braving the endless damp concrete caverns of the Sandton City car park.

He followed way-out signs, exit signs, neon signs depicting walking stick figures until, eventually, he came to a pair of enormous glass sliding doors that opened automatically in welcome as he approached.

And he was in a different world. Marbled floors with brass inlays, sumptuous carpets, stainless steel light fittings and acres of plate glass windows. The African heat held at bay by gigantic air-conditioning units that kept the temperature at a constant twenty degrees Celsius. The people all walked with a purpose, many of them with cell phones seemingly attached to their faces as they conversed simultaneously with their companions walking next to them and those separated by the ether.

Garrett felt drab in his tired old clothes. Washed out next to all of the noise and vibrancy. As if he were a ghost walking amongst the living. Or a time traveler. He stood still amongst the throng, simply watching, getting his bearings. He did not notice that, while everybody else was getting jostled and pushed by the crowds he was a rock in a pool of calm. People gave him a wide berth without even knowing that they were doing so. Bait fish around a barracuda. He decided to walk until he saw some sort of information signage and moved forward abruptly. The baitfish parted in front of him, driven aside by the palpable force of his presence.

As it happened, he needn't have worried. The mall was well signposted and he found his way to the office tower with no problem. He took the elevator up to the floor that Manon had given him and found Brian's offices at the end of the corridor. A discreet sign on the door read 'Davies Security Consultants'. He opened the door to be greeted by a small reception area dominated by a leather Chesterfield and a dark wooden desk behind which sat a blonde, over made up, receptionist. She was busy talking. She had a pair of those almost invisible headphones on that allows the wearer to talk to someone and keep their hands free. Like some sort of special forces operative. Or Madonna on stage. Garrett hated them. They lacked the essential honesty of a telephone handset. Also, you were never entirely sure if the person was talking to you or answering the phone and you could end up having a meaningless and embarrassing three-way conversation that led nowhere.

So, Garrett simply decided to act as if the receptionist didn't exist and walked down the corridor that ran off the reception area. He vaguely heard the receptionist squeak behind him. A high-pitched urgent sound like a hamster was being stood on.

'Davies. Where are you?' bellowed Garrett. 'Come on out you spineless Pommie bastard.'

A door on the left of the corridor burst open and a small man barreled out. Hands held low in front of him, slightly crouched, nostrils flared and eyes slightly slatted. A man who was used to becoming instantly combat alert. He stared at Garrett for fully two seconds, his face tight with anger before he relaxed.

'Garrett. I don't fucking believe it, my old mukka.'

He rushed forward and gave Garrett a hug. Like many small men he moved with force and aggression. Even his hug was at full strength and Garrett could feel his ribs creak under the pressure.

'Jesus, man. You look like shit. Fucking long hair, unshaven. You some sort of hippie or something?'

They broke embrace and stood looking at each other for a while.

Garrett grinned widely. 'Hell, Brian. You look like a mister. Suit and tie.' Davies grinned back; teeth white. Straight.

'Fuck me,' shouted Garrett. 'You've had your teeth done. You're beautiful, man.'

They hugged again. Two schoolboys at the beginning of term.

'Come on, Garrett. Let's go for a drink. You hungry?'

'Can always eat.'

They took the elevator back down, ignoring the receptionist on their way out although her squeaks of distress followed them until the doors closed.

Brian took them to one of the ubiquitous steak houses in the mall that proliferated around Johannesburg like Starbucks infested any other major city. For the same price as a sandwich in England, Garrett had a steak with all the trimmings. He ordered water to accompany. Surprisingly, so did Brian.

'You not drinking?' He asked the small man.

'Nope. Not since…well. Not since.'

'Me neither.'

'How's the sleeping?'

Garrett shrugged. 'All right. Sometimes.'

'Nightmares?'

'Always. And not only when I sleep.'

'Me too, my friend. Me too.'

'So, Brian. You're the dog's bollocks now. Your own company. Expensive suit. New teeth. Give me the low down.'

'Nothing much to tell. After you bottled out on us in Sierra, everything went to shit. They ran out of money; no pay came through so the boys and me sort of helped ourselves to a bit. Things got a little tense and we ended up fighting our way to the border. Got through to Liberia. Lost most of the boys on the way. Eventually got a plane out. Hitched a ride with some mad South African who was running guns into the region. Got here. Nowhere else to go so I just stayed. Got into security because it's all I know. The rest is boring.'

'Manon said that you owned a detective agency.'

'No. She just can't understand the fucking difference. I wouldn't know how to be a detective. I've hired me some serious muscle. All ex-military. Kitted them out with the best equipment. We protect payrolls, industrial property, that sort of shit. It pays the rent. Barely. I take it that you've seen Manon?'

Garrett nodded.

'You still in love with her?'

Garrett said nothing. Stared at the remnants of his steak. A small piece of gristle. Some blood.

'Jesus, you poor sick fuck. She's a fucking nun, you asshole. Give it up.'

'Can't you talk without swearing?' Asked Garrett quietly.

Brian shook his head. 'Of course I can't, you fucking useless dickhead. How long have you known me?'

They both laughed and the seriousness of the moment passed.

'But really, Garrett. She told you this missing orphan crap?'

Garrett nodded.

'Look, my boy. I grew up in an orphanage. It's fucking shit, I tell you. Ran away all the time. Joined the army on my sixteenth birthday. Be the best.'

'You don't believe her?'

'It's not that. She wouldn't lie. I just think that she's wrong. Too emotional. You know. She's been through a lot. Every kid lost is a personal thing to her. She's just gotta realize that you can't save them all, especially the ones that don't want saving.'

'What do you think that I should do?'

Brian leant back in his chair. 'Go through the motions. Put her mind at rest. Go and see all of the other

Children's homes and speak to the people in charge. See the Archbishop.'

'She says that you can't get to see the archbishop.'

Brian laughed. 'She can't. I'd like to see them stop you.' He stood up. 'Look, I've got an appointment. Where're you staying? You got digs?' Garrett shook his head. 'Right then,' continued Brian. 'You're bunking with me. No ifs, no buts. Here,' he gave Garrett a card and a key. 'On the back is my home address. Hold on.' He took the card back and wrote on it. 'That's the alarm number. Type it into the keypad after you open the door. I'll see you later tonight'

They shook hands and went separate ways, Brian paying on the way out.

***

The Sweetie man drove one handed, whistling a simple tune as he did so. Jaunty. The same rhythm repeated in different keys. His name was painted on the side of his truck. But not his real name.

His real name was Khethukuthula Hlanganani but he had been called the Sweetie Man, or mister Sweets for so long now that most people honestly thought that his name was Sweets. He ran a small cash and carry outlet from a double garage at his house. Mister Sweets Cash and Carry.

The difference between him and the larger traders were twofold. Firstly, he delivered at no extra charge and, secondly, he obtained the majority of his stock from mister J.V. Harribia in Durban. In turn, mister Harribia obtained his stock directly off the ships that were bound for Somalia. The bags of meal and rice emblazoned with the World Food Program logo and underneath, gift of Switzerland or, From the People of the USA. Mister Harribia brought tons of stock every week for less than ten cents in the Dollar. He passed a large percentage of this saving onto mister Sweets. So, when it came to pricing on basic foodstuffs no one could beat the Sweetie Man.

Sweets had got his nickname from his habit of always carrying with him a number of large bags of cheap boiled sweets that he would hand out liberally to the children wherever he was trading. As a result, they would often run next to his truck when he was driving through the townships shouting, Sweetie or Sweets at him. He would always oblige, stopping and handing them out to all comers.

A short man. Graying hair. Double chin on a face that was somehow much fatter than his body. A bass laugh and a smile that showed off his many gold-filled teeth. He was a man well-liked by all. And when he stopped to deliver, he could always rely on the locals to help him with any of the heavy work because, although he was fit and healthy, his left arm was bent and shriveled. It had been since the early eighties when, during the apartheid years, he had been arrested by the security police and questioned as to his cousin's whereabouts. He had genuinely not known where his cousin was; if he had, he would have told, having always held a rather intense dislike for the man. This line of reason had held no water with the two semiliterate Afrikaners that had been in charge of eliciting information from him. They had beaten him with a baseball bat, breaking his arm so badly that it mortified and almost had to be amputated. There were days when mister Sweets wished that it had been, such was the constant pain.

They had released him a week later when they discovered that they already had his cousin in custody. He had been there for well over a month. Another reason to dislike him, thought Sweets, he owes me an arm. In all fairness no one had ever seen the man again. Such was the way of things in the dark days. Detention without trial. A shovel and a few feet of dust. He wasn't missed.

But now life smiled on Sweets. He had his own business, a truck, a house and, next year, he would buy himself a car. Something nice. A Mercedes or Audi. German. Nothing said success quite like something German.

He pulled his truck into the parking lot at the Honeydew Children's Home. He always enjoyed delivering here. The nice sister Manon would always make him a cup of sweet tea and the children would flock around him like butterflies to a flower. Not caring about his shrunken arm, not even noticing or, if they did, coming straight out and asking, what happened to your arm? Always he had a different story; sometimes he said that a lion had eaten it, sometimes a bad wizard had stolen his real arm and replaced it with this one. But at the end he would always give them some sweets and pat their heads. It was good to feel so well liked.

The only one that he was unsure of was the guard, Petrus. He made Sweets nervous. Petrus was well known by all as man to respect. And to avoid if possible. Although, of late, as he had grown a little older and he no longer picked fights wherever he went. Now he affected indifference, meeting violence with violence but never courting it. Sweets thought that it was probably the presence of the sister that had changed the warlike Zulu. Her presence was a balm to all souls. Pure, beautiful and full of peace.

He climbed out of his truck and rolled up the back. Before the door was even fully open the children had arrived. Voices high and excited. Crowding close. Hello mister Sweetie. Hello Sweets. Hello.

He picked up a huge bag of gumdrops and started handing them out.

***

Garrett had taken twenty minutes to find his car and, after he had finally got out of the labyrinthian parking garage, fired up the satnav, got pointing the right way and driven to Brian's address, a further forty minutes had passed. When he pulled into the gated townhouse complex where Brian lived, he could still clearly see Sandton City in his rear-view mirror. A walk of perhaps fifteen minutes.

He parked in a designated space outside Brian's garage that was attached to his house. Then he unlocked the house door, disarmed the alarm and went in, carrying his bag with him.

Although not large the interior of the house was stupendous. Staggeringly opulent. And unless the ex-SAS soldier had suddenly developed some sort of taste, obviously furnished by a professional. Furthermore, a professional who had been given a blank check. The entrance hall led to a large open plan living area; a copper cowled fireplace stood in the middle of the room separating the sitting area from the dining. Behind that lay the kitchen, a work of art in stainless steel and glass. Glass fronted refrigerators, thick glass counter tops, glass cupboard doors. Recessed lighting refracted through all of the glass and painted prismatic rainbows across the travertine marble floor. A hand carved African Teak table dominated the dining room. The wood dark and heavy, the chairs carved with a lighter hand, leather cushions on the seats. Woven wall hangings decorated the walls and offset the bright African colorings of the sofas and wingback chairs in the sitting area. Bowls of Ostrich eggs, austere metal sculptures and vases filled with arrangements of driftwood and feathers were scattered around the room, each one artfully placed so as to drive your attention to the next piece until your eyes finally came to rest upon the prize: an oil on canvas, perhaps three feet by two feet, displayed on an easel. A savage image, the colors a dark and brooding mix of red, green, black and brown.

The artist had applied the paint using a palette knife with such force that, in some areas, he had actually punctured the canvas. It was not a beautiful piece but there was something compelling about it. Primal. A visceral thing. It took Garrett a while to work out what the image was actually depicting. But when it came to him it was obvious. A man in full combat gear, a machete held in his right hand, his head thrown back. His mouth wide open in a scream. And in the bottom corner of the canvas, in white paint, the signature. Brian Davies.

CHAPTER FOUR

Mister Sweets pulled the truck into the car park next to the beer hall. He delivered here early every Wednesday morning; eighty bags of maize meal and twenty cases of *sheshebo* spicy tomato and onion mix. As with all of his customers in the Alexandra Township, Sweets allowed a further ten percent discount to the owner. This discount was not passed on to the customers nor was it to be enjoyed by the proprietor. The ten percent went to Dubula, the local hard man who collected every Friday afternoon. Neither mister Sweets nor the owner contemplated lying about their respective turnovers. The simple reason for this was that neither one of them wanted to be dead. Not even a little. And people that attempted to skim from Dubula ended up in pieces. Spread all over Alexandra.

By the time that Sweets had unloaded, there was already a gaggle of children clustered around the truck, hands held out, high piping voices. Sweets. Sweeties. The trader handed out handfuls of the primary-colored confectionaries and shooed each child off after they had received their share. But as he was doing so, he was looking over their heads. Searching for someone. Someone who would never beg so crassly. A boy that would never debase himself by chanting for Sweets. A serious little man-boy with a sister. A boy who always carried with him a sharpened yellow and silver screwdriver. And surely enough, when all the other squealing children had left, mister Sweets saw him, standing by the gates. Looking in the other direction. Feigning indifference. Far too adult to clamor after gum drops and gummy bears. Sweets called out. 'Hey, Vusi. How goes it?'

The boy walked briskly over and shook Sweets's hand. They reversed grip, the African way. 'Hello, mister Hlanganani.'

Vusi was probably the only person that Sweets knew that addressed him by his real name. A fact that both amused him, and endeared the boy to him. It was typical of his serious demeanor that he would never address someone by their nickname.

'So, Vusi, how is your sister?'

'Still coughing, sir.'

'Hold on. I have something for her.' Mister Sweets went to his truck, opened the glove box and took out a packet. 'Here, give these to her.' Vusi started to open the packet. 'No, no. Open it when you get home. Give them to her. And here, for you.' Sweets gave Vusi a whole unopened bag of gumdrops. Vusi bowed in thanks and left. Mister Sweets smiled. He liked that little boy. He liked him a lot.

Vusi spent the rest of the day trawling Louis Botha Avenue and the area around it. He found a tray of stale buns behind the bakery and, in the trash section of the Mister Rooster fried chicken, three cartons of expired orange juice. He put his bounty into a plastic packet along with any small pieces of wood and cardboard that he found for his fire.

The sun was going down when he returned to the shack. Thandi had refilled the water bucket from one of the public taps and was lying on the floor. Her cough had worsened and she was not looking well. Vusi opened the packet that mister Sweets had given him. Inside was a roll of mentholated cough drops and a ten Rand note. Vusi never cried no matter what hardship he was subjected to but the trader's small act of kindness brought a prickle of moisture to the boy's eyes. Adversity could be ignored but compassion slipped easily through his defenses.

Thandi sucked on the cough Sweets. They seemed to help her congestion. Later that evening they feasted on buns and gumdrops. And once again, Vusi fell asleep, the screwdriver clutched ready in his right hand.

***

After a sunrise breakfast with Brian, Garrett decided to leave early. He wanted to see at least two of the orphanages today and have a chat to the people in charge. The first one that he figured on seeing was on the outskirts of Pretoria, about an hour's drive away. The second was in Krugersdorp, sort of on the way back but still another hour's driving. Not for the first time he blessed the man that had invented the satnav as he followed the many twists and turns to get onto the main highway to the city of Pretoria. He stopped to re-fuel before he hit the main road.

The harsh African sun reflected off the white-gray concrete highway and assaulted Garrett's eyes like a laser. He squinted as much as he could without actually closing his eyes and reminded himself to buy a pair of sunglasses at the first opportunity.

The concrete surface rumbled loudly under the wide off-road tires and set up a resonance that made Gar-rett's jaw ache. The noise combined with the sunlight led to a grinding headache within less than fifteen minutes. Garrett pulled in at a roadside service station and picked up a packet of ibuprofen, washing down four with mineral water before he had even got to the till. Then he noticed a rack of sunglasses. They were cheap but claimed to have Polaroid lenses so he picked a pair in the style of Rayban Aviators and paid for them along with the pills and water. Then he sat in the Jeep with the engine running, air conditioner on full, for five minutes while the painkillers took effect. He picked the price tag off the sunglasses, put them on and got back on the road.

As he approached the outskirts of Pretoria the satellite directed him, via a myriad of back roads, to the Sunlight Children's Home Pretoria. In contrast to Manon's place of work this was situated on a smallholding. A plot of dry earth with a rambling whitewashed bungalow in the center.

There were obvious extensions to the original building erected from corrugated iron sheeting with plastic covered windows. But the area was neat and tidy. Whitewashed stones lined the driveway and it was obvious that the dusty garden had been recently swept, the marks of the broom's bristles still etched into the thick dust, the air hot and still.

As he drove down the driveway the Jeep kicked up a cloud of red dust that hung motionless behind him. When he stopped the car and got out the dry heat hit him like a hammer blow and he felt the sweat on his body evaporate instantly. Garrett turned to look at the dust cloud that he had created and marveled at its stillness. Nothing moved. There was no sound. It was as if he had been transported to some alien world where there was no life. No movement except from himself. Then he heard a dog bark. And children's voices and, all of a sudden, the place was teeming with sound and life. Kids ran out of the front door towards him, dogs came from around the back of the building, barking and jumping. Tongues lolling, impossibly long, from panting mouths.

Behind the children came an old man. Dressed in a black suit, so old that it was now a shiny dark green. Bent over he was, and walking with the aid of a stick but his huge size still apparent. His head bald, shiny as a teacher's apple, his beard long and white but for the area around his mouth that was stained a dark yellow from the pipe that seemed surgically attached to his lips. Clouds of smoke billowed around where he walked, like some sort of rain god. Thor. Or even Odin. And when he stopped and spoke his voice reinforced the image. A deep, gravely baritone. His words clipped, precise. English not his native tongue.

'Good day, my son. How may we be of help?'

Garrett walked towards him and held his hand out. 'My name is Garrett, sir. I am a friend of sister Manon.'

The old man grasped Garrett's hand. A rough leather glove stuffed with pebbles. His handshake was eye-wateringly firm.

'Come inside, young man. It is cooler in than out.'

They walked back inside, the children and dogs thronging around them. The kids wide eyed and staring at the newcomer. 'Come,' he continued. 'We will sit in the kitchen. Agnes will make us some tea.'

He waved the dogs and children off with his stick as they walked down the dim corridor. 'Go. Go away. *Voetsak*. The grown-ups are busy.' The noisy throng melted away leaving behind a strong smell of dog that competed on even terms with the tobacco smoke.

The old man pushed open the door and ushered Garrett into an enormous kitchen. Two ancient coal stoves stood against the far wall and the center of the room was filled with a rough wooden trestle table that was placed diagonally across. Twenty or so mismatched chairs were positioned around the table and at the one end sat a large colored woman in a bright pink dress. Around her head she had wound a turban of purple and her fingers were covered in silver rings. She was probably the hugest female that Garrett had ever seen. Her massive bosom rested on the table in front of her and the flesh bulged around the silver rings like over baked bread rolls. She was chopping carrots, her movements deft and economical, belying her vastness. When she looked up at the old man her smile lit up the room like a lighthouse in a storm. Her teeth strong and white, her face a symphony of laughter lines and happiness. She stood up to greet Garrett. She was taller than he had suspected. Fully six feet. A towering work of art in bright pink. 'Hello, sir. My name is Agnes.'

Garrett hurried around the table to grasp her hand. 'I am Garrett.' She held his hand for a while and looked deeply into Garrett's eyes, her haze almost hypnotic. But not aggressive. Searching. And then she nodded in approval. 'You have traveled here from afar, young sir.'

Garrett nodded. 'From Johannesburg.'

She laughed, still holding his hand. 'Further than that.'

'London?' asked Garrett.

She nodded. 'Further than that even. Much further. But you still have far to go. Never mind, sit down. Agnes will make you some tea and it will all seem better.' She turned to the old man. 'You too, Hartvig. Sit.' She finally let go of Garrett's hand and swayed over to one of the stoves, collecting a teapot full of water on the way.

While Agnes busied herself fixing the tea Garrett told the old man about sister Manon and her suspicions that something was awry with the missing children. However, Hartvig's response took him by surprise.

'I have met sister Manon. A lovely child. God has blessed her with both beauty and principles. However, in this she could never be more wrong. '

'How do you know?' Asked Garrett.

'Well,' answered the old man. 'For a start, no children have gone missing from this home. Not for the last ten years. Not ever. And as for her missing ones, it is a sad and simply fact that sometimes these street children that we save prefer their lives on the street. There is no great conspiracy, no ring of kidnappers or such. Simply the knowledge that not all enter God's house willingly. Tell the good sister to concentrate on her flock. Tell her that sometimes the wolves of temptation and sin descend upon us and take some of our sheep away and there is nothing that we can do about it. It is natures, and God's way. In time they will return…or they won't.'

Agnes placed a tray of buttermilk cookies on the table and a mug of tea in front of each of them. The tea was bright orange, stewed rather than drawn, made with sweetened condensed milk, the steam as fragrant as boiled sweets. It was delicious and Garrett complimented her. Hartvig puffed furiously on his pipe, drawing the smoke deep into his lungs like a cigarette smoker. 'Used to have tea like that on the whaling boat back in the day. As strong as the word of the Lord and as sweet as any of his angels. Better than a shot of rum.'

Garrett raised an eyebrow. 'You served on a whaling ship?'

'Chief mate. Until the early seventies when whaling stopped in Durban. I turned to the cloth then. Dedicated my life to the Lord. His strength has kept me young. How old would you say I am?' Hartvig jabbed his pipe at Garrett.

Garrett gave it some thought and then chopped off about a thousand years. 'Seventy five?'

'Ha. Ha and ha. Eighty-three. And as fit as a fifty-year-old. The Lord's doing.'

Agnes raised her one eyebrow and gave Garrett a wink. 'Any more tea?'

'No thank you,' Garrett declined. 'Places to go.'

Hartvig leaned forward and shook Garrett's hand without rising. 'Good luck my boy. And remember to tell Manon, tend to her flock.'

Agnes led Garrettt from the room, her hips brushing the door on each side as she sashayed through. When they got out of the front door she leaned over to the young man. Conspiratorially. 'He's a liar you know.'

'Really?'

'*Ja.* He's eighty-nine. Takes off six years every time. Thinks that I don't know. Silly old man.'

'But you love him.'

Agnes shrugged. One shoulder only. Like a small girl denying that she had a boyfriend. 'He is a good man.'

Garrett gave her a hug and walked to the Jeep. As he put the keys into the door Agnes called him back with a hiss and a crooked finger. He strode back to her side. 'He forgets sometimes. He doesn't mean to. He is almost ninety after all.'

Garrett didn't respond.

Agnes looked guilty. At odds.

'Some of the children have gone missing.'

Garrett drove back through his own dust. Before he got to the highway, he passed a big white van coming the other way, on the side written in red, Mister Sweets Food Wholesalers.

Soon the Jeep was on the main road heading towards Krugersdorp. Driving on the rumble inducing concrete highway. But the cheap sunglasses were doing their job and Garrett had worked out how to plug his iPod into the sound system so the seven speakers were pumping out one of Berwalt's overtures played by the Gavle symphony orchestra. Garrett liked Berwalt, considering him to have been a composer well ahead of his time. Even now unjustly ignored. Brian could never understand why Garrett listened to classical music, and the fact that he favored such obscure composers irritated him all the more.

The Dentist was more of a German heavy metal fancier. Bands like Rammestein and Totenmond. Vicious, grinding music. Every bar a call to arms. Whereas Garrett found his classical music a balm for his soul, cool and comforting. They both, however, agreed that all other modern music was shit. Three and a half minutes of over-composed triteness vomited up by whoever the next Bieber clone was.

The Gavle orchestra started the second movement. And the road rumbled beneath him, drawing him closer to the next Sunlight Orphanage.

***

The Krugersdorp branch of the children's home was built on a steep hill, so from the front it seemed small. An average three-bedroom house. But when Garrett pulled into the driveway it became apparent that the house continued down the hill in a World War two concrete bunker style. This home had a different feel to the last one. Empty soda cans crunched under the Jeep's tires and plastic supermarket bags festooned the barbed wire fence in a post-apocalyptic version of Christmas. Flapping in the breeze like colorful birds caught in a multitude of snares. Blues, reds and yellows, beating out their lives as they tried to free themselves from the rusty strands of steel.

First, he tried the doorbell, a small steel button recessed into the door. But when he didn't hear a corresponding ring inside the house he knocked as well. A plump middle-aged man with a large round, fleshy face and a tiny retrousse nose answered the door fairly quickly. The effect was entirely disconcerting. It was as if someone had stuck a doll's nose onto an adult size human being. He had a heat rash or perhaps simply a large crop of pimples on the right-hand side of his face. And the hand that he proffered in greeting was limp, flabby and lifeless as an old slice of microwave pizza. But his voice was liquid gold. A light tenor, pleasing to the ear and soul alike.

'Good afternoon, good sir. I am father Cornelius. Is there any way in which I may assist you?'

Garrett nodded. 'I am a friend of sister Manon. I wonder if we could have a quick chat, father.'

The father nodded. 'Follow me,' he said.

The house was badly lit and smelled institutional. Boiled cabbage and harsh antiseptic.

'Come. We shall talk in the common room. The children are in a prayer meeting with sister Dorcas while I was taking time to catch up on some of my paperwork.'

The priest led the way to a room that hosted a haphazard scattering of threadbare armchairs, cushions and blankets. In the one corner was a small old-fashioned television set with a makeshift set of bunny aerials sticking out of the top. A wire coat hanger and some aluminum foil. Round face sat down in an old wingback and gestured towards another. Garrett sank into the chair that had been indicated and started his tale immediately, not wishing to spend longer than necessary in this depressing place.

The priest listened intently while Garrett spoke, his hands steepled together as he leant forward in his chair.

At the end he nodded, his look thoughtful, his face round, pink and porcine.

'Yes. We have had a few children go missing.'

'More than a few,' noted Garrett. 'Twenty or so in recent months.'

The priest shrugged. Weary. 'I wouldn't know about that. Whenever one of ours goes missing we wait for twenty-four hours and then we inform the police.'

'Do the police ever find anyone?' asked Garrett.

'Not really. But sometimes they return of their own accord or I assume that they find a life elsewhere.'

'Or they die.'

The priest leaned forward even further. 'What was that?'

Garrett stood up. 'Or they die. I'll show myself out, father.'

As Garrett strode from the house, he knew that he shouldn't be blaming the priest for his frustration. The father was doing a job few others would. But how, he wondered, could people accept the loss of these children so easily. At what stage did they become meaningless? Mere numbers in the balance sheet of life. Present. Not present. Dead. Alive.

He slammed the door behind him and stood breathing deeply for a while until he noticed the five men grouped around his Jeep. He could see straight away that this was trouble and his body immediately jumped up a level, raising his adrenaline, restricting the flow of blood to internal organs and flooding the muscles. Step one; scan the rest of the area to determine if this small group was the only threat. Step two, approach the source and ascertain the level of threat.

Garrett walked up to the group. Hands by his side. Expression confident but not aggressive.

'Can I help you gentlemen?'

One of the group, a black man, six foot, stood forward.

'Reckon you can, boy. Give us the keys for the Jeep and then we'll take it from there.'

Garrett ran his gaze over the man. He was obviously the leader. The leader always speaks first. He was armed. Garrett could see the butt of a semi-automatic pistol sticking out of the waistband of his shorts. A quick second glance confirmed it to be a Star 9mm single action. The hammer was down so it wasn't cocked and locked. Of course it may still have a round in the chamber but Garrett would bet against it. The rest of the group clustered behind the leader in a V formation. Like flying ducks. The analogy brought a smile to Garrett's face

'What's so funny?'

Garrett shook his head. 'Nothing. Look, I'm very busy. Could we move this whole thing along?'

The leader drew the Star and pointed it at Garrett's face. 'Give us your keys and then we will decide what to do to you.'

Garrett had been shot a total of eight times before. All of the incidences occurred in the first few years of combat. Since then, he had experienced only minor injuries. That was because his body had learnt. Reactions had been honed; scalpel sharp. Thought was no longer involved. Muscle memory was everything. To think was to die. His reaction was instant and complete. No holding back. With his right hand he grabbed the top slide of the weapon and pushed back hard. At the same time, he grasped the bottom of the pistol and ejected the magazine before depressing the slide stop and whipping the top slide off the receiver. This left the leader with a handful of wood and metal with no discernable function whatsoever. Garrett, however, had a weapon. The top slide was six inches of hardened steel weighing in at a little over half a kilogram. He held it gripped in his fist, a half-inch nub of steel protruding out each side to strike with. Using an overhand right he smashed the tip of the slide into the bridge of the leader's nose, shattering the bone. He sank to the floor like a corpse.

Spinning hard, Garrett struck the man to the left of the leader in the hinge of his jaw, the blow striking with enough force to splinter the lower mandible and detach it from the skull. He then stepped back and to the right and jabbed the end of the slide into the third assailants Adam's apple causing him to drop to the floor, clutching his throat in panic as his airway closed up. A quick front snap kick to the head ensured that he stayed where he was.

Then Garrett stepped back. Reassessing. Thought catching up with action.

He stared at the remaining two men and shook his head. 'Go home. It's finished.'

Neither of them moved. And then the one reached behind his back, lifted his shirt, and drew out a machete. Twenty-three inches of high carbon steel with an eighteen-inch blade.

The force of memory brought on by the sight of the weapon made Garrett take a step back. ... *the children lay on rush mats on the floor, their foreshortened arms wrapped in bandages*...he held up a hand towards the man with the blade, his face white as a shroud. 'Stop. Go now. Please.'

The assailant mistakenly took Garrett's reaction as a sign of weakness. Fear.

The blade glinted in the sun. Blood, thick and purple dripped off the handle. Around him, screams of agony. Gibbering. Begging for quarter. But there was no quarter. There was no mercy. And the blood sprayed high...retribution.

The man raised the machete above his head.

And the beast roared and smashed down the gate. Garrett simply stepped forward. Pushing up against the blade-wielder and thereby negating the man's advantage. You cannot swing a machete at someone who is close enough to you to dance.

He grasped the arm holding the blade and then whipped his head forward in a vicious head butt.

Ordinarily Garrett would have then stopped there, but the beast was howling. With the steel slide still grasped in his fist Garrett hammered a series of short punches into the man's ribs. Every strike accompanied by the sound of bone cracking and splintering, puncturing lungs and internal organs. The fifth man turned and ran. But Garrett cocked his arm and threw the steel slide at him, hitting him on the back of the head and knocking him down. Then he wrenched the machete out of the unconscious blade-wielder's hand and walked over to the prostrate fifth assailant. He stood above the man for a while, chest heaving with emotion as he stared down at him. His green eyes wild, untamed and terrifying.

And, as the beast slunk back into its cage, Garrett returned to the Jeep, opened the door, threw the machete onto the back seat and drove off. But the memories had been shaken loose and his whole body had been flooded with their poison...*and the little girl smiled at him and raised her arm. A bloody stump wrapped in a dirty bandage*...he would never be free.

CHAPTER SIX

Dubula stood at ease. Legs apart, hands behind his back, thumbs interlocked. A small trickle of blood ran down his cheek from the cut above his eye. The master's rings often opened up the skin when he showed his displeasure. But Dubula did not mind. He knew that the master's anger burned hot but not for long. Anyway, was it not a father's job to discipline his children as and when he felt? And Dubula considered the master to be his father as much as if he was related by blood.

He had taken the bodyguard from the streets and given him life. Clothes beyond comparison. Meals that contained meat every day. And most importantly, power. Power to command. Power to have an effect over his own life. To change his own destiny. No longer a terrified boy living by his wits and inherent viciousness and eking out a living, day to day. Dubula was the master's dog, and that made him happy.

'Five armed men. He defeated five of my men. Ruined them.'

Dubula stood. Still.

'Did he have help?'

The bodyguard shook his head.

'Then how did he do it? This is a fuck up. You were meant to give him a warning. Break a leg. Arms. Send him home. Instead, he breaks my men. How could you let this happen?'

'I am sorry, *ubawo*, father. It will not happen again. I assumed that five would be enough.'

The master shook his head. 'Tell me, my son. What exactly happened? You have talked to the men…the ones that lived.'

Dubula took a deep breath. He was not a man given to subtlety or subterfuge. He tended to speak the truth, to tell things as he heard. An honest man. But he knew that his answer would incite the master to an even more incandescent rage. Nevertheless, he told what he had heard from the three surviving men that had accosted the foreigner.

'I spoke to them after I picked them up. We avoided any problems with the police. Got them home quickly. Samuel was in charge. I gave him a Star 9mm from the stores. He took four men of his choice with him. I told him to hijack the foreigner's car and damage him severely. Maybe even shoot him in the knees. But when Samuel drew his weapon, the man cast a spell on it and it fell apart.'

'What!' shouted the master.

Dubula shifted uncomfortably. 'The man made the gun fall to pieces.'

'Bullshit.'

'I believe him, sir. When I got there the weapon was in pieces and lying all over the place.'

'What next?'

'The stranger struck Samuel with a fist of steel. Breaking his head. Then he smashed Wellington's jaw off his face. Then he struck Joshua in the neck and *bulala*, killed him. Bradford took out his machete and attacked the man but the blade simply bounced off him. Then, once again using his fist of steel he struck Bradford in the ribs and crushed them, causing his death. Never before have I seen such a thing. It was as if a car had run the man over. Finally, he struck down Sipho from afar without even touching him. And then he stood over Sipho and cursed him. Even now, he is dying with fever. Sipho says that the foreigner is not a man. He is *Umptyholi*, a beast in a man's flesh.'

The master felt a thrill of superstitious fear before he cast it off.

'Rubbish. He is just a man. Next time we will not make the same mistake. You see, my child, we cannot afford to let this man raise any more questions about our operation. It is too lucrative. We must stop him at all costs.' He stroked Dubula's cheek. Smearing the ruby red blood as he did so.

'I will talk to our man. See what he can do.'

***

The Jeep was parked outside the Honeydew orphanage and Garrett sat in the front seat. He lit another cigarette and wondered if he could have played the scenario out differently. He could have simply given the men the car keys. He could have run. But to where? And anyway, the more he went over the incident the more he was convinced that it wasn't a mere car-jacking. The assailants weren't after the Jeep, they were after him. When someone wants to steal a car then that is pretty much what they do. But twice the leader had referred to what they were going to do to Garrett after he had given them the keys. In a true hi-jacking situation it works the other way around; a threat of violence and a promise of reward if you comply. This had been all violence. It was made plain that whatever Garrett did they were going to punish him. So, it was a warning. That could mean only one thing. Manon was right. Someone was taking the children.

Garrett slid out of the Jeep and walked over to Petrus who was lounging in the shade, eyes half closed like he was about to fall asleep. '*Sawubona*, Petrus.'

'*Sawubona, Isosha.*'

Garrett smiled. The guard had just given him a nickname, The Soldier. He nodded his approval and Petrus grinned back at him, his face still a picture of somnolence apart from the flashing white teeth. But Garrett could see, behind the hooded exterior his eyes were actually bright, alert. A man who saw more than he let on. He tapped out a brace of Gauloise, lit them and passed one to Petrus. Then he squatted down next to the man and they smoked in silence for a while, the blue smoke curling lazily around their heads in the windless late afternoon.

The sun was scheduled to set at around seven o'clock and, already, an hour before, it was only a few inches above the horizon. The low level combined with the dust laden air caused the glowing ball of gas to show as bright red with streaks of orange. Around it the cloudless sky went from silver to the deepest of azure blue. Large flights of mossie sparrows winged their way noisily through the tepid air to nearby farmers' fields to feed on the ripening grain, the shrill sound of *cheerup cheerup* accompanying any change in direction.

Using his cigarette to point, Petrus brought Garrett's attention to a spot high in the sky above the chattering swallows. A harrier-hawk, riding the thermals without moving its wings. Omniscient. Alone. At first it seemed that the bird of prey was simply flying. Going from one place to another, using the least necessary energy. But then Garrett saw that it was actually gliding around to place itself in front of the sun. A fighter pilot placing himself into a position of the fullest advantage. As soon as he was in position he dove, wings tucked in to his side, steering with tail alone. There was a puff of feathers and seconds later the sound of impact and the Hawk peeled away, his dinner clutched in his claws. The mossies continued on their

way. Unconcerned. The flock had survived. The loss of
one member was meaningless. Insignificant.

'So, talk to me, *Isosha.*'

'About what,' asked Garrett?

'Whatever you want to. Tell me why you are here.'

'I would have thought that you already knew.'

Petrus grinned, allowing smoke to trickle out of his
mouth as he did so. 'I know. But stories heard second
hand are sometimes just that, stories and not facts.'

So, Garrett told him. Of the missing orphans and of
more. Of the past. The wars and the killings. He spoke
as he had never spoken before to anyone, even Manon.
Petrus listened, and they shared cigarettes, understanding and much more. The sun set and the evening grew
dark. For a while sister Manon had watched them from
her window, and had left them alone, sensing Garrett's
need to talk.

Eventually Petrus nodded. 'I know about the missing children.'

'You do?'

'Of course. I wouldn't be much of a guard if I didn't
notice that the people that I was guarding had gone
missing.'

'And?'

'And nothing. There are not so many. They normally don't return from school. Or some slip away on
a Sunday after church. I would also run away if they
made me pray and go to church every Sunday. We tell
the police and the school and that is the end of it.'

Garrett shook his head. 'No. There is more. Someone is taking the children, kidnapping them. Until today I may have agreed with you. But those people that attacked me. That was a warning. A clumsy one but a warning nonetheless.'

'Maybe.'

'Definitely,' stressed Garrett.

'Well then, are you planning to stop looking?'

'No.'

'Then they will come for you again. Next time ask one what this is all about before you smash them to bits. It will simplify things.'

Garrett smiled ruefully.

'But before you continue, *Isosha*, let me ask you one thing. What if you are right? What if there is more to this and someone is taking the children. What then…will you destroy them? Will you do what you did before, in the dark days of the war? Will you do that?'

Garrett drew a shuddering breath and fought to control his emotion. The question was a fair one. Harsh. But fair.

'I will protect the children.'

Petrus shook his head. 'No. You cannot protect the children. There are too many orphanages and they are too far apart. So, tell me what you will do.'

Garrett could make out Petrus's eyes glittering in the dark, his expression earnest. Firm.

'I will find the people responsible and I will punish them.'

'Yes,' agreed Petrus. 'Because, *Isosha*, that is what you do. You punish.'

Garrett said nothing. There was nothing to say.

'One last thing, *Isosha*. What if the people who are responsible are the same people who keep the orphanages going? Will you still kill them? And if you do what will happen to the rest of the children? They will be cast out. Homeless. Tell me, my friend. Will you kill the whole flock just to save one sparrow?'

And Garrett held his head in his hands.

Because he honestly did not know the answer.

CHAPTER SEVEN

Garrett lay in bed. It was unlike him to sleep past sunup. However, he wasn't sleeping, he was merely lying still. Not thinking, just breathing in and out. The barest of autonomic bodily functions needed to stay alive. Heart beating slowly. After he had spoken to Petrus, he had said goodnight to Manon. Then he had driven back to Brian's place. Once again, the dentist had arrived home late, after Garrett had sacked out. There were things that he needed to think about. Important things. Life changing things. But instead, he simply lay still.

Petrus was right. He had to decide exactly what he was going to do. If the children were being kidnapped for some foul reason, then how would he react? Was it up to him to decide on the perpetrator's punishment? Would he simply report the whole thing to the police and, if so, would they bother to do anything? Could they do anything? How big could this whole thing be? But debate with himself as much as wanted, one thing was abundantly clear; if he did nothing about it then nothing would ever be done. That decided he climbed out of bed.

***

They called themselves 'The Finders of the Children of the Lady of the Cedars of the Lebanon.' Ostensibly they worked hand in hand with the Catholic Church. Particularly when it involved the homeless, the destitute or the infirm. They were a privately funded group, a mixture of upper middle-class whites and working-class black women. Some would say do-gooders, some busybodies. But those who had been helped by these women, those who had been given food, or clothing or a place to stay; they would call them angels.

This Friday afternoon they were visiting the Alexandra Township, giving alms in the form of food and clothing. Nomusa Bongani, a plump middle-aged matron knocked softly on the cardboard sheet that formed a makeshift door to the lean-to. There was no answer, but she could hear a faint coughing. Weak but persistent. She pushed the cardboard to one side and went into the dwelling. Lying on the floor was a young girl of perhaps seven years of age. Her thin cotton dress drenched in sweat. Nomusa leant over her and felt her forehead. She was oven-hot. Her tongue hung from the side of her mouth like a panting dog and when Nomusa tried to talk to her the little girl babbled in fever driven delirium.

Nomusa went outside and called for Missus Seagal. Annabella Segeal was the nominal leader of the group more for the fact that her husband was a wealthy plastic surgeon than for her own leadership qualities. However, that notwithstanding, she was a caring person who put in many hours of genuine hard work. She also spent a lot of her time telling people how much good she did but this did not negate the acts of charity in any way. It simply made her a complete pain in the ass.

After questioning the people that lived around the cardboard lean-to and discovering that the child had no parents, the ladies carried her to Missus Seagal's Range Rover and laid her on the back seat. Thirty minutes later the plastic surgeon's wife pulled into the parking lot of the Honeydew Sunlight Orphanage.

Petrus carried the child to the small private room at the back of the converted factory that served as a sick room and Manon wasted no time in calling the church doctor. Within the hour the girl had an electrolytic drip in her arm. The doctor explained to Manon that she was severely dehydrated due to chronic diarrhea and the cough would clear up as soon as her strength increased.

'She's sleeping naturally now,' the doctor said. 'When she wakes, she may show signs of disorientation. This is normal. Keep her warm and well hydrated. Fruit juice, watered by half. Some dry biscuits and toast until the bowels stop acting up. Maybe some chicken soup, can't go wrong with chicken soup. Any worries, give me a call.' He shook hands with the sister and left.

Manon sat with the girl for the next hour when she woke. She stared around the room for a while. Eyes wide. Puzzled. Not scared. Finally.

'Where is my brother?'

'I'm sorry, my sweet. You were very sick so some people brought you here to get better. We don't know about your brother.'

The little girls face puckered up. Her eyes glazed with tears. 'I want my brother. He will be worried about me.'

Manon took her hand. 'Don't worry, little one. We will find your brother. What's your name?'

'Thandi. I live in Alex with my brother. He made a door. He's very strong. His name is Vusi.'

'Okay, Thandi. You wait here. Don't worry. I am going to call someone and they will find your brother for you.'

Thandi nodded.

Manon walked through to the front of the building to find Petrus. He was in his usual spot, leaning against the wall, eyes half closed. Cigarette dangling from his lips. The sister explained what she needed done.

'No problem. I know where the church ladies found her. I'll go there now and find this Vusi.' He set off down the road. His stride deceptively long, muscular shoulders rolling as he walked. A thin tendril of smoke swirled around his head as from a lit fuse.

***

Dubula opened the door of the black Mercedes S500 and stepped outside. The roasting air brought an instant sheen of sweat to his face after the frigid cool of the climate control. A dust devil swirled across the dirty parking area picking up plastic packets as it danced. Yellow and blue and red partners pirouetting together in the dirt.

He glanced around the lot looking for him. He knew that he would be there. He was there every Friday. And then he saw him, standing in the shade of the building trying to appear casual. Lounging. One hand on hip. Dubula hid his smile and beckoned for him to come over. They shook hands.

'Good day to you, Vusi,' he greeted the boy.

'*Sawubona, umnumzana.*' Vusi returned the greeting formally. Showing great respect.

'So, Vusi. The usual please. Twenty Rands to protect my car. Half now,' Dubula took a roll of money from his pocket and stripped off a ten Rand note. 'Half when I get back.'

Vusi bowed and went and stood in front of the car, his hand resting on the handle of the screwdriver in his pocket, his chest puffed out with importance. This was a man's job.

Dubula walked into the beer hall. A group of teen-age *skabengas*, street thugs, were clustered around the entrance. Baseball caps on backwards, oversized jeans at jailbait half-mast. Fake Nike's, shoelaces loose so when they walked, they had to shuffle like zombies. Dubula scanned them and they averted their eyes. Hands in front of crotches like a dog covering its genitals with its tail in the presence of the alpha. The big man stopped to speak to them.

'Hey, you shits, watch my car, okay? And if any harm comes to my car or to the boy, I will hunt you down and roast you over an open fire. Okay?'

There was a frantic nodding of heads and a chorused, '*Yebo*,' of agreement. They knew that this was no idle threat.

Dubula gave them a thumb up. He enjoyed Fridays. The end of the week was money collection day. *Shebeens*, illegal drinking halls, gambling joints, whore houses, even legitimate shops. All paid a percentage to the master. And Dubula was in charge of collections. In return the businesses received a form of protection. Protection from the wrath of the master as well as protection from both other gangs and any attempt at competition.

This protection was not as dubious a perk as it might sound. Only two months previously a Chinese gang had attempted to take control of a number of the gambling joints that flourished in SOWETO and surrounds. They had come in hard and fast. Torching one of the joints and badly beating another two owner-operators. Then they sent a polite note to the master. It was along the lines of, let's talk. There is room for all of us and no need to fight. The master had agreed and asked to meet at their premises. Their head office turned out to be situated on a smallholding close to Rustenburg some hundred miles or so from SOWETO. They had a number of houses for management and smaller single room dwellings for the muscle. The master had hit them with overwhelming and completely unexpected force. Fifty men armed with assault rifles, RPG's and machine guns. They had driven straight through the electric fences and destroyed the place. Every building burnt to the ground. Twenty-eight Chinese were killed, including five women and three children. Even the pets were exterminated.

For the next couple of weeks, it became life-threateningly unfashionable to be of Chinese extraction as the master cleaned up. Another seven people were put to the gun. And now everyone was under no illusion when it came to what they were paying their monthly ten percent of turnover for. And, as such, Dubula was treated by all as an honored guest. Tea was supped. Biscuits eaten and business talked in hushed and respectable tones. The big man even carried a briefcase. He was a businessman. A far cry from the boy on the streets.

Despite what the people thought of Dubula he was not a violent man. Instead, he was simply a man capable of great violence. He had killed his first man when he was very young and he had gone on to kill many more. But he had only done so when necessary and he had never enjoyed it. Bar the first one.

His mother had been unemployed for over four years. His father was merely a giver of seed. He had left before Dubula had been born. In an effort to keep her three children, Dubula and his two older sisters, from starving, his mother was forced to become an *injakazi,* a street whore. And in Africa there is no more dangerous profession. By the end of the first year, she was HIV positive and after another three was in the first stages of AIDS. But still she plied her trade at any opportunity. Servicing up to ten men a day with unprotected sex. By now both of Dubula's sisters had succumbed. Malnutrition combined with filthy water and constant diarrhea had killed both of them. They had literally wasted to death. Most people in the western world are unaware of the fact that diarrhea is one of the leading causes of child deaths in Africa. Far higher than AIDS. But we see no brown ribbons at award ceremonies. Diarrhea is not trendy. We remain ignorant. So, one might say that Dubula's sisters died of western ignorance.

Be that as it may, by this stage Dubula's mother was so weak that she could only tout for business that came very close to her hut. And she would take on anyone. Men diseased with syphilis, the infection so far advanced that the palms of their hands and the soles of their feet were covered with the dark brown syphilis rash and their genitals were a crop of seeping wounds. And Dubula would lie quietly in the corner of the hut, under a blanket, while these rotting men would pound on his mother as she earned enough coin to keep them alive for one more day.

Until one evening, a man had finished, stood up, pulled his trousers up and made to leave. His mother had called out, asking for her money. But he had reacted violently. Backhanding her with a full-blooded sweep of his hand. He struck her flush on the side of her face catapulting her wasted body into the wall with such force that Dubula actually heard her rib bones crack. He reacted instantly, running out from underneath the blanket, a slim-bladed paring knife in his hand as he did so. The blade was small, perhaps three inches long, but it had been honed to a scalpel like degree. It slid into the man's torso, somewhere between the fourth and fifth ribs. The man picked up the boy by the throat and started to squeeze the life out of him. But it was no easy task as Dubula wriggled and thrashed about, kicking and punching.

Eventually one of his kicks struck the handle of the knife hammering it even further in. Far enough to skewer the heart. Blood bubbled out of the man's mouth and he sank to the floor. Dead. Dubula carried on kicking him for a while until he was utterly exhausted. And then he lay down on the floor next to his mothers body, pulled the blanket up to cover the both of them and slept until the morning. He was seven years old.

Many more men had died since.

And now Dubula carried a briefcase.

The owner of the beer hall bustled up, bowing in respect as he walked. Dubula could smell the tea brewing. Yes, he liked Fridays.

***

Garrett had filled the Jeep's tank again and was heading to a house in the suburb of Sandhurst, the wealthiest area in South Africa. He was happy with the Jeep; it was comfortable and had all of the mod cons but it drank fuel like an Irishman downs Guinness on St. Patrick's Day. Not that it mattered with the petrol prices being so cheap. He had spent the morning on the phone tracking down the head of the Catholic Church in South Africa, a Cardinal Voysie. That had been the easy part. Getting an appointment to actually see him was a little more difficult. Eventually Garrett had resorted to an out and out lie, claiming that he was an English lawyer representing a large charity based in London and was looking at donating a vast sum of money to the South African Church to support its various outreach programs. The Cardinal's personal assistant, Bishop Mandoluto managed to squeeze Garrett in, midafternoon at the Cardinal's house for a quick informal meeting.

The satnav beeped and a Joanne Lumley sound-a-like informed him that he had reached his destination. The gates to the house were nothing short of stupendous. Dark hardwood slabs fully twenty feet high. Running along the top, two foot of electric fencing that joined the wall surrounding the property. Garrett buzzed his window down in order to push the intercom button next to the gate. He could hear the fence as it hummed and clicked. A full ten thousand volts of high-tech deterrent. Before he even touched the intercom it crackled into life. 'Can I help?'

'Yes,' affirmed Garrett. 'Two thirty appointment with His Most Reverend Eminence. I'm from London.'

The gate rolled to the side, whispering on greased ball bearings. A modern portcullis. The marble chip driveway curved out in front of him, a bow of glittering white, cutting through six acres of landscaped magnificence. Proteas, strelitzias and hydrangeas teemed in the flowerbeds, above them dense purple bougainvillea, and bright red bottlebrush trees added another layer of color. And high above them stately, lilac blossomed Jacaranda trees swept the skies and filled the air with the scent of honey and musk.

Garrett brought the Jeep to a crunching halt in front at the house, the four-wheel Bridgestone's making a sound like a rainstorm on fabric. He left the keys in the ignition and strode up to the front door that was a mini replica of the gate. Perhaps ten feet of teak with an off-center swivel hinge. It swung open as he approached. A young man in a well-fitting gray suit greeted him. Holding out his hand and walking forward. 'Good afternoon, sir. I am Bishop Mandoluto, we spoke on the phone.

Garrett shook his hand in the western way and found his grip to be firm and dry. Confident. 'Your Excellency.'

'Please follow me. His Most Reverend Eminence is busy training at the moment.'

'Training?'

'Yes, sir.'

Garrett could see that no further information would be forthcoming so he simply followed the Bishop. The opulence of the house was staggering. Original oils of the type normally only seen in museums. Statues of bronze and marble. Furniture that would grace the rooms of any royal dwelling and carpets from every part of the Ottoman Empire.

They walked down a long corridor, through double doors and finally reached their destination. Huge windows ran down the length of the room, looking out over the garden. On the opposite side mirrors reflected back the sunlight. He could tell as he walked that the wooden floor was sprung. But there was no *barre* so it was no ballet studio.

Running down the center of the room was a marked area measuring approximately fourteen by two meters, the last two meters on each end marked with white hashes. Garrett recognized it immediately as a *piste* or fencing strip. However, even if he had not, it would have been apparent by looking at the two men in full fencing kit, engaging in a bout.

Bishop Mandoluto leaned towards Garrett and pointed. 'Closest to us is His Eminence,' he whispered. His voice low but precise. A man used to conversing quietly.

The two men were using sabers and, although they were not wired up, they were keeping score, relying on each other's sportsmanship to declare *touché* or *pas de touché*. The Cardinal was good. Very good. Better than the other man whom Garrett took to be the coach as he was dressed in black. The Cardinal had the reach on him, by a good yard. The holy man was probably six feet seven in the shade and the instructor perhaps a foot shorter. Combined with perspective it made the coach look about two foot high. Or the Cardinal eight feet. Or perhaps like they were standing twenty meters apart.

Saber bouts are notoriously quick to finish and this one was no exception. It lasted perhaps eighty seconds and the Cardinal won five points to nil. They both saluted and stepped apart, the Cardinal stripping his mask and gloves off as they did so. He approached Garrett; his hand held out in front of him. Garrett knelt down on his left knee and kissed the ring. 'Your Grace.'

'My son.'

Garrett stayed on his knee until the Cardinal gestured for him to rise. With the mask no longer covering his face the Cardinal was revealed to be a man of surprising countenance. His large beaked nose flanked by small stone black and eyes topped by bushy charcoal eyebrows. A small moustache and a goatee surrounded a pair of very red lips, full, wet and sensual. He radiated a force of will. Power. The unshakable strength of belief.

'You do not dress like a lawyer.'

'No, Your Grace.'

The Cardinal smiled. His eyes bored into Garrett. All knowing. Garrett started to speak. He could not lie to this man. Every second that he stood in front of him without telling the truth he demeaned himself. But the Cardinal held up a finger to his lips. 'Do you fence?'

Garrett nodded. 'A long time ago, Your Grace.'

'Suit up. Plastron and mask should suffice.'

The instructor came forward with a mask and a plastron, an underarm protector that provides protection on the sword arm side and upper arm. Garrett strapped it on and then, holding the mask under his arm, selected a saber from the pair offered by the instructor. He donned the mask, squatted a few times and swung the saber left and right. Took a few breaths and approached the *piste*.

The instructor stepped up and raised his hand.

'This will be a five point bout. First to five wins. Standard saber rules apply.' He dropped his hand.

Garrett and the Cardinal saluted the instructor and then each other before assuming their positions. The Cardinal advanced, forcing Garrett back. The soldier felt clumsy, untutored next to the Cardinal's fluid movements. But Garrett had fought before, both on the *piste* and for real, with two-foot lengths of razor-sharp high carbon steel as opposed to the lightweight, plastic pointed toys that they now wielded.

And when you have fought for real you enter a room that normal people never go. It is a room full of terror and panic and dread. Full of darkness and blood. The reek of offal and the stink of the beast. It is a room that gives a man the ability to conjure up reserves of speed and endurance that no normal man can. And once you have visited there you can always bring it back.

The Cardinal scored first. A classic *Moulinet* off Garrett's extension. A flashy, impressive cut, but slow. Slow enough to show that the Cardinal had no respect for Garrett's capabilities.

Garrett took a deep breath and opened the door to the room. Sound faded, focus sharpened, heartbeat sped up. Massive quantities of adrenaline stretched the microseconds out into seconds. He started with an *appel*, stamping his foot hard on the ground to distract followed immediately by a flunge, jumping high into the air and striking with the edge of the blade to the Cardinal's mask. The next three points went the way of the soldier in embarrassingly quick time using a combination of compound attacks and in fighting.

They saluted once again and removed their masks. The Cardinal approached Garrett with his hand out, held ready to shake and not to kiss. Garrett hesitated momentarily before grasping the holy man's hand.

'It is customary for people to shake hands after a bout,' said the Cardinal. 'So be not nervous about protocol, I am a person before I am a Cardinal.'

'Your Grace.'

'Come. We shall drink some tea and you can tell me why you are here. Truthfully, this time.'

***

Vusi was pleased. It had been a good day. Mister Dubula had given him twenty Rands for guarding his car and then the man who owned the beer hall had called him over and given him a plastic bag full of buttered bread slices and some small packets of sugar. To make sugar sandwiches, he had told Vusi. He couldn't wait to get back to Thandi to show her how well he had done.

He started running as soon as he saw that his new door had been pulled off at the hinges. Thandi would never have done that. Something was wrong. He burst into the lean-to. His little sister wasn't there. The water bucket was still there so she hadn't gone for water. He ran out and went left to the area by the trees where she always went to squat. There were others there, relieving themselves, but no Thandi. His heart hammering in his chest he started asking around. Whoever he saw. Where is she? Where is my sister? Finally, he came across someone that had seen her being taken away. An old toothless woman who stitched clothes for the locals.

'They took her this afternoon,' she said. 'The church people. They took her and put her in a white lady's car. She was sick. They had to carry her.'

'Where did they go, *umame*?'

She shook her head. 'I don't know, my child. Maybe to the hospital, maybe to the church, maybe to the orphan house.'

'I must find her. I must find her and bring her home so that I can take care of her.'

Vusi tied the plastic bag to the loop on his tattered jeans and started jogging. He would go to a church. There were lots of churches. He would find one and ask the holy man where Thandi was. And he would tell him and then he could bring her home. And she could have sugar sandwiches. As many as she wanted.

***

It was a short drive back to Brian's house and Garrett was hungry so he stopped at a likely looking burger place to load up on sustenance. There was a sign outside what looked to be a standard, plastic tables, paper tablecloth establishment boasting, 'the biggest burgers in town.' Under that a smaller sign told everyone to, 'ask about our live oysters.' Garrett did so and was served up a bizarre combination of half a dozen live oysters accompanied by a beef burger the size of a baby's head. It was one of the best meals that he'd had in a long time. The oysters a fresh taste of the sea, lifted with a little lemon juice. The burger, rare, the bun homemade, crispy on the outside, soft in the middle. Pickle, tomato, onion. Seasoned with salt and pepper. The flavors honest and unadorned. For some reason the chef had stuck a small flag on a toothpick into the top of the burger. It said, 'burger.' There were no flags in the oysters.

Garrett sat outside at a pavement table where he could smoke. Took time over his meal, enjoying it, mulling over his meeting with the Cardinal. The man of the church had given him a full twenty minutes and had listened intently, asking questions at the right time, compassionate, concerned. At the end Garrett realized that he had told him far more about himself than he had meant to. Far more than he was comfortable with. The Cardinal had assured Garrett that he would have someone look into the matter of the missing orphans even though he was sure that it was of no real import. The general consensus amongst everyone involved seemed to be that, from time to time, orphans go missing. Like cats. Or odd socks. The lack of empathy left Garrett with a vague feeling of unease. Disquiet. It was as if society had drawn a line in the sand and the orphans had fallen on the wrong side. Unessential. The ones that they took care of, there merely as a sop to conscience rather than through concern and kindness.

He paid for his meal and left a good tip. He also pocketed the little 'burger' flag. As he climbed into the Jeep, he considered going to see Manon but rejected the idea. There was nothing to tell her of any import, and being close to her made his soul ache. Their knees touching. Breathing the same air. The heat off her body. The smell of her hair. And the ever-present silver crucifix between them. Looming as high as a wall. Higher than understanding. Higher than human love.

***

'I couldn't find him.' Said Petrus. 'Kids like that, living in Alex. It's like they're invisible.' The guard lit a cigarette. 'I found where they lived. Not much more than a cardboard box. I will go back tomorrow. Try again.'

'Thank you, Petrus.' Manon touched his shoulder. She could see that the normally taciturn Zulu was upset. The usual look of casual arrogance was gone from his face. Replaced with reticence. Melancholy.

'You know, sister, that place should not exist. What happened? What happened to our dream of a new South Africa? Sometimes I wonder what we fought for.'

Smoke trickled from his nose. His mouth. As if he were simply too exhausted to expel it.

'There are more shacks now than there were under the Apartheid regime. An abandoned factory burnt down last week. There were forty families squatting there. Over two hundred people. Almost all died. It's not right.'

Manon said nothing. There was nothing to say. In the melting pot of South Africa, one did what one could and that had to be enough. She left Petrus to his musings and went to tell Thandi the bad news.

The little girl sat on the end of her newly allocated bed in animated conversation with two of the other girls. Her recovery had been almost miraculous. Within hours the drip had replenished her vital fluids and by that late evening she ate a full meal of maize porridge and gravy. This morning she had eaten a large bowl of maltabella malt porridge with butter and sugar. The doctor had checked her out after breakfast and recommended that she go to school with the other children the next day. Keep her occupied. Youth was a cure for most ailments.

She accepted Manon's news about her brother without comment, confident that they would find him. After all, they were grown-ups. Manon spent the next twenty minutes with her while she chose a new second hand dress from the charity box. She wanted her to look her best for her first day at school. It was yellow. With frills. Faded but whole, the material still thick and unworn. The newest, nicest thing that Thandi had ever owned. She couldn't wait to show Vusi.

***

Garrett walked up to the door at Brian's place. Even before he let himself in, he was aware of the overpowering smell of burnt toast. When he opened the front door, the air was full of rank, purple smoke and the stink of burning caught at the back of his throat. A physical presence.

Brian sat at a barstool next to the toaster, empty wine bottles strewn around him. Three. Four. Another, half finished, stood at attention on the glass kitchen surface. As Garrett watched, two pieces of charcoal toast popped out of the toaster. A pyromaniac's Jack-in-the-box. Brian removed them carefully from the machine. His movements precise. Particular. As seen in recovered stroke victims. Or the very drunk. He pushed the foot pedal of the stainless-steel kitchen bin. The lid jerked open like a hungry hippo and Brian threw the toast in. Dropped the lid. Then he inserted two more slices into the toaster and pushed the reset lever to the bottom.

'Hey, mate,' said Garrett. Quietly.

Brian's head bounced up. 'Hey, Garrett.'

'What you doing?'

'I'm feeding the bin. They like burnt toast. Love it. Their favorite food. I'm feeding it.'

Another pair of burnt offerings raised their heads to be snaffled by Brian and proffered to the ever-hungry stainless-steel mouth.

Brian picked up the bottle and downed it, spilling a good amount down his neck and chin. Red wine. The blood of Christ. Garrett lunged forward and caught the bottle as it slipped from his friend's fingers. Placed it safely on the floor.

'Wine finished. Gone. Be a good friend, Garrett. Get more.'

'I thought that you'd given up.'

'Fuck you.'

Garrett ignored the insult. Drunken friends are allowed leeway. He glanced around the kitchen. 'There is no more wine.'

'Is.'

Brian pointed carefully at a door that Garrett had assumed to be the broom closet. 'In there. Down a steps. Wine cellar. Lots. Give it to clients. Lots'

Garrett opened the door. A switch on the left. Flick. Light. A narrow corridor and a short flight of steps opened into a small but well stocked wine cellar. Garrett simply grabbed the bottle closest to him and turned to leave. But as he turned the bottle slipped. Smashed on the floor. It was the least of his problems so he grabbed another and went back into the kitchen. Handed Brian the bottle.

Brian squinted at the label. 'Good choice. 1972 Nederburg Baronne. Highly recommended with burnt bakery products.' He laughed. Loud and high. A child laughing at the dark, hoping to drive the monsters away. Brian struggled with an opener. Slipped and cut his thumb. The blood flowed rich and dark and velvet. Pooling on the thick glass kitchen surface. Garrett grabbed a dishcloth. Tore off a strip and bandaged the cut.

Brian stared at the small pool of blood. 'Six liters. That's about ten pints.'

'What you talking about, mate?'

'That's how much blood we have in us. How much life.'

Garrett nodded. 'Apparently.'

'Bullshit.'

'What?'

Brian stood up and threw the unopened bottle against the wall. It exploded. Left a shape on the wall like a melting purple chrysanthemum.

'Bullshit. I was in Burundi once. Shot a guy in the leg. Just missed his dick. He sat down and bled out. Took him about four minutes. I gave him a cigarette. He thanked me. I'd just shot the fucker. Thank you, he said. Looked like he was sitting in a pool of old engine oil. Pints of it. Fucking pints and fucking pints. Gallons.'

'What's wrong, Brian?'

Brian stared at Garrett like he was a stranger. His eyes red rimmed. Watery. 'I'm not an evil person.'

'You're a good friend, Brian.'

'Not evil. No one ever called me *Popobawa*. Never.' The dentist's eyes rolled back into his head and he slumped to the floor. Unconscious before his head hit the tiles. Garrett carried him to bed.

CHAPTER EIGHT

The next morning when Garrett awoke and went through to make himself coffee Brian had not shown his face. He could hear him in his room. Moving about. The muted sounds of someone getting ready. Buzz of shaver. Running water. But after half an hour the room grew quiet and Brian did not emerge. Garrett figured that he might want some time alone so decided to go for a run. He left the townhouse complex and turned left, running at an easy soldier's pace. A loping stride that ate up the miles. There had been times when he and his men had run like this for days on end. With full battle pack. Burundi. Burkina Faso. Angola. Sierra Leone. The names flashed through his mind like a litany of horrors.

As Garrett ran, he drew some strange looks from people. After a while it struck him that he didn't look like a jogger. More like a man on the run as opposed to a running man. This was because Garrett had no use for trainers or running shoes. His clothes were practical. Long khaki trousers. Cotton shirt in similar autumn shade. Handmade Altberg combat boots from

Yorkshire in England. No Lycra, skimpy shorts or neon colors. Simply a man. Running.

He ran through fenced off suburbs. Eight-foot-high electric fencing. A boom. Bored guard. Armed with a pump action shotgun. Mossberg or Remington. Waved him through without stopping. A man. With combat boots. Running.

After three hours the air felt like it was burning his lungs. He had forgotten that Johannesburg was 5500 feet above sea level. He turned and headed for home. When he got back in, Brian had left. He made himself breakfast. Brown bread thickly sliced. Peanut butter spread with teenage abundance. Calories. Energy.

His cell phone rang as he was getting out of the shower. Stripping water from himself using his hands. He answered. It was Manon. Her voice was tight, like she had a weight resting on her chest.

'Garrett, the children finish school early on Saturdays; they should all be back by now. But they aren't. The new girl, Thandi, she isn't here.'

'Give me eight minutes.'

***

Garrett arrived in just over seven minutes after the nun's call. Hair still wet. Shirt drying on his back.

Manon was pale. Petrus non-committal.

'Tell me.' Said Garrett.

Manon spoke. 'When the children returned for lunch Thandi wasn't with them. I phoned the school and they say that she isn't there. Gladys says that she saw Thandi being picked up by a man in a big car.'

'Call Gladys.'

Petrus went inside and returned with a small girl. Perhaps six. Wearing a dress that had once been a bright poppy-red but was now the color of boiled ham. She carried a doll with no arms. The lack of limbs caused the beast to grunt in the darkness.

Gladys looked afraid but Garrett smiled and picked her up and her fear was dispelled. 'Hello, my flower. So, tell me, did you see someone pick Thandi up?' Gladys nodded, the fingers of her right hand in her mouth. Doll in her left. 'When was this?'

'Today.'

'Okay. What time today?'

Gladys looked puzzled. 'I don't know. I do not have a watch.'

'Well, was it early or a little later?'

'It was morning teatime. We had milk and biscuits and then we went to play and then the man in the big car came to the fence and called us. I didn't go because I couldn't find my ball but Thandi went and she spoke to the man and he stayed in the car.' Gladys pointed at the sky. 'Look. A bird. And then Thandi got into the car and the man took her. Maybe she has gone to a nice big house with a swimming pool and servants and new clothes and a baby brother and a mommy and a daddy.

Maybe.' She sucked her fingers for a while. 'The bird has gone. See?'

'Gladys. What did the man look like?'

The little girl thought for a while. 'He had a big car and a baby brother for Thandi.'

Garrett sighed. 'That's nice. Anything else?'

'No. Can I go now? My dolly is hungry.' Garrett lowered her to the ground and she scampered off.

'Where is the nearest police station?'

'Close,' answered Petrus. 'Down to the end of the road. First left, over the crossroads and first left again. I will come with you.'

Garrett shook his head. 'No. You and Manon go to the school. Speak to the teachers. See if anyone else saw anything. And then search the area.'

Garrett climbed into the Jeep and drove the short distance to the police station. Parked outside in the gravel topped designated area. The station was a low-pitched bungalow. A cross between a ranch house and an army barracks. The front door armored glass. A reception area with wooden benches against the wall. Stained, blue needle-punch carpet tiles on the floor. Walls painted a mucus-green gloss up to armpit height and then matt bile-yellow above. A ceiling fan squeaked away, whining about the heat but doing nothing to dispel it. A charge desk ran the width of the room. On it, a dead spider plant.

A woman lay sprawled on the one bench. Blood dripped from her head. Sporadically, she would let out a yelp of pain followed by a long drawn-out moan. Two black police officers sat behind the counter chatting to each other in low voices. They ignored her utterly. Judging by the pool of blood on the floor she had been there for over half an hour.

Garrett walked up to the counter and rapped on it. One of the policemen stared at him for a while and then turned back to his companion. Both of them were in full combat gear. Blue overalls, matching blue flak jackets with webbing and R5 assault rifles strapped to their chest, steel butts folded. Nine-millimeter semi-autos rode on their right hips. Helmets, Ray-bans and tactical gloves lay strewn on the countertop. They were both big men. Made even bigger by their attitude. Their swagger. Garrett pointed at the bleeding woman. 'What about her?'

One of the policemen leaned over the counter. 'Shut up,' he bellowed at the woman. The other laughed. Genuine amusement. Big full-throated guffaws petering out into little hiccups of mirth.

'Maybe you could get her some water,' suggested Garrett.

The laugher shook his head.

'Do you have a vending machine around?' Asked Garrett. 'I could get her a Coke.'

The laugher pointed to the corner of the room. There was a lighter, cleaner rectangle on the carpet. A broken plug socket in the wall above it. 'There was a machine. It is gone.'

'Where?'

'Someone stole it.'

Garrett raised one eyebrow in disbelief. He gestured at their outfits. The weapons. Armor. 'Brave man to steal from you.'

There was a long pause. Both policemen stared at him. Eyes dark. Dead. And then they both laughed. The one so much so, that he literally fell onto the floor and grasped his sides.

'Brave man. Yes. Very brave.' He stood up and slapped his palm on the counter. 'Very brave,' he repeated. 'Good looking too.'

Through the door Garrett could see a pickup truck parked out back of the station, the Coca-Cola vending machine lying on its side in the load area. He wasn't quite sure why the two cops found the situation so hilarious but it was obvious that it was their truck. Hence, their vending machine.

The less amused of the two beckoned Garrett over.

'Come, funny man. How can I help you?'

Garrett told of the missing orphan, Thandi. The policeman shrugged.

'Sorry. We can do nothing. She is not missing for another forty-eight hours. Even then, these sort of ex-street children go missing all of the time. It is no big issue.'

'She is about eight years old.'

'Eight. Eighty-eight. No difference. She is not yet officially missing.'

'But there was an eye witness,' argued Garrett.

The policeman looked up from picking his nails. 'Well, that makes a difference. Where is this witness?'

'She is back at the orphanage. One of the other little girls.'

The cop shook his head. 'One street-child saying that she saw another street-child being abducted. A likely story, funny man.'

'They aren't street children. They're orphans. Anyway. She saw what she saw. A man in a big car took Thandi away.'

'Very unlikely, sir. Now we bid you goodbye, as you can see,' he gestured at the bleeding woman. 'We are very busy.'

The one policeman came around the counter and walked Garrett to the door. His manner had changed. No joviality. He propelled Garrett through the door, one hand on his shoulder.

'Go, funny man. We cannot help you. You see, you have made a mistake. Go,' he glanced around and then repeated himself. Shouting. 'Go!'

Garrett went.

***

The three of them sat in the small kitchen. The door and windows were wide open to create a through draft that drew the cigarette smoke from the room. Garrett was at a loss, as were Manon and Petrus. This was not the soldier's area of expertise. And the more Garrett ran through his options the more limited and helpless he felt. They had questioned everyone that they could at the school and then searched the surrounding area thoroughly but to no avail.

Mister Sweets had arrived with a delivery in the late afternoon as well as a gift of scented soap for Manon. He too had joined in the search, driving around the whole area and asking questions. To no avail.

And then there was the way that the police reacted. He thought that they seemed suspicious. However, when he had discussed the incident with Petrus, the guard had assured him that it all seemed pretty normal. Corrupt policemen, stealing from their own station. Bleeding victims sitting unattended in charge offices. Neither the will nor reason to even attempt to take Garrett's alleged abduction seriously. With over five hundred violent crimes a day to deal with Garrett could understand why. His problems were so far down the list as to be almost non-existent. He needed someone that he could question. He was a soldier. Soldiers fought battles. But he had no one to fight. So, he sat in the kitchen and the day turned to dusk.

***

Vusi had walked all day. He had visited three churches but only one person had talked to him. The other two had chased him away. *Voetsak*, they had shouted. Bugger off.

At the third church there was an old lady who was sitting outside, in the church garden. She had spoken to him. He had explained to her that the church ladies had stolen his sister and he was trying to find her so that he could take her home. To their home. With a door. She had told him to go to Randburg, Wolmorans street, behind the supermarket. There he would find the church mission. This is where they took the homeless people.

So Vusi walked all day. But when he got to the mission it was filled with men. Only men. Men, old before their time. Faces scoured by the outdoors, pared down to essential lines like crude paintings. Every slash of the artist's brush a story of defeat. Of hardship. And suffering.

A young girl with a ring in her nose and purple hair had told him that he should try the children's orphanage in Honeydew. So, he had started to walk there.

But the sun had gone down and he had left the road and wandered off into the veldt to try to find somewhere safe to spend the night. For this was Joburg and at night the crazies came out. Especially on a Saturday, the night after payday. Drunkards, drug addicts and worse. But Vusi knew how to hide. He found a small copse of thorny bushes and crawled into them, curled up into the fetal position and lay still, his screwdriver in his hand. Tomorrow he would wake early and find his sister. Tomorrow he would take Thandi home.

CHAPTER NINE

To most of the people in SOWETO he was known as Mister Big. Those closer to him were allowed to refer to him simply as Big or Mister B. He was fifty-three years old. Eighteen months ago, he had looked closer to thirty-three. A big man in all aspects of his life. Three hundred pounds of muscle overlaid with a good quantity of sleek fat, a sign of his wealth. His ability to afford meat meals whenever he felt like it. His suits tailored to fit his bulk. Shoes, off the shelf but the very best of quality. The Rolex was real but had not been paid for. The gold chains around his neck had.

His laugh was large and his sexual appetite was as voracious as a lion. He was a man amongst men and had fought his way up from the very bottom. Running with street gangs back in the evil days of apartheid. Fighting the white security forces and opposing black gangs with equal dedication and ferocity. And in a land where violence was an everyday occurrence, he had made a name for himself as one of the most violent. He had personally killed more men than he had fingers and toes and, as a result, he was the acknowledged king of the darker side of the southwestern township or SO-WETO. Illegal gambling, unlicensed drinking houses and protection all fell under his auspices. Armed robberies, hijacking and crimes outside of the township fell under someone else's umbrella. Someone whom even Mister Big talked of with a voice lowered in respect. A man that few had ever met or even knew that he existed. Many had met his second in command. A man whom, behind his back, people called The Dog. To his face, however, they called him Sir and bent their knees as in the serfs of old.

But that was eighteen months ago. Now Mister Big's suits hung on him like a king's robes on the court fool. Limply draped over his wasting frame. The Rolex looked outsize on a wrist as thin as an old lady's. Spare flesh drooped from his face in empty folds. Skin, once a glossy black now the color of old car tires. His chest was covered in skin infections, warts and ringworm. Sores in his mouth were so painful as to make eating an almost impossible task.

He had seen doctors. At first only white doctors as was befitting his standing in society. No traditional healing for him. He was a man of the future. A modern man unfettered by superstitions and the old ways.

But, by the time that he had eventually gone to the doctors for help he was in the final stages of the filthy disease. The slimming disease they called it. The curse of Africa. AIDS. At first, he had not believed them. It was impossible. He had always chosen healthy looking girls and, to make sure that he was never infected, he almost always showered afterwards. But the white doctors were insistent. And to make matters even worse they could provide him with no definite cure. Two years of life they had given him. As if it were theirs to give.

He had refused their drugs and called in a local traditional healer. A man of great repute. After a long consultation he had told Mister Big that there was only one cure. He had to penetrate a virgin. Preferably a young virgin. The younger the better. Seven or eight being the optimum age. This female child should be kept in Big's own bedroom and taken every day for at least a week. This would draw the poison from the dying man's body. He warned Mister Big that the cure did not always work because many times the child would die after two or three penetrations. And this would be even more evident with a man such as Big who was well known and respected for the size of his member. Big had called for his most trusted advisors and told them what he needed.

And now he sat. A dying man in a one point eight million Rand house in Diepsloot Extension. Waiting for a child to fuck.

***

Garrett woke early and broke his fast with Brian. Eggs. Scrambled. Half a dozen each. With buttered bread. The toaster no longer worked. Burnt out after Brian's drunken bread-burning. Instant coffee, three heaped spoons, three sugars and three of creamer. In the army they had called it triple-three. A guaranteed heart starter. Cigarettes. Smoked without talking. Companionship. Real. Quiet. Comfortable.

After eating Brian left with a, 'Later.'

Garrett sat for a while. Hands steepled. Thoughtful. Then he went to his room to grab an extra pack of cigarettes and the keys for the Jeep and headed to the orphanage to pick up Petrus. He had decided to interview the headmistress once again and if he was going to interrogate a local then he wanted backup in the form of someone who was more in tune with the culture than he was.

The guard was in his usual place and when Garrett beckoned, he grabbed his blanket wrapped assegai and jumped into the Jeep. As they took the short drive to the school Garrett filled him in. Petrus was skeptical.

'We already spoke to the headmistress. She knows nothing. How could she?'

'I don't know. But I don't know where else to turn.'

Petrus shook his head.

'What?'

'Not sure that I trust that logic.'

Garrett laughed as he pulled in through the school gates and parked outside what he assumed was the administration building. Petrus was correct. There was little logic involved and much more desperation than there should be.

The school was a mixture of red brick and prefabricated stand-alone classrooms. The admin block, a shoebox shaped bungalow noticeable by the fact that many of the rooms had window-mounted air conditioners. They thrummed away like a thousand beehives, dripping condensate onto the dusty earth as they did so. One of them had a loose fan that hammered rhythmically against the casing. A blacksmith at work. The noise preferable to the appalling heat.

Inside the building was simple. Utilitarian in the extreme. A concrete floor covered in cracked linoleum tiles in varying shades of blue-gray. One bright orange tile randomly placed in the middle of the corridor that ran the length of the building. A color-blind caretaker. Or a frugal one. Buzzing neon lights, only half of them working. A row of cardboard-thin doors. Six on each side of the corridor. One of the doors sported a frosted pane of cracked glass. Garrett figured that would be the reception to the principal's office. He was correct.

A large Formica covered table dominated the reception area. On top, an old computer, circa nineteen eighty something, a single phone and a manual typewriter. Behind the table sat a comely young girl. Perhaps eighteen. Perhaps older. She had her index finger plugged firmly in her nose. Delving deep. She looked up as they entered but continued to explore her nasal cavity with uninterrupted vigor. Unembarrassed. Unfettered by western ideas of propriety. After a short while she removed her finger and wiped it delicately on the side of the typewriter.

'Hello, sirs. How can I help you?' Her smile was wide and white and unaffected. Friendly.

Garrett nodded his hello. 'We would like to see the headmistress, please.'

The girl pointed at an interleading door and then got back to work on her nose. Forehead crinkled in concentration.

Garrett knocked and walked in followed by Petrus. 'Good morning, headmistress. My name is Garrett. I hope that you can help us.'

The headmistress was a blade of a woman. She wore her hair natural. Unstraightened, showing streaks of gray and cut close to her head. Large plastic rimmed glasses with massive lenses pushed down on an impressive nose. Badly applied rouge gave her the look of a fever patient, cheeks bright with red spots.

'I was hoping that you could tell us more about the disappearance of Thandi.'

The headmistress was shaking her head before Garrett had even finished his sentence. 'I know nothing about that.'

'Ma'am, any small detail could help. Did any teachers see anything? Has anyone seen the car before?'

'You are not the police. I know nothing. I am a very busy woman. You must go now. I am sorry.'

'Please?'

She pulled her diary towards her and began flipping through it, ignoring the men completely. The interview obviously over.

Garrett grimaced ruefully and turned to leave the room but Petrus shook his head.

'She knows something.'

Garrett snorted. 'Earlier you said she didn't.'

'She knows.'

'Please, ma'am. If you know anything. For the sake of the children.'

The headmistress kept her head down. Silent. Petrus tapped Garrett on the shoulder and gestured for him to move aside.

'Let me speak to her.'

Garrett nodded and walked to the back of the room, next to the door.

Petrus walked around the desk and placed his hands on the woman's shoulders. Then he leant forward and spoke quietly, his lips touching the older woman's ear. Garrett could not hear what he was saying but the effect was almost supernatural. Her face crumbled. Tears welled from knowing eyes, cutting channels of brown through a bright red landscape as they oiled down her cheeks. Fear muddied her features. A child's finger painting done in shades of terror. But she shook her head and Garrett caught her quiet reply.

'*Ungazi.* I do not know.'

Petrus whispered again. Urgently. Visible pressure on the woman's shoulders. His voice audible to Garrett only as a mixture of sibilance and glottal stops. But still she shook her head. And a low sound escaped from her tightly compressed lips. The sound of someone calling for help in a nightmare. A release of air that mixed with fear to make a mindless, meaningless noise.

Abruptly Petrus stood up and walked to the door, beckoning Garrett to follow him into the corridor.

'She knows,' said the guard. 'She knows but she is too afraid to tell me.'

Garrett raised an eyebrow in disbelief. 'Too afraid? I don't think that I've ever seen a woman so terrified. What did you say to her?'

Petrus looked slightly ashamed. 'Bad things. But we had to know. Anyway, she is more afraid of the person that did this than she is of me. And I tell, *Isosha*, that is not something that happens often.'

'So. We're back at base. What now.'

Petrus grinned. 'I think I know who it is.'

'How?'

'By not telling she has told me. Well, to be more precise, she has narrowed the field down to a handful of men. Maybe three or four who could terrify her more than me.'

'That's good news.'

Petrus shook his head. '*Eish*, not really. These are all bad men. Very bad men. If we irritate any of these men, they will surely fuck up our lives.'

'You scared?'

Petrus stopped walking, drew himself up to his full height and started haughtily at Garrett. 'I am Zulu.'

'So, not scared.'

'Well. Maybe just a little. Zulu means brave, not stupid.'

Garrett unlocked the Jeep and they climbed in.

CHAPTER TEN

Brian shook his head. 'I'm not sure about this, Garrett. I know of all of those men that Petrus is talking about. We're talking about serious players here. Hard men with even harder men working for them. Shit, man. Even the smallest fish that you're talking about has at least ten or twelve guns under him, the biggest, twenty or more. You do not want to fuck with these dudes. Especially with no proof.'

'I understand, my friend. All I'm asking is that you lend me a few of your guys for backup. I'm willing to pay top dollar for the privilege. Couple of nights.'

Brian swore under his breath. 'If these dudes link any of this shit back to me I'm well screwed. All right for you. You can just fuck off back to Scotland. I gotta live here.'

Garrett said nothing. The silence stretched out. A friend in need. A brother in arms. An unspoken appeal.

'Oh, fuck it,' said Brian. 'I'll ask for a few volunteers. Fifty dollars an hour each. And, Garrett, this is protection only. I don't want my boys getting me into a war. I can't afford it. Okay?'

Garrett nodded. 'Got you.'

'You're wasting your time, you know. These fuckers are bog standard criminals. They wouldn't be involved with child kidnapping. It's not their thing. Robbery. Protection. Hijacking. That's their sport. Not kids.'

'Thanks, mate.'

'Yeah. Fucking orphans. Ten to one they're just running away. Shit, man.' Brian shook his head in disgust. 'Waste of fucking time.'

***

A dry breeze blew fitfully across the range. Intermittent little gusts of heat that picked up dust and grass seeds and puffed them across the land, obscuring the targets like battle-smoke. Heat mirages shimmered in the air, elongating the short scrubby thorn trees. Reflections in a fun-house mirror. Late afternoon sun pushed deep shadow in front of it. Black and gold.

If one had to choose one of the most difficult circumstances under which to do some long-distance target shooting then this would be it.

A man lay prone, a Russian Dragunov SVD sniper rifle propped on a piece of wood in front of him. A 6-25x50mm Apex tactical long-range scope fitted to the rifle. In a box next to him fifty standard issue Russian 7.62 x 54mm rimmed ammunition. Out of a box of fifty there were ten rounds left. Thirty spent cases lay in a neat pile next to the box. The other ten cartridges were in the detachable magazine of the Dragunov. Two-man sized police silhouette targets were set out on the range. One at six hundred meters and another at nine hundred meters. The closer target had a ragged hole punched out in the center of the torso. Minute of angle grouping at six hundred meters. The further target was, as yet, untouched.

The Dragunov sniper rifle has developed an almost mystical name for itself over the last couple of decades. Wrongly accredited with battlefield kills at close to a mile in the Second World War it is actually only capable of seriously accurate grouping up to six hundred yards. After that it can only do accurate damage in the hands of someone who is so good as to be almost supernatural. The shooter took a deep breath, let it out, and squeezed off ten spaced shots. Every shot registered in the 5 X section in the middle of the target. A grouping of two minutes of angle at just under one thousand yards. Supernatural.

The man collected the ejected casings, added them to the existing pile, rolled out a large cloth, field stripped and cleaned the rifle on it and then put it back together. Movements familiar. Beyond second nature. After that he jogged downrange and took down the targets. Everything was placed in the locked boot of a black Audi A4. Before the man got into the car he knelt on the ground, bowed his head and prayed. Fervently. For over ten minutes. Then he climbed into the car and drove back to Johannesburg, satisfied that he had not lost his skills but not happy that he had been called on to use them once again.

***

Garrett was impressed. Brian had organized three volunteers. Men of a type that Garrett was wholly familiar with. Of average height and build, perhaps a little thicker set. Their postures solid. Confidence bordering on arrogance. Eyes bright with anticipation. Men who had seen action before. And plenty of it.

They all wore dark clothing of similar cut. Almost a uniform. Knee length coats concealed shoulder holsters containing the South African made BXP submachine gun. A nine-millimeter weapon that Garrett had used before and that he rated very highly. A two-stage trigger pull, partial for single shot and fully for automatic fire. It also came with a variety of muzzle devices including a silencer and a grenade launcher. Each man carried two 40mm fragmentation grenades for the launcher as well as a Star nine-millimeter sidearm and a six cell Maglite torch that could double as a baton if necessary.

Brian had also brought with him a tog bag of assorted hand guns for Garrett to choose from. The soldier had eschewed all of the more exotic weapons and settled for a Colt model 1911A1 with a Canadian

Para Ordnance frame. He preferred this to the bog-standard Colt due to the higher magazine capacity, fourteen rounds as opposed to seven. It was a dependable weapon and fired a big slow round that would put a dent in someone's day no matter where you hit them. He stuffed it into his belt, Mexican carry. Two extra magazines went into his jacket pockets. Also, nestling in the small of his back, the machete. Petrus carried only his assegai and didn't even try to hide his sneers when he looked at the white men's guns. Brian may not have wanted a war but he had ensured that his men were prepared for one.

Petrus had singled out three suspects and had decided that they should take on the weakest first for no other reason than they might just be lucky. Suspect number one was a man called Mister Butshingi. Like many of the local gang lords he went by a street nickname. The people called him *Inkanyamba* or The Tornado. Petrus reckoned him to be a minor crime lord with four or five guns under him. He lived in a fortified house on the outskirts of the Alexandra Township outside Sandton, Johannesburg. Petrus's plan was simple. They would park the Jeep next to The Tornado's wall. Throw a thick blanket over the electric fencing, pile over the top and storm the house. Anyone who got in the way would be subdued, preferably without the use of deadly force but no chances were to be taken.

They drove slowly down Marlborough Avenue. Garrett and Petrus in the front and the three volunteers in the back. They had waited until a couple of hours after sundown and the air was thick with smoke from the thousands of fires that burned in the nearby township. Cooking fires. Fires for warmth. Some fires simply piles of damp rubbish that forever smoldered, never quite bursting into flame but also never going out. As thick as a London pea-souper and as rank as swamp gas it provided perfect cover.

The house stood on a corner plot. Massive and tasteless. Built to impress with not even a nod given to form or line. A yellow brick monstrosity that screamed its bank balance out to the poorer, smaller dwellings around it. Garrett pulled up alongside the wall that ran next to the driveway, away from the streetlights. On closer inspection they decided not to cover the electric fence so as not to set off the alarm and instead to take the risk of shock by simply jumping over it. This they did with no mishap. Silent shadows in the murk and gloom.

Without warning two colossal Rottweilers ran at them. Coming out of the smog like demons, lips pulled back to expose inch long fangs. Saliva ropes swinging from mouths of shining red. Petrus's assegai rose and fell and the dogs lay still.

Garrett took point and they crept round the side of the house, skirting the pool and what looked like an outdoor sauna room. The back door was ajar, creamy yellow light spilling out into the fetid night. Security lax. Trusting to the high wall, electrified fence and the fact that no sane person would enter The Tornado's house without express invitation. Garrett kicked open the door and went in fast. There was a man standing at the kitchen table. In front of him the flotsam and jetsam left over from the makings of a Dagwood sandwich he had been constructing. A shoulder holster. Black semi-automatic. Garrett struck him with the butt of the 45 above the bridge of his nose and he went down with a soft expulsion of air. Another man walked in at the same time and Petrus hit him in the temple with the back of his assegai, dropping him instantly. They leap-frogged over the still bodies and went down the corridor. Garrett gestured for the three volunteers to go right as he and Petrus went left. Garrett went down the corridor towards a set of double doors that he assumed led to the sitting room. Behind him he heard the thump of other doors being kicked open followed by the wet meaty sound of fists striking flesh. He pushed open the double doors and strode in.

The sitting room was a large gaudy affair. Rococo style mirrors and gold leaf being the central theme. Casino meets Byzantine whorehouse. A massively fat man dressed in tight shorts and a vest lay back on a reclined La-Z-Boy. A barrel of Kentucky fried chicken balanced on his chest. In his greasy paw, a huge jug of beer. Football was playing on a seventy-two-inch plasma TV. AmaZulu verses Moroka Swallows. Ama-Zulu were two nil down.

Garrett pointed the Colt at the man's chest. 'Don't move.'

The fat man stared at Garrett for a few seconds. His gaze calm. Unruffled.

'I wasn't planning on doing so. It's Friday night. I never move on Friday nights.' He gestured at a chrome and glass bar that ran the length of the room, the shelves behind it packed with a vast selection of rainbow-colored liqueurs and various spirits. 'Help yourself to a drink, sit down and tell me what you want. And put that gun down or I shall have to get up and tear it off your skinny self and I really don't feel like doing that right now.'

His podgy fingers delved into the bucket of chicken and transferred a leg to his mouth. Lips shiny with chicken fat. A fine coating of the Colonel's secret herbs and spices stained the front of his tight vest. He turned his attention back to the game while he pulled meat off the bone. Teeth, surprisingly small and white. Delicate.

Garrett hesitated for a moment and then stuck the 45 in his belt and went over to the bar. He selected a bottle of Moskovskaya vodka and glanced at Petrus who nodded. He poured a tumbler full for the guard and then took a bottle of mineral water from the glass-fronted fridge for himself.

'Ice?'

'In the gold bucket.'

Garrett added a generous quantity of ice to the tumbler and proffered it to Petrus. As he did so the three volunteers came into the room. The fat man looked momentarily worried but only for a fleeting second. Garrett was impressed by his composure. A man obviously used to command but equally used to working at the coalface. A man with little fear.

'Anyone in the house apart from the guards?' Garrett asked the volunteers. They denied with a collective shaking of heads.

The fat man put the chicken bone back into the bucket, pulled out another piece and began stripping it of flesh.

'So. Why are you here?' He asked, snuffling slightly around a full mouth.

Petrus stepped forward. 'Did you or any of your men kidnap a child from the Honeydew school a couple of days ago?'

The Tornado shook his head. 'What for?'

'We don't know. For someone else. Sex. Who knows?'

The fat man chuckled. 'Sex? Please, I like my women real. Big and experienced. I can afford the best. What I want a child for? You think I got AIDS or something?'

Garrett cocked his head to one side. 'Sorry, what do you mean?'

'AIDS. Fucking a virgin, especially a young one, cures AIDS.'

'No, it doesn't.'

'Does so. It's a proven fact. I already told you.' The fat man peered into the bucket and scowled. 'You know, I think that these Kentucky people breed especially small chickens. No meat, just batter and fat. Tastes good though.' He looked up at the soldier. 'I don't know you. I know the type. Fuck me, I am the type.' Then he pointed a greasy finger at Petrus. 'You, I know. And you should know better than coming here and fucking up my Friday night. Do you really think that I am going to let you get away with this?'

Petrus shook his head. 'No.'

'So, what now?'

Petrus dropped his glass of vodka on the floor, stepped forward and held up his assegai. The blade reflected back in the floor to ceiling mirrors, dull red with the blood of the Rottweilers. 'I am going to stick this in your fat belly and let out your insides. Then who cares what you think?'

For the first time the fat man failed to mask his emotion. 'Please don't. No harm has been done. Whose blood is on the blade?'

'Dogs.'

'Not a problem. I can buy new dogs. My guards?'

'They are alive.'

The Tornado shook his head. 'Fucking useless. Look, we can come to an arrangement. How can I help?'

'Tell us who is kidnapping the orphans from the Sunlight Children's Homes.'

'I have no idea what you are talking about.'

Petrus leant forward and pushed the assegai against the fat man's bloated gut. The blade was so sharp that it split the vest and drew a trickle of blood.

'Please, no. I swear. I know nothing. If I did, I would talk. Anyway, who cares about orphans? They probably just ran away.'

Petrus glanced at Garrett. The soldier nodded. 'I believe him. Let's go.' Petrus and the volunteers left the sitting room and walked towards the front door. Garrett bent over, close to The Tornado. Eye to eye.

'If I hear that you have lied to me, I shall return. I will kill you, your family, your friends and anyone who you have ever dealt with. Do you believe me?'

And the fat man nodded. He believed.

CHAPTER ELEVEN

To go against the church is to go against God. And to go against God would negate his every reason for living. But sometimes the holy fathers demanded more than he thought that he could bear.

He stared at the rifle that lay on his bed with revulsion. In his past life he would never have believed that an inanimate object of wood and steel could elicit such depth of feeling. And when he picked it up and held it, he knew its every angle. The steel, smooth as silk, the odor of gun-oil, the sweat-stained wooden furniture and the dull satin finish of the telescopic sights. He ran his hands along the length of the barrel. Caressing. Hating. Like a weak man who returns to the same whore again and again. Cursing his own weakness. But the church had spoken. And its demands must be met. Its orders obeyed.

He vividly remembered the day that he had first obtained the rifle. Taken off the body of a FRELIMO soldier that he had killed in an ambush. He had fallen in love with the venerable old sniper rifle from the moment he had first picked it up. It seemed a part of him.

An extension of his own body. Unlike the hated stand-ard issue G3 rifle with its excessive recoil and tendency to jam during a fire fight due to its shoddy workman-ship and the resultant inability to be able to field strip it and clean it correctly. Two weeks later a South Afri-can Special Forces advisor had gifted him with a new Schmidt & Bender telescopic sight to replace the twenty-year-old Russian PSO1. He had practiced with the Dragunov at every available moment and, after a short while, it became apparent to all that he was an unusually gifted marksman, able to achieve hits at dis-tances beyond even the inflated claims of the weapon's manufacturer.

And then that day had come. His squad commander had laid an ambush on the main road between Dondo and the Gorongosa national park. Intel had reported that there would be three truckloads of weapons and ammunition passing their position at around four that afternoon. The ambush was in the form of an American made M19 anti vehicle mine that was buried under the road by burrowing in under the tar surface. Totally un-detectable. This would take out the first truck, blocking the road so that the eight RENAMO guerrillas could attack and subdue the remaining two trucks and capture the weapons. The commander had placed him on a hill-ock some six hundred meters out from the ambush point so that he could provide covering fire and act as a stopgap.

The first truck had detonated the mine as per plan but then, as often happens in combat situations, the rest of the plan had gone to shit. The first truck was full of weapons, as they had thought, however, the second and third trucks were both carrying FRELIMO government troops. Fresh from R&R and keen as hell. Twenty-four of them. The cadre of eight RENAMO guerrillas broke and ran when faced with such overwhelming odds.

But the shooter on the hill with the Russian rifle had remained calm. Tracking from left to right he dropped seven soldiers with his first ten rounds. The next magazine of ten ended nine more lives. With the odds now being equal the guerrillas reformed and fought back, killing the rest of the government soldiers and taking no casualties. The operation was a resounding success due mainly to the shooter on the hill. A young boy who had just celebrated his fifteenth birthday. And from that day on the boy, who had just become a man, was no longer known as Afonso Diogo Mandoluto. Instead, he became known to all as 'The Long Gun'.

And over the next five years The Long Gun was responsible for the cessation of almost one hundred lives. He became a man admired and feared in equal measure. He also became a man haunted by the souls of the departed. Every night they would stand in silent queues. Waiting patiently in the shadowy recesses of his consciousness. Their horrific injuries never healing. A constant reminder of the savage death that he had delivered. Every night he tried to hide from them. To avoid their accusing looks. Their silent accusations. But wherever he turned they were there, close enough to touch. No longer separated by the distance that allows a sniper to remain aloof and unattached. Faces blurred as if seen through telescopic sights. Hands grasping. Imploring. Beseeching.

And the next day he would take his long gun and go forth and add to their number.

So, when South Africa had signed the Inkomati accord and withdrawn all overt support for RENAMO he had used it as an excuse to leave the cause and travel to the land of his father. Portugal. It was in this gentle country that he had found The Lord. He entered the *Seminario dos Passionistas* in Barroselas, Northern Portugal and, from his first week there, was marked as a young man to watch.

His dedication to both God and the church was nothing short of fanatical. He prayed and preached with a fervor that was driven by the red-hot blade of his own guilt. His love for the teaching of the bible was a tangible thing. He drove himself mercilessly and, at the end of his first three years after he was ordained a Deacon he was sent to Rome to study at the foot of the Holy Father Pope John Paul II. Within two years he had obtained a doctorate in sacred theology. By the age of thirty-eight he had become one of the youngest bishops in Europe. It was then that he had asked to come back to Africa. A full circle.

And now he sat in a room with 4.3 kilograms of steel and wood and asked himself. If I hated it so much then why did I go to such lengths to keep it? Why did I not throw it into the ocean? He may well have asked why he did not simply cut off his own arms. But he knew that the Lord worked in mysterious ways and his was not to question them. So, he bowed his head and prayed. He prayed for the people. He prayed for the church. And he prayed for himself. For His Excellency, bishop Afonso Diogo Mandoluto…The Long Gun.

***

When they arrived back from the Tornado's house Brian had insisted on taking Garrett and Petrus out to dinner. Garrett had driven, under instruction, to a restaurant in Muldersdrift. A magnificent thatched and vaulted pastiche to colonial Africa. The center of the restaurant boasted a massive BBQ pit from which, roasted cuts of meat from seemingly every animal under the sun were served up. Besides beef, lamb and pork there were large spears spitted through sizzling slabs of warthog, giraffe, ostrich, crocodile, kudu and springbok. Most of the patrons were drinking *dawa*, a blend of white spirits, honey and slices of lime. Brian ordered a brace for Petrus and he and Garrett settled for Perrier.

The service was excellent and the atmosphere festive, but despite the mountains of food that kept arriving at the table, Brian merely picked at his food. His gaiety forced. Brittle. The conversation restricted to inconsequentialities. The weather. Politics. Formula one racing. Garrett ate his full and Petrus worked through piles of bleeding beef with a great show of lip smacking and sighs of pleasure. He eschewed the more exotic game with a sneer of distaste. If beef were available, he told Garrett, then a Zulu would not bother eating anything else. Over the course of the meal, he must have put away over four kilograms of steak. No salad, no potato, no vegetables. Simply huge quantities of rare roasted flesh.

It had been a long, long while since Garrett had eaten merely for pleasure. For the taste and texture of food as opposed to merely refueling his body. The simple pleasure of eating more than you needed because you were purposefully indulging yourself. He had lived a monastic lifestyle, a lifestyle of abstinence for so long that he had forgotten what it was to indulge himself. But he took great pleasure in watching his new friend eat with such passion. Unbridled joy in such a simple act. And for a fleeting few seconds Garrett felt a flash of jealousy before it was washed away by a wave of common sense.

After Petrus had eaten his fill, they ordered coffee and dessert.

'So,' said Brian. 'I take it tonight was a bust?'

Garrett shrugged. 'Maybe not. The fat dude said a strange thing. He said that he didn't have AIDS so why would he need a young girl.'

The dentist took a sip of his coffee and grimaced.

'Fucking stupid bastards think that you can cleanse yourself by raping a young child. In fact, a recent study showed that almost twenty percent reckoned that sex with a twelve-year-old wasn't even rape, just sex. You know, there are twenty thousand reported rapes a year in this country. Twenty fucking thousand. And that's just reported, the actual figure is probably two or three times that. Man, it's like everyone here is either coming from or going to some sort of sexual encounter.'

Garrett looked at Petrus for confirmation or denial. The Zulu said nothing as he ladled sugar into his coffee, eventually stopping when his spoon could stand upright. Then he sipped some of the syrupy liquid with evident pleasure.

'It's more complicated than that,' he said. 'Yes, it is quite acceptable in the more rural areas for a twenty-year-old man to have sex with a twelve-year-old girl. Just because western culture deems it rape does not necessarily mean that rape has occurred. In fact, a young girl of twelve or thirteen can gain a lot of status by dating a twenty year old plus guy. Also, AIDS has broken the normal family structure. Families are now headed by young teenagers who are in charge of toddlers. The parents are dead. If a girl wants to trade her *ikheke* for security then why stop her? Who would suffer? Not the liberal know-nothing who tries to assert their culture on ours. No, the children would suffer. Rape is only rape if you think that it is.'

Garrett raised an eyebrow, not wholly comfortable with Petrus' sweeping statement, however, he refrained from comment. 'And the curing AIDS thing?'

Petrus nodded. 'Many people believe this. I don't know why, not once have I ever heard of it working.'

'So, if a man with AIDS takes a young girl, is that rape?'

Petrus shook his head. 'No. That is murder.'

'Could people be kidnapping the children to sell as cures for AIDS?'

'Maybe,' conceded Petrus. 'But two that went missing were boys.'

'Wait,' Brian butted in. 'This is a good theory. The majority were girls. It could be simply that the boys ran away. The girls were kidnapped. Think about it, it makes sense. It's far more likely for a boy to run away than a girl. Fuck me, I ran away all the time. Can't actually remember a girl that did the same.'

'You could be right,' said Garrett. For the first time he felt like progress was being made.

Later, they dropped Petrus at the orphanage. He stayed in a small lean-to at the back of the building. One room, outside toilet with a shower over it so that you had to sit on the crapper to wash. Cold water only. Concrete floor, a single rug woven from plastic shopping bags. In the corner a bucket for dishes. A paraffin

Primus stove for cooking. Traditional *icansi* or sleeping mat as well as an *isigqiki* or wooden headrest that doubled as a low stool. Utilitarian in the extreme. Not dissimilar to Garrett's croft in Scotland.

When they got back to Brian's place the dentist left almost immediately, leaving Garrett alone with his thoughts and the music of Louis Moreau Gottschalk. Afro-Caribbean influenced compositions blending well with the surrounding night. He made himself a triple-three coffee and lay back on the sofa. The syncopated melodies flew around the room like a tropical bird released from a cage. Bright and colorful. Its flight path varying and unexpected.

He wondered, not for the first time, why he continued to harbor such intense feelings for Manon. *Sister* Manon. People say that one cannot control love but that wasn't true. Love was simply an emotion. And emotion can be controlled. But only if one had the will. Perhaps she was his Flagrum. A scourge for his own self-flagellation. A hair-shirt of the mind.

He remembered his first stirrings ever of pubescent love. A matron's assistant at his boarding school. The place was a bastion to Spartan living. Early morning runs and ice-cold showers. A school designed to bring up boys healthy, strong and ready for service. Miss Carmichael. Janice. Hair as blonde as cobwebs. A figure both full and lithe as only youth can provide. Lips a slash of scarlet and eyes a smoky gray. She wore no perfume and, sometimes when she was close, you could smell her. Cheap soap and female musk. Heady. Exhilarating.

And if you climbed out of the dormitory window, scaled the wall and followed a suicidal route along the crumbling battlements, there was spot that overlooked her bedroom window. If you were patient, still, you could watch her undress. She would always leave her bra on until last. Blouse first to go. Then skirt, stockings. Panties to reveal a shockingly dark wealth of pubic hair, lush and springy. Secret. And then her bra. Breasts full and heavy. Nipples erect in the under heated room. Sometimes she would run her hands over her nipples and her lips would part. Her tongue wet and pink. But never more than that. Garrett was the only one who ever saw her. Apart from him the climb was too dangerous for even the most testosterone driven teenager. But Garrett had welcomed the danger. Accepted it as a price to pay for the privilege of seeing Janice naked.

Many years later he had seen her in London. A chance meeting. They had a drink together. She was older than her years. Sallow. Bitter. A chain smoker with a voice like sharkskin. She told him that she had known that he used to watch her. Perv at her, she had said. He wasn't embarrassed. He was sad. Sad that she didn't understand. Sad that his princess of the night had turned into a charlady. She had groped at him under the table. Clumsy fingers grasping at his cock. He paid for the drinks and left. He could still hear her laughter in the street.

Was his love for Manon merely another way of climbing the battlements? Changing reality? If she ever accepted him would the end be the same? Clumsy fingers and ignorant laughter? The music filled the night with magnificent symphony. And Garrett drifted slowly off to sleep, not leaving the sofa.

CHAPTER TWELVE

Vusi stood under the tree across the road. Shadow and cover. Hidden from the tall imperious Zulu man who stood guard in front of the orphanage. This might be the place. He had seen children leave early in the morning, they all held hands and walked together. He had followed them. They had gone to a church down the road. He had waited. One hour. Then he followed them back. Thandi was not with them but they may know where she was. He was going to have to be brave.

The small boy-man put his shoulders back and crossed the street, walking straight up to the guard. He stood as tall as possible and addressed him as an equal. He hoped that the guard could not see that his leg was shaking so much that he was struggling to stand upright.

'*Sawubona, ubaba.*' Vusi greeted Petrus.

'*Yebo. Sawubona, umfana*, little boy.'

Vusi bridled at the form of address. 'I am not a child. I am a man.'

Petrus bowed. Not a trace of amusement on his face. '*Ngiyaxolisa, umufo*. My apologies, fellow. How can I help you?'

'The church ladies stole my sister. I am here to get her back.'

'I see,' said Petrus. 'And why do you think that she is here?'

Vusi said nothing. It was taking all of his self-control to simply stand where he was. He was exhausted and scared and very, very hungry. He had lost the only member of his family that was still alive and the tall man in front of him filled him with anxiety. Then, to his shame, he felt his eyes well up and hot tears rolled down his cheeks. 'Her name is Thandi.'

Petrus went down on one knee and put his arms around the little boy. And, for the first time since his mother had died, Vusi cried.

CHAPTER THIRTEEN

Thandi was missing her brother. She had no one to play with. But she did have her own bedroom with a chair and its very own bathroom. And, a never hereto experienced item, a TV set. Never before had she been exposed to such luxury. One of the men had shown her how to use the TV but she had not really understood and was too polite to ask him to repeat himself. So, she watched the channel that he had left it on. Reruns of classic black and white movies. The lack of color puzzled her. Not because she was comparing it to color television. She could not, as she had never seen one. She was comparing it to real life. Thandi wondered where this colorless world existed. It must be sad, she thought to herself. Never to see the purple of a Jacaranda, the silver of an old person's hair, the yellow of her favorite dress. Although she did admit to herself that the men were very handsome and the girls, with their black lips and white faces and gray dresses, very beautiful.

Earlier that day an old man had unlocked her door and stared at her for a long time. She had greeted him as *Baba*, father, and she had stood up in his presence to show her respect because he was so very old. And sick. But he had said nothing. Simply stared at her as his breath rasped painfully in and out. Someone cutting wood with a saw. She felt sorry for the old man. But mainly she wanted to go back to sister Manon, and her friends and…family? But there was no one to tell.

So, she lay on the bed and watched. The beautiful colorless lady on the TV was unhappy because her house was burning down. And the man with the moustache didn't give a damn. It was all so sad.

And then the door opened again and the old man came into the room. He closed it behind him.

On the television the flames grew higher.

***

The next night. The same three volunteers. A similar plan. Go in hard. Go in fast. Find the truth. Avoid a war. This time they were going to a house in Eldorado Park on the Southeast border or SOWETO. An aspiring middle-class area that seemed at odds with the type of character that their target was reputed to be. He was a Venda called Zwanga Madima, street name, Taxi Man. So called because he owned a fleet of taxis as well as controlling the routes that other drivers used. Tolls to use those routes were paid to him. If not, vehicles were burnt, kneecaps smashed. Families visited. In London, cab drivers had the knowledge; here they had the Taxi

Man. Both were as essential to success, the only major difference between the two being life and death.

The Taxi Man's house stood alone, a new-build surrounded on three sides by empty plots. Garrett parked the Jeep a street away and they approached on foot. Walking casually, weapons under coats. When they were close to the house they ducked into the shadows and waited while Petrus did a recce. After four minutes he came back and briefed them.

'Ten-foot wall all around. At the back they haven't finished connecting the electric fence. Security lights but there's a big bougainvillea that makes shadows. Should be easy to get over without being seen.'

Garrett gave a thumb up. 'Lead the way.'

***

The range finder showed five hundred and seven meters. The X27 clip-on thermal scope was powerful enough to pick up individual features even at over half a kilometer in full darkness. The Gunworks universal suppressor ensured that no one would hear the gunshot. The Long Gun lay prone on the flat roof of a partly built low-level apartment block. It provided a clear view of The Taxi Man's house. He had followed Garrett to the residence and then driven back to his vantage point.

He watched the five men climb over the wall and disappear from sight until they were into the garden and visible once again. He scanned ahead and saw no guards. Like The Tornado before, security was relatively lax, relying on the fact that no one would dare attack a crime boss unless they were certifiable. But then, on the edge of his vision, he saw a man. Standing in the shadows. Dark clothing. Pistol grip shotgun in his hand. Mandoluto tracked back and framed Garrett's face in his sights. The soldier had taken point and was going to walk straight into him. The Long Gun concentrated on his target. Hand steady. Breathing slow. He tightened his finger. The shot was perfect, but he could not take it. He could not pull the trigger. Faces leered out of the dark. Pushing into his field of vision. Long dead faces. Blood. Bone. Gristle. He tried again but he could not get his trigger finger to obey. And then it was too late.

***

Garrett stepped around the corner and walked into a man holding a shotgun. Both of the men reacted instantly. The guard whipped up the shotgun, flicking the safety off as he did so. Garrett grabbed the man behind his neck, arched his back and dragged him into a vicious head butt. The guard slumped to floor without a sound.

'Shit. That was close.' Garrett ran his fingers through his hair with a shaking hand. 'Fuck me.'

Petrus grasped his shoulder and squeezed. 'Well done. I'll take point.'

One of the volunteers chuckled. No humor. Merely reaction. They walked around the side of the house towards the back door. Single file. Five little Indians. No dogs. Unusual. Petrus stopped.

'What?'

He pointed at a metal stanchion sticking out of the ground. Perhaps two foot high. A small round mirror attached to its side. He had just walked past it. 'What's that?'

'Fuck it,' Garrett swore. 'Infrared. We've been rumbled.'

As he spoke a concussion rent the air. He felt the whistle of shot as it shrieked past his head. Heard the sound as it struck the volunteer behind him. An axe hitting wet wood. A grunt as he went down. Petrus ducked, throwing himself to the ground. Garrett drew and fired at the source of the shot, pulling the trigger of the Colt as fast as he could. Thirteen rounds hammered off in a little over two seconds. Behind him he heard the growling purr of one of the volunteers BXP submachine guns as he burnt off thirty-two rounds at a rate of seventeen rounds per second. Someone was firing back at them. Shotguns. Dull booms as opposed to high velocity cracks. Massive muzzle flashes lit up the darkness. Eject empty magazine. Reload. Move forward. Target. Black shape against white wall. Three shots and man down. BXP growling again knocking two more shapes off their feet. Petrus rising from the ground. Flash of steel. Blood spraying high. Silence.

Petrus hit the back door hard, springing it open. Garrett followed him in. Some sort of utility room. Dog bowls. Big ones. Four of them. Shit. Boerbulls. Massive hounds, heads the size of two footballs. Barking and biting. Growling. The BXP snarled back at them, scattering blood and fur and chips of bone. Garrett vaulted the dead bodies and found himself in a large kitchen. Two men. One in dark clothing the other in a vibrant orange tracksuit. Nike trainers. A chest full of thick gold chain. Heavy medallions. Both men had their hands up. One volunteer had followed Garrett and Petrus into the house. The other had stayed outside to care for his compatriot.

Garrett trained his gun on the two men. 'Where are the children?' His question was greeted with a look of total non-comprehension.

The man in the orange tracksuit turned to Petrus. 'What the fuck is the white man talking about?'

'The children. The ones that have been abducted from the Sunlight Children's Homes. What do you know about them?'

The man shook his head. Denial. But there was hesitation. Slight but discernable. Garrett rammed the barrel of the 45 against the man's forehead. Hard. Splitting the skin.

'Tell us or die.'

The man squinted at the barrel but said nothing. Garrett flicked the pistol to one side and pulled the trigger. The blast nudged the man's head to one side. The lead slug ripped his ear off.

'Talk or die. Last chance.'

He stared back at Garrett. Eyes small and red. A bull terrier. Maybe a komodo dragon.

'Fuck you, whitey.'

Garrett shot him in the center of his forehead and then turned the gun on the man next to him. On the floor the body in bright orange twitched and shivered. A bizarre break dance. Hit that perfect beat, man.

'Anything to tell us?' Asked Garrett.

The man nodded. 'Mister Big. Just rumor. One of his guys took a little girl from somewhere. That's all. Don't shoot me.'

Garrett glanced at Petrus who nodded. 'Makes sense,' he said. 'He was the next on the list. Shit. I was hoping that it wouldn't be him.'

'We'll hit him tomorrow. What do we do with this guy?'

Petrus swung his assegai like a sword, slicing through the man's neck. He dropped to the floor, his face a mask of surprise. Petrus watched him until his life's blood bubbled away and he collapsed in a heap. Small and ragged in death. Garrett raised an eyebrow.

Petrus shrugged. 'Had to. He would have told Mister Big for sure. Then he would be waiting for us and we would be well and truly fucked.' Then he snorted. A mirthless grunt of a laugh. 'We're fucked anyway. Nobody attacks Mister Big and lives.'

'There's always a first time for everything.'

'Why?'

'I don't know. It's just what everyone says.'

The Zulu wiped his blade on the fallen man's shirt. 'Well, everyone is wrong. Let's go.'

They left through the front gates. The volunteer who had been shot limping along with them. Two buckshot pellets in his left leg. Lucky. Smiling.

And just over half a kilometer away a man lay on the roof of a half-finished building and dry scrubbed his face in shame and prayed.

CHAPTER FOURTEEN

Brian was literally frothing at the mouth. Small flecks of foam bubbled at the corners of his lips.

'Jesus fucking wept. For fucks sake, Garrett. Don't start a war, I said. Protection only, I said. I specifically did not say, kill everyone in the entire fucking neighborhood and get my boys shot to shit at the same time. I know, because I would have remembered saying it. I fucking would have remembered saying, kill fucking everyone and make sure that my boys get shot as well. I would have fucking remembered.'

'Look, I'm sorry, mate. But it's not all that bad. It was only a flesh wound...'

'He was shot fucking twice. Getting shot twice is not a flesh wound, it is getting the fucking shit shot out of you.'

'It won't happen again.'

'Fucking sure it won't happen again, my china-plate. Because it ends here. No more using my boys. Now you want to go up against Mister Big? Garrett, listen to me, Mister Big shits bigger than us. Mister Big is bad. He is untouchable. It's over. Tell sister Manon that it's finished. Seriously, Garrett, this will get you killed. These are bad fucking men; you have no idea what will happen to you.'

Garrett stared at his ex-sergeant for a while. No one talked. Heavy breathing. Visible anger from Brian.

And then Garrett said.

'I am bad men, Brian. I am what happens to other people. They do not happen to me,' he leaned forward, green eyes unhooded. The abyss looking back at you. 'I happen to other people.'

And Brian took a step back. *Visions of darkness. Slashing machetes. Men screaming like animals. Less than animals. Less than human. Popobawa.*

'Sorry, mate. Relax, okay? We'll talk later, relax.'

And the beast crawled back into its cave.

***

Mandoluto pulled his cincture tight. The knots cut into the flesh of his torso. A reminder of his weakness. A punishment for his failure to do his duty. He dressed in his usual dark gray tailored suit, the cut emphasizing his broad shoulders, narrow hips. Prowling, feline athleticism.

It was five thirty in the morning and, as he did every morning, he had a breakfast meeting with his most reverend imminence cardinal Voysie. It was here that he would tell him of his failure.

He sat down opposite the cardinal. Before him, a bowl of Pronutro; a South African high-energy cereal that tasted like a blend of Soya and sawdust, no sugar, a bowl of stewed fruit, black coffee, water. The cardinal was already seated. His imminence said a short grace and they ate. Food before talk. Always. When they were finished a servant cleared the table and brought a fresh cafetiere of coffee.

Mandoluto took a deep breath. 'I have failed. I could not pull the trigger.'

The cardinal said nothing for a while. Stared intently at the younger man opposite him. Eventually.

'Yes, my son. You have failed. You have failed me. You have failed yourself. You have failed your church. And you have failed your God.'

Mandoluto's eyes brimmed with scalding hot tears of shame. 'Help me, your eminence.'

'Where will he be tonight?'

'If our information is correct, he will be attempting to question mister Big. A crime boss in charge of the greater part of SOWETO's crime.'

The cardinal nodded. 'I know of him. He has contributed quite generously of late. I haven't actually met him. Not sure why the sudden generosity to the church.'

'Perhaps he has found the Lord.'

The cardinal smiled softly. 'Perhaps, my son. More likely that he has contracted some form of dread disease and seeks repentance. Covering all of his bases, as our American friends would say. It would be a pity to lose such a benefactor, would it not?'

Mandoluto stood from his chair, walked around the table and went down on his left knee.

'Bless me, your eminence. Help me to be strong.'

'May God grant you strength and courage. Bless you, my son.'

Mandoluto kissed the cardinal's rings and left the room.

The cardinal picked up the phone.

***

'I will go alone,' said Garrett as he racked back the slide on the 45. Then he ejected the magazine, thumbed in another round and slapped it back. One up the spout. Cocked and locked. Ready to rock and roll.

'They'll kill you.'

Garrett looked at Petrus. The paraffin lamp in the guard's one room living quarters cast shadow from the ground up. Every face a child's horror movie.

Manon sat on the edge of the bed. Pale. Quiet. Pools of darkness hid her eyes.

'Don't go, Garrett.'

'I have to.'

'Why?'

Garrett smiled. Grim. Sardonic. 'If not me, then who?'

'Okay,' said Petrus. 'I'll go with you.'

Garrett raised an eyebrow. 'Any particular reason?'

'Yes, your eloquence overcame me. Anyway, who said that you had the monopoly on stupid?'

The soldier laughed and then his face grew serious. He leant forward and grasped the Zulu's shoulder.

'Thank you, my friend.'

They left the room in silence. Garrett did not belittle Petrus's offer by questioning it. He was a man. He could make his own decisions.

As they drove towards SOWETO Garrett took stock of their situation; he had a 45 with thirty rounds of ammunition and a machete. Petrus had his assegai. When Garrett had suggested that he bring his rusty shotgun the Zulu had refused. Better to die with steel in your hand than with plastic, he had claimed. Garrett thought it better not to die at all. But then here he was. He had asked Brian for more weapons but he had refused. Adamant. As a result, they had not even bothered to formulate a plan. They would arrive, try to sneak in, question mister Big and then take it from there. God protects fools and angels. Garrett hoped so.

***

Mister Big tried not to cough. It was too painful. Never before had he experienced such agony. He felt like his body had been scourged and rolled in salt. His skin hung in loose folds on his body. A human Shar-pei. His tongue and mouth were full of deep lesions, his head a ball of pain. His breath came in short shallow gulps and his diarrhea was so chronic that he had started to inadvertently soil himself. And now he had just learnt that a man, a foreign white man, was coming to his house to punish him for taking an orphan. A homeless, parentless, meaningless child. The irony was delicious. Every day that he lived had become a curse. But still, he was not the sort of man that would let a threat like this go unopposed. He called Washington, his second in charge, his command a wheezing bark. And he told him. When the man comes tonight, let him get over the wall and then finish him. Outside, in the garden. Not in my house. Pull the fuses for the security lights on the left, back corner of the plot. He will come over there. Take eight men and ambush him in the hedges before the swimming pool. There may be one or maybe two of them but still, do not underestimate them. I have been told that these are very dangerous men. Washington nodded his acceptance of the order and went to arm his men.

The clock ticked, slicing little moments of pain off mister Big's life.

***

The Long Gun lay flat on the top of the water tower that overlooked mister Big's mansion. A full magazine in the Dragunov, the same sight set-up as the night before. The target environment lay just over six hundred meters away. The sun had gone down and Mandoluto sipped on a plastic bottle of mineral water. He emptied his mind of trepidation and filled it instead with a vision of the stained-glass windows of his church, lit up by the morning sun. The glory of the Lord in full Technicolor. He would not fail.

***

The security lights mounted on the back corner of the property were not working, leaving the area in deep shadow. Garrett had parked the Jeep up against the wall and they had climbed over the electric fence by simply jumping from the roof of the vehicle. There had been a light rain just before the sun had gone down and now that it had dried out the air was alive with mating flying ants. Half an inch long with wings so flimsy that they fell off as soon as they brushed against anything and the insect was left to crawl around for a couple of hours, mating frantically until it died. Garrett had seen swarms of them before but never as thick as this. He brushed a handful from his face. Born, eat, fly, fuck, die. Garrett thought that it sounded like a pretty fulfilling life. Turning his thoughts back to the moment, he crept slowly across the garden, heading towards the house.

***

Mandoluto focused on Garrett, his features hazed slightly by the inordinate number of flying ants in the air. He had already compensated for bullet drop over the distance and there was no wind to speak of. Then he raised his barrel up and scanned ahead. He saw them. Counted. Eight. Four on each side of the path that the two intruders were taking. All carrying sidearms. It was time.

Our father …his finger tightened, taking up the slack. *Who art in heaven*…the rifle recoiled and the brass case flew in a glittering arc into the night.

***

Garrett had spent over fifteen years of his life fighting in various armies. He had been wounded a number of times, once close to death. And, over time, he had developed a sense that had kept him alive when most others around him had passed on. It was not as much as a sixth sense. Nothing as overt as that. It was merely the tiniest, faintest feeling. Some small niggle in your subconscious that said; something is wrong. And when you feel it, you have to react instantly.

He threw himself to the ground, dragging Petrus down at the same time. As he did so the air above them was torn apart with the whip and crackle of small arms fire. A group of men came charging out of the bushes at them, pistols blazing away like an old cowboy movie. And then the lead man was picked off his feet and thrown back in a mist of blood, like a giant had flicked him in the chest. In rapid succession the other ambushers were hammered to the ground. Marionettes, strings being cut. No accompanying sound of gunfire. Simply the wet sound of lead punching through flesh. Blood arcing blackly through the night air. Twitching corpses. Flying ants picking greedily at pools of viscous red warmth.

***

Mandoluto collected up the spent cartridges and put them into his pocket. Then he wrapped the rifle in a towel and placed into an Adidas holdall. That late afternoon, before he had left, the Cardinal had come to him and said, "'And all thy children shall be taught of the Lord; and great shall be the peace of thy children. In Righteousness shalt thou be established: thou shalt be far from oppression; for thou shalt not fear: and from terror; for it shall not come near thee. Isaiah 54:13,14."

My son, if little children cannot be saved, then how can any of us expect to be? For too long has the Catholic Church turned its back on the children. No longer. Go forth, my son, and do God's work. Protect the soldier at all costs for he is a servant of the Lord even if he does not know it.'

So, The Long Gun had done the Lord's work. And tonight, and every other night, in the twilight of his dreams, there would be eight more pleading souls crying out to him.

***

Garrett and Petrus lay prone, faces pushed into the lawn.

Eventually Petrus spoke. 'What the fuck was that?'

'I have no idea. Someone took out the uglies with a silenced sniper rifle of some sort.'

'Is it safe to move?'

'Definitely,' replied Garrett. 'I've never seen shooting like that before. Incredible. If the shooter wanted us dead, we'd be ant food by now. Looks like mister Big has got more on his plate than just us. Come on. Let's move.'

The two of them sprinted for the back door. It was unlocked so they both barreled in, Garrett with 45 held ready. The kitchen was empty. The soldier crept through into the hall. Shadow. Threw himself to the floor. The concussion of a shotgun. Shockingly loud in the confined space. A gout of flame rent the air above him. He returned fire. Double tap. The shadow went down. He waited a while, ears ringing. Eyes smarting with the afterimage of orange flame. Body tense. He gestured to Petrus to take point.

The Zulu ghosted past Garrett; assegai held at high port. The house was dark. Silent but for the faint noise of a television set coming from one of the upstairs rooms. Music and voices. The rain in Spain. Audrey Hepburn. My Fair Lady.

The end of the corridor opened out into a huge open-plan area. Clusters of sofas were placed around the room forming smaller conversation-friendly areas. A water feature trickled soundlessly down the one wall into a pool of colored water. In the far corner of the room was a double bed, fully made up with a mountain of pillows piled against the headboard. On the edge of the bed sat a man, his head low. Hands clasped between his knees. His breath a harsh grinding drone. Gray face like melted rubber. Slack and lifeless. Apart from him the room was empty.

He looked up at the two intruders. 'So, you have come for the child.'

Garrett nodded. 'We have come for all of the children.'

The sick man shook his head. 'There is only one. She is upstairs. She is unharmed. I did not…could not…' he coughed. Deep wracking and painful.

'Where are the others?' Asked Petrus.

'We only took one. Why would I take any more?'

'To sell. To others with the disease.'

'I would not trade in children.'

'But you took this one.'

'Yes, but as I said, she is unharmed. Go and check, third door on the left at the top of the stairs. The door is locked, just turn the little knob on the handle to open.'

Garrett took the stairs four at a time and hurried to the door, unlocking it and rushing into the room. Thandi was lying on the double bed. On her stomach, feet in the air, watching a small portable television. She looked up at Garrett.

'Hello.'

'Hello, Thandi.'

'Have you come to take me home?'

Garrett nodded.

'I miss my brother. Can we take the television?'

Garrett nodded, 'Don't see why not.'

He unplugged the unit and put it under his arm, the 45 still held in his right hand. They walked back down the steps and into the lounge area. Petrus and mister Big silently watched them descend.

'This guy knows nothing about the other kidnappings,' said Petrus. 'He simply needed a virgin child and figured to take an orphan so no one was that bothered.'

Mister Big laughed. The sound wet and unpleasant. 'Just my luck, hey. I picked one of your orphans. So, what now?'

Thandi waved at mister Big. 'Bye-bye, *Baba*, father. I go home now. Thank you for the TV.'

Big waved back. 'Goodbye little one.'

Garrett gestured to Petrus with his head. 'Come on. Let's blow, leave the old guy, he's been punished enough already.'

They walked towards the front door. As Garrett opened it mister Big croaked out.

'Wait,' he held his hand out to Petrus. Beseeching. '*Madota, minasiza.* Help me. Please.'

Petrus glanced at Garrett who nodded. 'I'll be outside.'

The Zulu walked over to the sick man. 'How can I help, *madala*?'

'I am dying. The pain is bad, but the feeling of weakness is worse. You have taken my servants; I have no friends, no family. Disease is my only companion.' He sat up straighter and looked Petrus in the eye.

'I used to be a man of power. Now, I shit my pants like a baby.'

'You want me to end it?'

'Please. A man's death.' He unbuttoned his shirt to expose his chest. 'Send me to my ancestors.'

Petrus nodded and knelt before the dying man in respect. '*Bayete, baba*. I salute you, father.'

And he stood up and lunged forward in one fluid movement. The scalpel-sharp steel punched through Big's chest and exited between his shoulder blades. Petrus twisted hard and pulled the spear back. The old man collapsed forward onto the floor. A slight smile on his face.

Petrus wiped his blade on the bedspread and left the house, leaving the door open behind him.

Dubula watched his master as he spoke on the phone. The master was angry. In fact, Dubula could not remember when he had seen his master so angry before. He knew because the self-control that he was showing was clear to anyone who was as close to him as the bodyguard was. His eyes were red with rage. The hand not holding the phone was clenched tight. But the ultimate give away was the smile. When the boss smiled with his mouth only then you knew that things were going to shit. A death's head grimace sketched across a mask of fury.

Dubula could not hear what the boss was saying; he stood at the other side of the room and spoke in a controlled, quiet voice. Another sign of his anger. At the end of the call, he replaced the receiver and stared at it for a while. Then, suddenly, he picked it up again, threw it against the wall, tilted his head back and bellowed. A formless animal roar. Dubula did not experience fear, but the sound of the master in full fury created…apprehension.

The master beckoned to Dubula to come closer. And when he was close enough, he started to talk. His voice barely above a whisper. A parody of reasonableness.

'My son.'

'*Yebo, Ubawao.*'

'My son, do you remember that man, the one that you called *Umptyholi*, a beast in a man's flesh.'

'Yes, father. I remember.'

'Well, that man, that you were meant to take care of and failed to do so, that man…is fucking up my business! Him and his pet Zulu have killed two of my associates. Good men. Men who pay us a fortune every month. Gone.' The master snapped his fingers. 'Dead.' He poked Dubula in the chest. 'That is your fault. And not only that, while he is poking his pink nose around in our affairs, we cannot risk getting any more stock from the orphanages. We are losing millions and all because you are too fucking useless to warn off one man. A foreign white man. And his useless Zulu.'

'I am sorry, father. I will take some men; I will find them and I will kill them.'

The boss shook his head. 'There is no need. I have already organized his demise. If you want something important done then do it yourself. Now fuck off.'

Dubula left the room. His face blank. Hiding his disappointment. And his shame. He was confident that he could find and kill the white man. The Zulu, Petrus, was a different matter. Dubula knew of the Zulu. Everyone who had lived for any period of time on the dark side knew of him. He was older now. But he was still a man to be respected. And when Dubula thought of Petrus, he experienced a feeling that he had not come across before. It was not strong enough to be called fear. But not weak enough to be called worry. If he had the vocabulary, and the desire to give word to his feeling it would probably be; foreboding. For, back in the days of Apartheid many people had tried to remove the Zulu. Many people. They were all dead. Dubula was a simple man with simple needs. But he did not want to be dead.

***

Thandi seemed no worse for wear despite her ordeal. She had been treated well and had brought back a new source of entertainment for all. Not only was she a hero, but she was now also the home's foremost expert on television. And she was with her brother, Vusi. Manon had squeezed the two new family members in even though, technically, there was not enough space. When Garrett had carried Thandi into the dormitory and set her down next to her brother he had instantly become Vusi's ultimate hero. And, after he heard Petrus address Garrett as *Isosha,* soldier, he had done the same. To him Garrett was The Soldier. A protector and savior that looked, not only over him and his sister, but over all children. *Isosha kakhulu,* the great soldier.

***

Garrett stood on the landing that looked over the dormitories and watched the two newcomers. The change in Vusi was incredible. No longer did he carry himself in an aloof and protective manner. His face grim with responsibility. Instead, he wore a constant smile. Every now and then he would look up at Garrett and give him two thumbs up. And, impossibly, his grin would get even wider.

Later, that evening when the children were readied for bed Vusi had shyly approached the *Isosha*. Garrett went down on one knee to bid him goodnight. Vusi threw his arms around him and held tight for a while. Then he stepped back and, from his pocket, produced a yellow and red screwdriver. He handed it solemnly to Garrett. 'Here, *Isosha*. You can have this.'

'Thank you, Vusi. But why are you giving it to me?'

The little boy smiled. 'Because I no longer have need of it.'

And then he ran off to bed leaving Garrett with a sharpened weapon and his thoughts. Garrett slipped the screwdriver into the side of his combat boot. It nestled there comfortably.

All of this should have made Garrett happy. And it did. However, it also filled him with frustration. There was so much more to do. He had saved a little girl and, most probably, her brother as well, but he was honest enough with himself to admit that he had done so by chance. A mere by product of his misdirected violence. It was not in Garrett's character to succumb to depression but he was struggling to maintain his focus.

As well as this he was worried. Things seemed to be running away with him. A boulder rolling down the hill, picking up speed, crashing into things, destroying without rhyme or reason. It was patently obvious that mister Big had known that Petrus and he were calling that night. No one sets an ambush just in case. It was also just as obvious that someone else in the know was watching the premises. But was that person friend or foe? Had they been protecting Garrett and Petrus or had they simply taken advantage of the situation to settle a score? Or to make a move on Big's business interests? One thing was for sure; he had to find out where the leak was or the next move that they made could well be the last. Although, in all fairness, Garrett had no idea what he would do next. He had hit a blank wall and there seemed no way around. But he also knew that this would not stop him continuing his search for the source of the missing children. It was merely another obstacle to be overcome. Whether that be by going around it or by simply crushing it would depend upon circumstance.

After the children were bedded down Manon asked him and Petrus upstairs for coffee and Belgian chocolates. The chocolates were courtesy of mister Sweets whom Garrett was convinced fancied the Sister. But who could begrudge the man his crush? His simple *joie de vivre* made him a pleasure to be around and he treated all about him with equal respect and diffidence, be they prince or pauper.

Manon was just about to pour the coffee when Garrett heard a car pull up outside. He went over to the window to see Brian get out.

'Hey, Brian,' he called, waving.

His friend waved back. 'Evening, Squire. What you doing?'

'Nothing of note.'

Manon and Petrus came to the window as well and waved. The dentist returned the salutation.

'Why don't you and Petrus come with me. I'm going to work and I'm sure Manon's got stuff to do.'

Garrett hesitated. Not that keen.

'Come on,' urged Brian. 'Be a come-with guy.'

Garrett relented. 'Okay.' He raised an eyebrow at Petrus who nodded his agreement.

With a wave to Manon, they trotted down the stairs.

As they were about to leave the building Petrus retrieved his blanket wrapped assegai from under the table in the reception area. He partially unwrapped it and drew out Garrett's machete. Garrett could see the weapon had been sharpened and oiled. Petrus offered it to the soldier. 'Here.'

Garrett nodded his thanks and tucked it into his belt in the small of his back, under his shirt. It rode uncomfortably high but it was concealed. It felt like the hand of an old acquaintance on his spine. Perhaps an uncle. Or schoolmaster.

Brian drove a black BMW five series. Garrett got into the front seat, Petrus in the back. Climbing into a jet fighter. The dash curved gracefully towards the driver and when Brian started the engine the instrumentation appeared on a head-up display on the windscreen, further enhancing the fighter image.

'Nice car,' said Garrett.

Brian grinned. 'I love this fucking car. Four liters of German power. Bulletproof windows all round. Kevlar armor in the doors and roof. Reinforced against landmines. Run-flat tires. Fuck the Pope-mobile, this is the real deal. And listen to this sound system.'

Brian fiddled with some buttons on the steering wheel and the sound of Kreator singing their song Betrayer came crashing out of the eight speakers like a wave of Teutonic invaders. Drums and guitar a frantic challenge. The lead singer screaming like a hyena on helium. Unpleasant. Thought provoking. Incendiary. As he pulled out of the orphanage grounds, he turned the volume down. An irritating mash of bleeding tortured sound in the background.

'Thought that I'd pick you up. Show you what I actually did to earn a crust. Reckoned you might find it interesting.'

'Well, I know that you're into security.'

'Yep. But not in the usual western sense of the word. I mean, my boys aren't doormen or such. Well, they do their share of protecting payrolls and what have. We stay clear of body guard work, factories, run of the mill stuff.'

'Doesn't leave much.'

'You'd be surprised. You know much about Hillbrow?'

'Drove through it on the way here. It's a complete shithole. Last time that I was here, in the early eighties, the place was amazing. Penthouses, nightclubs, restaurants. Now it's worse than any war zone.'

Brian nodded agreement. 'It is a war zone. That's why I'm involved. Same old stuff, my mate. Different African country. Different war. Different reasons. But this time I'm going to make some serious money out of it.'

'How?'

'Hillbrow started going into proper decline a few years back. I mean, real fucking Beirut stuff. Cops couldn't walk the streets for fear of petrol bombs chucked out of windows. If you took vehicles in, people would lob fridges full of bricks at you from the twentieth floor. I tell you, that hits your cop car, it will put a serious dent in your fucking day. So, the Rainbow nation decides that it's lost interest in Hillbrow, what with blood red being the only color of the rainbow that's prevalent there. No more cops, no army, no nothing. Obviously, the Nigerians reckon it's Christmas so they move in fucking wholesale. That's mine and that's mine and fucking that's mine and I'll take this building and that hotel and this bank and if you don't like it eat this. Bang, bang, all mine.'

'I don't get it. How do make money out of this?'

'I've become a property baron, mate. Bought three blocks of flats, well, two and a hotel. All above board and real-deal. Cost me fifteen thousand pounds all told. That was a few months ago. They were full of Nigerian drug dealers and squatters. I hired myself a group of likely lads, kitted them out with the best and set about convincing the itinerants that I was a serious fucking health hazard.'

Brian slowed down and took an off ramp from the M1 that led into Empire Road and then Hillbrow.

The sun was going down and, in true Highveld style, yet another bleeding sunset regaled the heavens with teenage poster colors. Deep reds, purple, silver and gleaming copper. The low-level sunlight picked up the permanent veil of smoke that covered the residential area. Tires burning on street corners, wood fires lit inside buildings designed for electric stoves. Diesel and petrol fumes. High-rise buildings with their entire contingent of windows blown out. Like the aftermath of a tactical-nuclear strike.

And then, every now and then, in shocking contrast a group of buildings, freshly painted, pot plants outside the heavily guarded entrances. Electric lights ablaze in the windows. More armed guards on all corners. Brian nodded at them. 'See. That lot is owned by Kobus Stanton. Totally fucked when he bought them. Chased out the scum, quick refurb, put his security on the streets. Rents the rooms out at two grand a month. There are over six hundred rooms in each apartment block. Do the math.'

Garrett did the math. Then he did the math again to make sure. If the figures that Brian was discussing were accurate then the three buildings would be bringing in an amount approaching four million Pound Sterling per annum. A staggering amount of money. He had been in wars that had been fought over for less. 'And your blocks? How many rooms?'

'Same. Just under two thousand rooms. But I can charge more for the hotel rooms because they all have their own bathrooms.'

'No kitchens though.'

'Put a cupboard and a hotplate in the corner. Instant fucking kitchen. Not talking top-level accommodation here. It's cheap, it's safe and it keeps the elements out. Natural and criminal. It's a perfectly acceptable place to live when it's sorted. And it's relatively cheap.'

'So, is it all going to plan?'

Brian held his hand up, parallel to the ground and rocked it back and forth. We've secured the one block but were a little overzealous when we did so. The building took a bit more damage than I would have hoped. We've got ninety percent control of the second block but the hotel is still full of Nigerian gangsters. I've got to be careful. Can't just go room to room because it'll fuck the place up so much that I can't afford to fix it up. It's a war of stealth. We make life unpleasant for them. Harass their customers and drug suppliers. Take out the odd one when we can. Fucking costing me a fortune.' Brian pulled the car onto the pavement. 'We're here.'

Garrett slid out of the BMW followed by Petrus. Brian was already talking to a group of eight men. They were of a specific type that Garrett knew well. All early to mid-forties. Five ten to six feet. One hundred and seventy pounds. Two were black, the rest white. Hair short. All well shaved. The group radiated an air of discipline and confidence. These were professional don't-fuck-with-me men. He didn't recognize any of the volunteers that he had worked with so recently. They all wore charcoal overalls and South African copies of the Rhodesian clandestine boots. The rest of their equipment was all Viper stealth kit. Top of the range assault vests, Kevlar body armor. Wrap around tactical goggles. Knee and elbow pads. M88 helmet. Leg style holsters carrying the Glock model 20 chambered for the 10mm round. With a sixteen round capacity this was a great handgun, provided you had big hands. Women need not apply. As a main weapon, six of the men carried the South African Neostead shotgun a 12 round, bullpup configuration that had two separate loading tubes so you could use two types of ammo. Perfect for close quarter tactical work. The other two carried the short barreled Vektor H5 .223, a pump action version of the South African R5 assault rifle with the thirty-five round mag. Brian hadn't stinted on equipment and, as a result, Garrett reckoned that he was looking at about forty thousand Pounds Sterling simply to kit these eight men out. He raised an eyebrow to Brian.

'Impressive kit.'

'Yep. Got another twenty troops kitted out the same or better.' Brian pointed down the street. 'Check it out, two guys on that street corner,' he swiveled and pointed in the opposite direction. 'Two there. Two round the back. This apartment block here in front of us, the one next to it and the ex-hotel across the road are mine.'

Garrett ran a soldier's eye over the three buildings. The one that they were standing directly in front of was attached to the hotel via a covered skywalk that arched over the road above them. The building on the right looked like it had taken a few direct artillery hits. Every window, save one, had been blown out. The single sheet of undamaged glass a mute testament to the vagaries of combat. It even had a set of curtains, dark and drawn. Smoke stains ran up the front of the building. Evidence of past fires.

'What happened there?' Asked Garrett, pointing at the severely damaged building.

Brian grimaced. 'Like I said, overzealous. The place had been taken over by a Nigerian drug lord. He ran a meth factory in the building and filled it with his soldiers. Also ran a whoring business out of it. We decided to go in hot and heavy. Room to room like you did in Liberia. You remember Liberia?'

He nodded. The siege of Monrovia. Brian had only been there for a short while, he'd been casevaced out the day before the siege had closed access down, courtesy of a bullet to the thigh. But Garrett had stayed. He and his men had been trapped in the city for eight weeks. The conditions had been dire. Nightly shelling from the rebels. No food or water. Living off rats and domestic pets that were so toast-rack thin that they were only good for boiling down into a thin soup. Every day the LURD rebels would push into the town and, every day, Garrett and his warriors, backed by President Taylor, would push them back out. Bitter house-to-house fighting that sapped your spirit and ground down your resistance until even the slightest sound caused your body to flood with fear induced adrenalin. Their exhaustion was absolute and they had lived in that strange zone between asleep and awake. A buzzing, fragile place where time seemed stretched thin, colors were dull and sounds muted. Before or since, Garrett had not known such utter fatigue. He doubted very much that the assault on an apartment block in the center of Johannesburg could have been in any way similar. But he simply nodded.

He remembered Liberia.

'Anyway,' continued Brian. 'Complete fucking disaster. We worked our way up from the lobby to the fifth floor, taking them out when we could. But they just moved up ahead of us. Left booby traps in the rooms, grenades tied to doors, that sort of crap. Lost two men. By the second day we were stuck on the tenth floor. Too much resistance. So, I hired a helicopter. Four of us abseiled out onto the roof. Fought our way down. Nothing fancy. Box of grenades. Room-to-room. Chuck in. Bang. Hose the place down with shotguns, move on. After two hours the helicopter came back and dropped us more ammo and grenades. Same again.

Meanwhile my boys were coming up from the bottom. Ended up we lost one more. Killed all the uglies. Thirty-two. Loaded them into the back of a truck and took them to a crematorium outside the city. Burnt the fuckers. Love this country. Cops knew, of course. Hard to cover up a firefight of that magnitude. Greased a few palms. Everyone suffered from sudden deafness and blindness; it's quite a fucking epidemic here. Problem is, we knackered the building big time. No windows and Sergeant Rock style holes all over the place. That's why we've been going the slowly, slowly route this time.

Look, guys. I'm going round the back. Have a talk to the boys there. Just do the rounds, you know. Do you mind waiting here?'

Garrett gave Brian the thumbs up. 'Sure, mate. We'll catch a smoke. Check out the beautiful scenery.'

Brian laughed and set of at a brisk walk towards the guards on the corner, trailed by his eight soldiers.

Garrett offered. Petrus accepted. The Zippo sparked and lit up. The wick needed trimming so the flame burnt high, orange and smoky. Both stood and smoked in silence, eyes moving constantly. Ready to pick up any would-be threat.

Garrett moved first. Fractionally before Petrus. It is a well-documented fact that if you stare intently at someone they can feel your gaze upon them. This is why Special Forces training teaches you never to stare at your target for too long before you take them out. It could compromise the kill. And if men have had their senses heightened by battle experience this trait is further enhanced. The bullet ricocheted off the concrete pavement where they had been standing. A volley of fire followed in quick succession as the men rolled on the floor. Handguns and rifles.

'Follow me,' shouted Garrett as he ran towards the base of the ex-hotel.

The tar on the road was chewed up by automatic fire as they sprinted across the street and threw themselves against the wall.

'It's coming from above us,' said Garrett. 'We're safe here as long as we stick close to the wall.'

Petrus swore. 'I dropped my cigarette.'

Garrett held his up, slightly bent but still intact. 'Still got mine.'

They both laughed. Tension release.

'Tell me,' asked Petrus. 'Why did we run here instead of simply getting into the bullet proof car?'

Garrett laughed again. 'Force of habit. When you're ambushed, always run towards the source of fire. Anyhow, I don't trust that car to keep assault rounds out.' Garrett leant out and looked up. Two more shots whined off the pavement and he whipped his head back.

'Why are these fuckers shooting at us?' He glanced across the road. 'Where's Brian?' Garrett took a last drag on his Gauloise. 'I think that we should go see who these pricks are and why they're shooting at us.'

Petrus thought for a few seconds. 'Isn't this building supposed to be full of Nigerians?'

'So?'

'No reason. Just pointing it out.'

Petrus unrolled his blanket. The assegai gleamed in the streetlight.

Garrett hitched up his shirt and drew the machete. They nodded at each other

Two men. With iron-age weapons. Against an unknown number of assailants with modern assault rifles.

Backs to the wall they shuffled towards the hotel entrance. A revolving door wedged shut with triangles of lumber. Two glass doors. One barred shut. The other hanging off its hinges. They went through the door fast. Service stairway to the side. Took the first flight at a sprint and then stopped. Still. Aware. Listening. Garrett pointed up.

'Slowly now. This place is crawling with uglies.'

They moved slower now. With purpose. The confidence of born warriors. Stopping at each flight and listening. Greeted only by silence, a fact that puzzled Garrett. Finally, on the tenth floor they heard conversation. Muted. Not quiet, simply muffled by distance. Garrett opened the door to the corridor slowly and smoothly. Inch by inch. The slow creep of death. As soon as it was wide enough, they both slipped through.

The corridor was dark. The only light coming from underneath two of the closed doors about halfway down the hall. They stopped outside the first and listened. Ear to door. Nothing. There was no need to get close to the next door. Although the conversation was still unintelligible it was obvious that there were at least two people in the room. Perhaps more. Garrett pointed at the silent door and Petrus nodded agreement. It made sense to recce the room where the threat was unknown.

Petrus leaned close to Garrett. 'Not slow. We walk in like we belong. Me first.' He turned the door handle and strode into the room. There was a man sitting on the edge of the bed. Dressed in boxers and a tee shirt. A naked woman lay on the bed next to him. He looked up.

'Fuck off. It's not your turn yet. I paid for the full hour.'

Petrus hit him in the mouth with the butt of his assegai, breaking off his two front teeth. He followed up with another blow to the man's temple causing him to fall forwards onto the floor and lay still. The whore jerked herself into a sitting position. Breasts bouncing as she did. The Zulu held a finger to his lips. Then he held the spear in front of her.

'No noise, no blade. Understand.'

She nodded.

'Good'

Garrett closed the door behind him and then searched the room. There was nothing save a roll of toilet paper next to the bed and a dry cake of soap in the corner basin. Cracked and dirty like old bone. No weapons. He looked at the girl.

'You speak English?'

'Yes.'

'How many men next door?'

She shrugged. It was a not altogether unpleasant sight.

'Tell me, or my friend will cut you.'

'I don't know. This one was the first. They pay for the night, not for the person. Maybe three. Maybe four. More? I don't know.'

'Did you hear the shooting?'

'There is always shooting. This is Hillbrow.'

'No, the shooting here. Close.'

'I heard it.'

'Was it from next door?'

She shrugged again and then kicked the man lying on the floor.

'This thing was fucking me. How can I tell where some shots are coming from?'

'Guess.'

'There was some from next door. Some more from higher up. I think.'

Garrett nodded. Acceptance. 'Fair enough.' He turned to Petrus. 'So, what do you think?'

'Probably only three. Maybe four. We can go back downstairs and call Brian. Or we can go next door and sort them.'

Garrett stepped over to the window and twitched the curtain aside. The streets were empty. Even the guards that were on the corners had disappeared. He pulled his mobile phone from his pocket and dialed Brian's number. Straight through to voice mail.

'Shit. Where the fuck is he? Okay, look, from the angle of the shots I reckon that some of them were definitely from higher up. We can't go onwards and leave these guys next door at large. Doesn't make tactical sense.'

'We take them?'

'We take them.' Garrett stared at the girl. Debating.

'I won't make any noise,' she said. 'This has nothing to do with me.'

They closed the door when they left. Gathered themselves outside the next door. Deep breaths. Rapid blinking to get some moisture to the eyes. Ready. Ready.

Garrett turned the handle and flung the door open. Visually swept the room as he moved forward. Four, five, six people. The light bright. Garrett's eyes took a half a second to adjust fully. One of the men in the room reacted instantly, swinging his firearm up. Bang. Bang. The concussion of gunshots. Something picking at Garrett's clothes, caressing his flesh with fingers of fire. Burning. Hot. Pain.

Machete swung. Throat. Blood sprayed across the room. Hot on his face. Wet and viscous. Men shouting. More shots. The vicious whine of ricochets. Overhand cut. Blade cleaving through clavicle and into chest. Twist to break the vacuum. Pull, move on.

Assegai blurred in movement as Petrus stabbed. Using his whole body. Blade penetrating through. Sticking out of the man's back.

Stillness. Save for the rasping of deep drawn breath. The silent shaking of adrenaline-fueled muscles.

The smell. Metallic. Meaty. The rank, moist reek of death.

A hand touching his side. 'You're bleeding.'

Garrett looked down. There were two holes in his shirt and, when he pulled it up to look, two corresponding crimson creases ran along the side of his torso. Rib bone. White. Peeking coyly through ragged flesh. Bleeding but not serious. He dropped his shirt back and ignored the wound.

'Come on. Check for weapons.'

Each of the bodies was equipped with a sidearm. All different. A street mix of 38 specials, 32's and 9 millimeters. The weapon that had missed Garrett was a Walther PPK chambered for the .380 ACP. James

Bond. He sifted through the weapons before he chose a 9-millimeter FEG, a Hungarian copy of the Browning Hi Power. Checked the magazine. Nine rounds left. Sufficient. He checked there was a round in the chamber, checked the safety was off. Then he looked out of the window again. Still no sign of Brian. Petrus sniffed with distain when Garrett asked if he wanted a pistol and he cleaned his blade on the curtains.

Garrett stood quietly for a while and thought. Something was wrong. Where was Brian? Where were the other guards? Where were all of the rest of the alleged Nigerians that were meant to be commanding the hotel that they were in? He beckoned to Petrus, cocking his head towards the door.

'Let's go. Quietly.'

They continued upwards. Floor by floor until they got to the top. All of the floors were empty. Quiet.

'They must be on the roof,' said Petrus.

The last section of stairway was cast iron. Rough steel treads and railings. They followed it to a gray, steel covered door. A handle. No lock.

Before Garrett opened the door he whispered to Petrus.

'Try to keep someone alive. I've got questions. Something's not right here.' The Zulu nodded. Garrett turned the handle and they went through. There was one man on the open roof. Crouching down. Staring over the parapet. AK47 in hand. As they walked through the door he spun around. Raised his rifle. And his head exploded.

Garrett and Petrus hit the floor and scrabbled over to the parapet, lying flat.

'Where did that come from?' Shouted Garrett.

He raised his head over the low concrete wall to snatch a quick glance. Saw nothing. They lay still for a while and then heard, faintly, someone calling from the street. Garrett popped his head back over the parapet. Saw Brian. Standing in the middle of the street. Flanked by his soldiers.

'Hey,' Brian shouted. 'What the fuck is going on? You guys all right?'

Garrett stood up and waved back. Then he pointed down. Brian gave the thumbs up. Garrett turned to see Petrus crouched over the body. Staring intently.

'What's wrong, Petrus?'

The Zulu shook his head. 'Not sure. I think that I've seen this guy before. Hard to tell.'

Garrett squatted down and peered at the ruined face. The bullet had hit the man in the back of the head, slightly off center. From another building. In the dark. A beautiful shot. The hyper-velocity slug had reacted exactly as it was meant to. Punching through the skull and then tumbling violently. Finally smashing through the face, tearing most of it off as it exited.

'Could be anyone. How can you tell? Got no face left.'

Petrus chewed his lip. Stood up. 'It will come to me.'

The two of them jogged back down the steps and into the street. Garrett was amazed that he couldn't hear the sound of sirens. But then, apart from the first fusillade of shots directed at them there had been only sporadic gunfire. And in a place like Hillbrow that wouldn't warrant any extra attention. Brian came running towards them.

'Jesus, guys. Are you alright?'

Garrett nodded. Brian looked at his shirt. Blood. 'You've been shot.'

'No. It's nothing.'

'I can't fucking leave you alone for ten seconds and you get into shit. Come here,' Brian threw his arm around Garrett. Affection. Rough.

'Listen, Brian. There's no one in that building.'

'What?'

'The hotel. There's no one there. Well, there was, six or seven people. And a hooker. But that's all.'

Brian looked puzzled. 'That's impossible. The place was packed with Nigerians. Only six or seven? Where are they now?'

Garrett drew his finger across his throat.

Brian looked shocked. 'You scribbled them?'

Garrett nodded.

'Fuck me. The whole lot?'

'No. Not the whore. She's still there. Oh, and some dude who was with her. There's also a body on the roof.' Garrett didn't mention how the man on the roof had been taken out and a quick glance at Petrus warned him not to either. He wasn't sure why he was keeping anything from his friend but some sixth sense told him to keep some things to himself for the meanwhile.

Brian turned to his men. Picked out five by name.

'Comb the building. Room by room. Go.'

The soldiers ran into the lobby, covering themselves as they moved forward.

Brian pulled a handkerchief from his pocket and handed it to Garrett.

'Your face.'

Garrett wiped his face with the cloth and it came away red with someone else's blood. He walked over to the BMW and used the side mirror. Cleaned up as well as he could. But blood still remained. In his pores. His laughter lines. The mirror also picked up the single unbroken window in the building behind him. Reflecting back the light. Like a shard of glass in a pile of coal.

One of Brian's soldiers came jogging out of the building.

'It's clear.'

Brian shook his head in bemusement. 'Well, let's not look a gift horse etcetera. Put two men on the entrance, two in the skywalk and one on the roof. We got ourselves a hotel.' He walked over to Garrett and put a hand on his shoulder. 'Let's get you boys home.'

And two city blocks away a man picked up a used cartridge from the floor, pocketed it, slid his long gun into an Adidas carryall bag and disappeared into the night.

***

No one talked on the trip back to the Children's home where Garrett had left his Jeep. Both Garrett and Petrus were feeling the after effects of combat. Slight nausea, dizziness. Discombobulation. Brian seemed deep in thought. Driving the well-known route on autopilot. His expression distant.

He pulled up outside the orphanage, left the engine running.

'Look, guys. I'm going back to Hillbrow. Sort the whole thing out. You gonna be alright?'

Garrett nodded. He and Petrus climbed out of the car. Waved goodbye.

Manon met them in the lobby.

'What happened? Your face, you're bleeding.'

Garrett shook his head. 'Not my blood.'

'He's been shot', said Petrus with a grin. 'But he's too tough to admit it.'

'Shot? Where?'

Garrett lifted up his shirt.

'Right,' said the sister.' Upstairs. My room. Wait there.'

The two men trudged upstairs. Manon arrived shortly after them. A bowl of steaming water and some bandages. Tape. Scissors and cloths. She didn't question what had happened, simply tended the wound. Cleaned it efficiently and taped a padded bandage over it. Then she used the water and clothes to clean the blood off Garrett's face. The smell of blood in his nostrils masked Manon's fragrance. The pain in his side offset her touch.

Garrett leant backwards so he could pull his cigarettes from his trouser pocket. He straightened the pack and offered. Petrus accepted. Manon not. The Zippo flared. Smoke drawn deeply. Releasing chemicals. Soothing the limbic system.

Abruptly, Petrus stood upright out of the chair. 'I remember.'

'What?'

'That man. The one with no face, I remember where I seen him. He was dressed differently. In uniform. Black overalls and full assault kit.'

'Where?' Urged Garrett.

'In the passenger seat of Brian's car. He works…worked for Brian. He was one of his soldiers.'

And suddenly, a lot of things made sense to Garrett.

CHAPTER SIXTEEN

Garrett parked the Jeep on Louis Botha Avenue. The outskirts of Hillbrow. Walked the rest of the way in. He was alone. He had left the Hungarian 9-millimeter in Brian's car but still carried the machete. Petrus had wanted to come with but he had refused him.

Gangs of young men were stalking the streets. Loud. Abusive. Their strident voices the equivalent of banging on pots and pans to drive away evil. Some approached him, all swaggering arrogance, only to pull away as soon as they got close enough to see his expression. His eyes. For the Beast was walking the streets and the lesser predators cowered obsequiously.

As Garrett stalked through the streets of Hillbrow's shattered night he went over the false notes of the past few days. Apart from Manon, who had known that he would be at the Krugersdorp orphanage where the five men had attacked him? When they had taken mister Big's house, who could have warned them that he was coming? Earlier on this very evening, why had he and Petrus been left so hideously exposed without weapons or protection? Where were the alleged Nigerians who controlled the hotel? Why did the other soldiers all conveniently disappear when the shit came down? The constant subtle attempts at misdirection. The shocked look on Brian's face when he had arrived. There was no way around it. His friend. A man he once called a brother. A man whose life he had saved countless times before, was trying to kill him. And the fact that he was trying to do so left Garrett with only one conclusion; Brian was somehow connected to the missing children.

A soldier's logic told him that, somehow, these buildings in Hillbrow were tied up with the whole thing. And in particular one specific room. The only room in the block with an intact window.

When they had taken the building Brian had specifically said that they had chucked a grenade into every room. Windows do not survive grenade blasts. In fact, windows in rooms next to grenade attacks did not stay intact. Someone had replaced the window. And hung curtains. That meant that someone wanted a secluded place in a no-go zone to hide something. Children perhaps? Garrett quickened his pace to a jog.

When he came into line of sight of Brian's apartments he slowed down and proceeded with caution. Seeking shadow. Ultra-alert. Four of Brian's soldiers were gathered at the front door of the hotel. Talking. Smoking. The odd laugh. Men at ease in an area of violence. The evilest sons of bitches in the valley.

Garrett slid through the night, flickering from one pool of darkness to the next. He went around the back of the building. Found a steel fire escape. Climbed it to the first floor and tested the fire door. Open, the lock long shattered. A corridor. No lights but bright enough to see. The room with the window was on the ninth floor. Near the East side of the building. Garrett took the steps, pausing every now and then to listen. Empty. Still.

Ninth floor. Garrett walked down the corridor. Doors to the left and right hung off their hinges or lay on the floor. Second to last door on the right. The room facing the street. The room with the window.

The door was locked. A Chubb padlock and steel hasp. Garrett ignored the lock and ran his fingers down the other side of the door. Standard hinges. He stood back and gathered his strength. Slow deliberate breaths. And then, strike. Lifting his booted foot to his chest he unleashed a kick at the top hinge, splintering the wood and smashing the door into the room.

The room was dark. He felt for a light switch next to the doorway. Found. Flicked. No children.

A steel framed single bed in the center of the room, legs bolted down. On it a dirt-gray sheet covered a thin mattress. On the floor around it, transparent plastic sheeting. Photographic lights on stands. A video camera on a tripod, pointed at the bed. Against the wall, a trestle table. On it, a DVD player. A TV. Full ashtray. Used tubes of KY jelly. A stack of three or four discs. Garrett walked over to the table. Turned the TV on. Hiss of static. Powered up the DVD player. Put one into the slot. The machine pulled the silver disc in. Hungry. Keen.

The camera pans across the bare room. The monitor flares in the low light. Someone adjusts the focus, the picture firms up.

A single bed. Metal. In the middle of the room. Bolted to the floor. Covered in clear plastic.

A little girl. Perhaps ten. Perhaps younger. Crying.

The high-definition lens picks up tears running down her cheeks. Raw, red-rimmed eyes. Fear. Animal. Primeval.

The sound of a zip. Of belt and trousers dropping to the floor.

Her breath. Large shuddering gulps. Starving of oxygen.

A man walking towards her, slowly. His swollen manhood throbbing in front of him. Nodding. A toy dog on a dashboard. Grabbing her by the hair and pulling her against him.

She screams.

The camera continues to record. In high definition. 1920 x 1080 pixel resolution. Until the end.

Garrett pressed stop. He leant against the table for support. A weight on his chest. Crushing. Lips numb with shock. The sound of his own blood crashed and surged in his ears. A sea of horror.

'You just wouldn't fucking stop, would you.'

Garrett spun around to face the door. Brain stood silhouetted in the frame. 10mm Glock in his right hand.

Garrett said nothing. His powers of reason had collapsed. The handgun was pointing at his face. Black. Unwavering.

'I told you to leave it. Orphans, fuck them. I told you. But no, save the children. Save the fucking children. Save the world. Look at me, I'm a saint.'

Garrett tried to speak. At first only a formless croak. And then.

'Why?'

'For the money, Garrett. For the money. I was fucked. Strung out. Another losing war for Brian. Another lost opportunity. Then the Nigerians approached me. Asked if I wanted to make some serious money. Easy money. It was for nothing in the beginning. Just provide them with a secure place, a bit of privacy. And then more. Before I knew it I was well in, mate. Fucking drowning in shit. But you know what? It doesn't matter. It makes no fucking difference. One, two, twenty. A thousand. No one cares. There're millions of them, Garrett. Kids die all the time here. AIDS, starvation, disease, murder. And for nothing. At least I had a reason.'

Garrett bit his lips in an attempt to bring some feeling back. His chest had cramped so much that he thought that he might be suffering some sort of heart attack.

'Jesus, Brian. No. Stop.'

'Fuck you. Fuck you, Garrett.'

Garrett shook his head. He noticed that Brian was weeping. His face wet with tears.

'Why did you leave us, Garrett?'

'What? When?'

'In Sierra Leone. You left us. You were our leader and you left us.'

'You were grown men. You survived. You became the leader.'

Brian shook his head.

'I didn't want to be the leader. I wanted you there. And we didn't survive. We died out there. Jamie, Scotty, Pedro, Samuel. Dead. You left us to die.'

'It wasn't my intention. I had to go. You know I had to.'

'No. No, you didn't have to go. You left because you are a coward. A fucking coward. So, you went a bit bush happy, killed a few too many, fell in love with a nun. You ran away. We had to fight our way through to Liberia. And then I ended up here. In this shithole of a country. Fighting again. I fucking hate this place, the people, the heat. The violence, the death. I just wanted one big score and then back to Blighty. Pubs with fire-places and real beer. People with a sense of fucking humor instead of a chip on their shoulder. Just one big score. Was that too much to ask?'

Garrett nodded. 'Yes, my friend, it was. You asked too much. You sacrificed too much.'

'Fuck you, I sacrificed nothing.'

'You sacrificed your soul.'

Brian flinched like he'd been slapped.

'I never touched the kids. I want you to know that. Never touched them. The guy who did the fucking. The killing. A doctor. Works in a private hospital in Olivedale. Doctor fucking Jakobs. He's the sick one, the evil one. Not me.'

Garrett shook his head. 'No.'

'Fuck you. Turn around. Face the wall.'

Garrett turned. Slowly. His legs leaden. Immobile. Like tree stumps. Hands limp. There was no chance of rushing Brian. He was a pro. He would get off three shots before Garrett had taken a step. He faced the wall. Tried to think of Manon's face. Her lips, hair. But he couldn't. Only the blank wall in front of him. He closed his eyes in an attempt to conjure up her image. Nothing. Blackness.

Behind him he heard Brian engage the hammer. Three separate clicks as it ratcheted back.

'Goodbye, Garrett. Goodbye, my friend.'

The weapon bucked in Brian's hand. The retort loud enough in the confined space to rattle the windows. Blood and gore splattered up the wall. Garrett's legs gave way and he sank to his knees with treacle-like slowness. Behind him, the thump of a body hitting the floor. He turned to look.

Brian lay sprawled on the floor. Gun still in his hand. The left side of his face missing. Spread across the wall by the high velocity round. Garrett stood up and walked over to him. He had shrunken in death. His body twisted at an awkward angle. His lips pulled back in rictus to show his perfect, white teeth.

'Goodbye, Sergeant.'

Garrett sat in the dark. He had driven back to Brian's house on autopilot, bringing with him the DVD discs from the room. When he had arrived, he had gone to Brian's cellar and found a bottle of brandy. Cape brandy, rough and smoky. He had picked up a glass from the kitchen but had not used it. He was drinking straight from the bottle.

He needed to think. To formulate some sort of plan. But the enormity of what his friend had been involved in swamped his normal cognitive abilities.

The level in the brandy bottle crept down. And the fiery spirit finally relaxed Garrett enough to think. He sat. He remembered.

Nineteen eighty-five. Angola. He, Brian and two American ex-rangers, had been hired by Gulf Oil to protect their oil storage installations outside Cabinda. One day on a routine patrol they came across the remains of a single engine civilian aircraft. A pilot, one passenger. They had been dead for many months. There were no overtly visible signs of the plane having taken hits so they assumed that it had crashed due to engine failure or pilot error. Remnants of passports found on the bodies showed the pilot to be South African and the passenger an American. Both had been armed, pistols in shoulder holsters. In a suitcase in the back of the plane they had found something else of interest. Two million dollars. Shrink wrapped in blocks of ten thousand dollars. Two hundred bricks of cash. They had split it four ways. After their contract came to an end Garrett had never seen the Rangers again. They took their share of the money and got out of the war game. He had taken his money and put it in a safe deposit box in a bank in London. And then in a box under the floor in his croft.

Brian had gone berserk. Over the next few months, he had taken leave and blown all of it. Women, casinos, chartered flights, horse races. It is possible to live a multimillion lifestyle on half a million dollars, but, as Brian found out, not for very long. But he had not begrudged his excess. Live fast, die young. Fight on.

Then Garrett lost touch with the cockney for a few years except for a brief time in Liberia. They were together for a couple of days there until Brian was injured, shot in the thigh and evacuated. And then, different wars, different parts of Africa. The next time that he saw him was in Sierra Leone, as his sergeant.

A South African mercenary recruitment company had contacted both of them on behalf of president Kabbah who was looking to put together a rapid response team of a dozen or so elite. The best of the best. When the recruitment company had done their research his name and the name of the cockney ex-SAS soldier had come up right at the top.

Kabbah had been true to his word and they had been issued with more than adequate weapons and transport. The ten others were made up of one ex-Rhodesian fire force soldier, two South African Parabats and seven locals. They were good. Very good.

At the start the president had taken personal care of them. Deciding for himself when and where they would be deployed and then basking in their inevitable successes. And in the beginning success had been easy to come by. The troops that they fought against, undisciplined and ragged.

After a while Kabbah had tired of his new toy and let them control their own destiny. Garrett turned the group into a roving reaction unit relying heavily on information from the Kamajors, groups of local tribesmen who fought on the side of the government. As Brian once succinctly put it, they find the shit and we clear it up.

And there was shit aplenty. Although Garrett had fought for most of his adult life he had never before, or since, come across such sickening violence. Such unbelievable inhumanity to fellow man.

The rebels fought under loose commandos designated as 'Fighting Units' and these units were named according to their favorite ways of killing. Thus, 'Burn House Unit' for the unit that used to lock civilians in their huts, alive, before they torched them. 'Kill Man

No Blood' unit who used to beat their victims to death but took great pride in doing so without spilling a drop of blood. 'Born Naked Squad', rapists and sexual deviants.

And, finally, a whole section of fighting units that were new to the conflict. Garrett and his men, now designated 'The Warriors' had not yet come up against them. They were a reaction to the government's new slogan, "The future is in your hands". In a brutal and sadistic counter-campaign the rebels had formed a number of fighting units designated, 'Cut Hands Commandos'. Their message was simple; support the government and you have no hands. They began a wholesale campaign. Chopping the hands off innocents, particularly those of little children. These commandos were led by people with nicknames like; Biggie chop hand, Captain two hands and Betty cut hands.

It was over this period that Manon come crashing into Garrett's life. Her essential goodness creating such a counterpoint to his current existence, that it seemed to possess him, mind and soul. A security blanket of decency and kindness for his tortured mind to cling to.

And also, the first time he saw the children. Horribly mutilated by the Cut Hands Commandos. Children as young as three years old with both hands chopped off. Sometimes entire arms lopped off at the shoulder. The sight of such terrible atrocities had literally driven Garrett to the very brink of insanity. All that he could think about was finding the people, the animals, who had committed such a monstrous crime against humanity. He had left five men to guard the mission and had gone on hot pursuit of the cut hand Commandos with Brian, two massive South Africans and three of his riflemen…

…the air was hot and sticky and full of biting midges. Jungle surrounded them, thick and verdant. Bright emerald green. Deadly. Perfect cover for an ambush.

The two South Africans were walking point. Their lightness of foot belying their massive frames. Kobus, the slightly bigger of the two at six foot five and around three hundred pounds carried a 7.62 FN Mag general-purpose machine gun, his body festooned with extra belts of ammunition. It was a sight that even the hardest of combatants would find terrifying. This, combined with his ragged black beard and badly broken nose had resulted in him being given the nickname, Daisy. An epithet that he accepted with surprisingly good humor.

The Warriors had been following the spoor of an alleged Cut Hands Commando that they had been told about by a local group of Kamajors. They were traveling North from outside the village of Meyesi towards Makimbolo. The spoor showed twenty plus rebels less than four hours in front of them and the Warriors were pushing hard to catch up. That night was to be a full moon and Garrett had decided that they would attempt to track through the night in order to catch up with the rebels and then, come daybreak, they would attack.

At around four in the morning Daisy held up a clenched fist. The unit dropped silently to the ground. Garrett and Brian leopard crawled up to the Afrikaner. He held his finger to his lips and then pointed ahead. It took Garrett a few seconds and then the full picture leapt out at him. They had almost walked directly into the middle of the rebels' camp. A sentry sat against the bole of a tree, his eyes closed, breathing rhythmic. Asleep. Garrett let his eyes rove over the scene. Using his peripheral vision to enhance his night seeing ability. Letting the rod receptors in his eyes take the brunt of the work as opposed to the color only cones. He counted the forms lying in the small clearing. Twenty-one. Daisy nudged him and pointed again. Across the clearing another sentry. This one awake but also sitting against a tree. Twenty-three rebels in all. The three of them slithered back. Away from the encampment.

Garrett spoke to the men. His voice low. Lips close to ears. Sunrise at five twenty. They would split into two groups. He, Brian and Daisy would circle around and come in from the West. The rest of the group would attack from their current position. No prisoners. Go in hard at first light, Garrett would signal by tossing a grenade into the encampment. Sentries first and then try to kill the rest before they woke up.

The next hour ground away with infinite slowness. Nerves stretched taut as piano wire.

The sun. A tendril of red above the horizon. The metallic ping of the safety lever detaching from the M61 grenade followed by the soft thud of the half-kilo lump of steel and explosive hitting the jungle floor. Three seconds later the air was rent with an explosion. Garrett shouldered his FN and double tapped the sentry opposite him. The 7.62 rounds punched straight through him and into the tree that he was resting against. On his right Brian was firing into the clearing, controlled double taps. And then Daisy opened up. The FN Mag spewed out death at a cyclic rate of one thousand rounds a minute. He worked the weapon back and forth across the encampment, shiny brass cartridges and steel links from the disintegrating ammunition belt fountained out of the side of the machine gun. Copper jacketed lead hosed out of the front. From the other side of the encampment the other Warriors were also dealing out death as aggressively and efficiently as possible.

And then silence. A soft ting-ting of the Mag barrel as it cooled down. A low moaning from one of the rebels. Ears ringing. Hearts hammering. Breath coming in short ragged bursts.

Garrett strode into the clearing.

'Come on Warriors. Check the bodies. If anyone's alive tell me.'

He took a pack of cigarettes out of his webbing, put one in his mouth. Zippo. Tried to light it with shaking hands. Couldn't. Brian leant over and helped, using his thumb to roll the flint. The wick flamed and Garrett lit up.

'Thanks.'

'No worries.'

Garrett walked down the row of bodies. Most of them torn to shreds courtesy of the Mag. Overkill. One moaning. Covered in blood. Still alive. Garrett knelt down to get a closer look. Two hits to the chest. Minutes at most. He put his face close to the rebel.

'Hey.'

'Hey', the rebel grunted in reply.

'You want some water?'

The man nodded. Garrett unclipped his canteen from his belt, held the man's head up and trickled some water into his mouth. He tried to swallow. Couldn't. Choked instead.

'What commando are you?'

'Betty cut hands.'

'Betty?'

'Our leader. Missus Betty.'

'Your leader is a woman?' asked Garrett. The rebel nodded painfully. 'Not very good, was she?'

The man chuckled. 'No, she got us killed.' He laughed again and then, as if someone had flicked a switch, he stopped living.

'Hey, captain.' Daisy called Garrett. 'Check this out.'

Garrett walked over. Lying in front of the Afrikaner was obviously the commando leader. A woman, perhaps in her mid-twenties, thick hair tied up with a red scarf. And around her neck, on a plaited leather necklace, the dried hand of a tiny child.

Daisy shook his head. 'That's fucking sick, man. Sick.'

Garrett pointed his FN at the dead woman's head, slipped the selector to full auto and pulled the trigger. And that was the first time that he had felt the beast stir within him. A part of him. Dark and vengeful. Unforgiving. Bent on retribution.

The next few days Garrett pushed his men harder than they had ever been pushed before. He was a man possessed. Two days after they had wiped out the Betty Cut Hands fighting unit the Warriors came across a small group of seven Kamajors. They were following a large cut hands commando of around thirty rebels but had stayed back as they felt that they did not have the necessary firepower to engage. They teamed up with the Warriors, placing themselves under Garrett's command.

Once again Garrett used the cover of night. Running hard they leapfrogged ahead of the cut hands and laid an ambush where the trail meandered through an old dried-up riverbed. Garrett, Daisy and the Kamajors on one side of the river, the rest of the Warriors on the other. Garrett had rigged a grenade linked to a tripwire across the trail and had told the men to fire only when the grenade exploded. No sooner.

Just past seven in the morning. The rebels had risen early, broken camp and continued up the trail. They walked together, bunched up in a gaggle. Talking and laughing. Children on a school outing. Off with teacher to maim and dismember.

A group of three hit the tripwire at the same time. Garrett was lying prone and he felt the thump of detonation in his stomach. Next to him, like an old insane relative, the Mag started yammering. The sound a cross between an ultra-fast hammer and paper tearing. Garrett fired into the bunched-up rebels, moving from right to left and back. Picking each target and moving on. Some of the rebels had gone to ground and were returning fire, their two to one numerical advantage allowing them to lay down withering sheets of fire. But the Mag played its music of death. And Daisy was an aficionado of the instrument. Long, controlled bursts of accurate fire. The rebel's AK47's hit back. The flat retort easily distinguishable from the vicious crack of the Warriors FN rifles. Garrett waited until that finely judged moment when a firefight is about to turn. The pendulum ready to swing either way, and he jumped to his feet.

'Warriors!'

As one his men charged in, firing from the hip as they ran. The Kamajors followed close behind. Mouths open wide. White teeth. Red tongues. Wide eyes. Elation, fear, anger, pride. All wrapped up in an internal package of white-hot energy that allows a man to run screaming into combat knowing that any step could be his last. Heady and exhilarating. Garrett knew of no better feeling.

The two groups of Warriors fought towards each other. Dust from the dry riverbed filled the air. Blue-white cordite smoke. Acrid and stinging. One of the Kamajors took a hit to the head, the 123-grain steel jacketed slug striking his skull at a little under 3000 feet per second. His feet flicked out in front of him and he did a perfect back flip. Garrett shot his killer twice in the chest and ran out of ammo. He ejected the magazine and fumbled the reload, dropping his spare in the dust. He went down on one knee to retrieve it and came face to face with a rebel who was busy cramming rounds into an empty magazine. Garrett picked up his FN and smashed the barrel into his opponents face as hard as he could. The steel flash hider slid along his cheek and plunged into the man's eye with a distinct popping sound as the orb burst. The rebel fell back screaming. Garrett reloaded, shot the man in the head and sprung back to his feet.

It was over. Bodies were piled in random groups. Lying over each other like a necrophiliac orgy. The iron smell of blood filled the air. Cloying. Sticking in the back of the throat like phlegm. The Kamajors were already looting the bodies. Boots were being tried on for size, wristwatches and personal jewelry disappearing into pockets.

The Warriors walked amongst the fallen and removed their weapons, casting them to one side, out of reach. Six of the rebels were still alive. Two of them only slightly wounded. The corpses were dragged to one side. The living lined up in front of Garrett. Those that could support themselves were on their knees. Three lay prone. Their wounds too dire to do anything else.

Garrett picked one, a young man. Twenties or so.

'You. What fighting unit are you?'

The rebel kept his eyes averted. 'We are Two Hands Cut Commando.'

'Why Two Hands?'

'Please, Sir. Because we always take both the hands. Never just one.'

'You cut hands off children?'

The man nodded.

'And women?'

Another nod.

'Do you keep any of the children's hands?'

With shaking fingers, the rebel opened his shirt. Around his neck, a copper wire necklace. Hanging from it two tiny wizened dried hands.

Garrett took a deep shivering breath. The machete made a rasping sound as he drew it from its stiff leather sheath. The oiled blade reflected the sun. And the deep green of the jungle.

'Hold out your right arm.'

The rebel started weeping. 'Please, sir. No.'

'Hold out your arm or I will burn your eyes from your head.'

The man held out his arm. Black from the sun. Thin. Muscles like cord. A diet barely above subsistence level. He looked up at Garrett.

'Mercy. Please, my master. Mercy.'

'What mercy have you ever shown, you cunt?'

Garrett swung. The hand leapt from the end of the man's arm like a live thing escaping captivity. Blood sprayed out of the severed stump. Dry dust turned red. Scarlet mud. The man sank to the ground clutching at the stump, keening formlessly. But it was not over. Garrett grabbed the left hand. Pulled it above the man's head. Swung again.

'Two Hands Cut!' He shouted and held the man's severed hand in front of him. 'Both hands you fucking animal. Both hands.'

The rebels that could move tried to get to their feet but the Warriors clubbed them down. Garrett turned to Daisy.

'Here.' He held out the machete. 'All of them.'

Daisy shook his head. Brian stepped forward.

'Listen, corporal. You will do as the captain says.'

Again, the huge Afrikaner refused.

Garrett turned to the group of Kamajors and held out the machete to them. One walked over. His face grim. He took the blade.

'We will do it. It is just. These men are less than animals.'

Garrett turned and walked off into the forest. The Warriors avoided eye contact. None of the rebels lived.

Later that day the Warriors were hunting again. Looking for their next battle.

The next six days were a wash. Endless trudging through forest. Village after village hunting down rumors of a particularly harsh fighting unit that went under the name of Captain Cut Hands. It was alleged by the locals that this particular commando also practiced ritual cannibalism. Fear of them was a tangible thing amongst the people. But by now Garrett's reputation had also spread and he and the Warriors were treated with a mixture of respect and trepidation. In a land where the removal of hands stood for evil it was hard to reconcile Garrett's crusade with righteousness. So the villagers stood back and watched. And waited. For this was Africa and patience is a way of life.

On the seventh day. Light rain. Almost a mist. Another formless track leading to another nameless village. Morale amongst the Warriors was low. Garrett had driven them beyond the call. Rations were low and the constant strain of imminent attack had worn them thin. Daisy was particularly morose. The brutality of the last weeks had shocked the unshakable Afrikaner. He had no qualms about machine-gunning down enemy soldiers but the brutal maiming that Garrett had insisted on did not sit well with him. As a result he had retreated into himself. An island.

The only person that still treated the captain normally was Brian. His cheeky-chappie sense of humor, his unquenchable enthusiasm and his boundless energy kept Garrett grounded. Human. He owed Brian more than he could quantify.

And then, muted by the thin rain and the thick jungle, the unmistakable flat retorts of an AK47. Measured single shots a few seconds apart. Not a firefight. An execution. As one the Warriors picked up paced and ran towards the sound.

They entered the village from the South. Spread out in a V formation. As always, Daisy on point. The raindrops on his ammunition belts sparkled like diamonds, turning the tools of death into costume jewelry.

The village was a poster for abject poverty. It never ceased to amaze Garrett that, in a climate where even spit would grow; the locals didn't seem capable of raising even the minimum of subsistence crops. The villagers, perhaps forty of them, were huddled in the clearing in the center. Around them twenty plus members of the rebel cut hands fighting group. On the right hand side of the clearing a large tree stump. Tied to it; two toddlers. Boys. Shirtless. Their wrists had been tightly tourniquet but blood and lymph still oozed from the fresh wounds. Their hands lay on the ground. Tiny. Pathetic. Like crushed insects. And next to them two villagers that had just been executed.

Garrett opened up first. Walking towards the rebels. Unhurried two shot taps. Aiming so as not to harm any villagers. The rest of the Warriors followed suite. And then Daisy. Short sharp bursts of fire. Each one less than a second long. Fifteen rounds. The cut hands did not even try to fight back. They simply dropped their weapons and knelt down. Still the Warriors had cut down twelve of them in that short time.

Garrett strode amongst them, his face white with fury. Brian ran forward and cut the toddlers free and, with the help of Jose, the medic, he bound their stumps and administered morphine. The mothers of the mutilated children came forward, sobbing quietly. Curtsying their respect as they laid claim to their offspring.

The Warriors lined the surviving rebels up. On their knees. Meanwhile the villagers dragged the rebel corpses to one side, stripping them of their clothing and weapons as they did so. Those that were close to death but hadn't quite crossed over were hurried along as the villagers gave physical expression to their fear. Their inability to fight back. They gathered around the wounded and kicked them to death. Silently. Faces blank. The air full of the meaty sounds of bare feet striking flesh. Over and over and over.

The village headman approached Garrett. His eyes cast down in respect. He stood in front of the captain waiting for his acknowledgement.

Garrett nodded at him. 'Yes, mister.'

'Please, sir. The rest?'

Garrett raised a quizzical eyebrow. 'The rest what?'

'Please, sir. I am asking that your soldiers please kill the rest of the cut hands.'

'You want them dead?'

The headman walked over to the line of kneeling rebels and spat on them. 'They are animals. Violators of children. Eaters of human flesh. This one here,' he pointed at a young man with a red beret on his head. 'This is their leader.' He spat again. The leader looked at him with a smirk on his face. There was no fear. Only smoldering anger.

Garrett stood still for a while. Thinking. Finally, he took a cigarette pack from his webbing. Extricated. Lit up.

'It is time for this to stop,' he turned to the headman. 'Get some wood. Start a fire here.'

He walked over to the cut hands leader and dragged him to the tree stump. Lashed his hands together, looped the rope over the stump and pulled tight, securing the man's hands to the chopping block. Then he waited while the villagers built a fire. The leader of the rebels started to sweat. The look of sardonic arrogance had been replaced with fear. But still only surface fear, not deep and visceral. The fear of someone who thinks that something may be going wrong but deep down does not really believe it. In this case the rebel could not believe that a white foreigner in charge of government troops would actually violate a prisoner of war. There were rules. He saw no dichotomy in his argument. The fact that he did not adhere to basic human rules and values was because he was superior. A people's leader. Above the rules.

When the fire was going strongly Garrett called the headman to him again.

'Do you have a steel spade or shovel.'

The headman shook his head. 'We have a steel hoe.'

'Get it.'

When the headman brought back the hoe Garrett placed the blade in the fire, leaving it until the steel grew cherry red. And then, without warning he spun, drew his machete and struck the cut hands leader's right wrist. His severed hand lay on the flat surface of tree trunk, fingers curled as if making a final effort to grasp at something. A second strike detached the left hand sending it spinning to the ground. Then he leant over, picked up the hoe and cauterized the wounds with the red-hot steel.

But it was far from over. Garrett had decided that the cut hand commandos had reached the end. He would no longer allow them to exist. The beast inside him howled and gibbered as he pushed against the boundaries of humanity in his quest for retribution. And then it broke free.

Garrett kicked the rebel leader in his chest, knocking him onto his back. The machete rose and fell two more times. Then the sizzling steel again. Stemming the flow of blood from the rebel's severed ankles. He screamed and thrashed around as the agony crashed over him in waves. Blood ran down his cheek where he had bitten through his lip as he convulsed. Garrett dragged the next rebel to the chopping block.

It took him over half an hour to do all eight rebels. They lay on the bare earth in front of him. Helpless, limbless freaks. Some unconscious, some wailing in agony and some mute. Faces gray with pain and shock.

The Warriors stood still. During the whole half an hour they had not moved, their discipline such that they did not intervene. But their humanity did not allow them to participate. Even though the rebels had done far worse and to many more.

Garrett beckoned to the headman who came forward on shaking limbs and then knelt before him. The old man could hardly bear to look at Garrett. For the man in front of him was no longer a man. His face, his arms, his uniform were drenched in blood. His eyes, green as the jungle, red rimmed with exhaustion and crackling with barely controlled insanity. He was *Popobawa*. The forest beast. And even though he had come to save them, the beast was known to be a fickle and could turn at any moment so he must be treated with the deepest respect.

And the beast leant over the headman and spoke to him in the tongue of the human.

'These men that I have punished. They must live. You and your village will care for them. And when their wounds have healed you will drive them away to live in the forest like snakes, crawling on the earth so all will know them for the evil animals that they are. And people will come from all around and piss on them and spit on them and curse them. You will send forth people from the village to tell all what happened here. Tell them and make them understand. If any more children are harmed then I will come for them. Do you understand?'

And the headman nodded. 'Yes,' he said. 'Yes *Popobawa*, I understand…

…Garrett stared at the empty brandy bottle in his hand. They had understood. But now, here, in the real world, not some stinking jungle, once again someone had harmed the children. And *Popobawa* was going to pay him a visit.

***

Garrett woke up. Still on the sofa. Mouth gummy. A head that felt constricted by steel bands. The smell of brandy in his pores.

Opposite him sat Petrus. Smoking. A wry grin on his face.

'Hey, you look like a rat that drowned in the beer pot.'

Garrett fumbled for his cigarettes. Tapped the pack. Empty. An imploring look at Petrus who offered from his pack. Garrett accepted. Lit. Deep inhalation.

'How long you been here?'

'Not long. Twenty minutes or so.'

Garrett pointed at the alarm pad by the door. 'And that?'

Petrus laughed. 'I don't usually let things like that bother me. So, what's up? Tell.'

And Garrett told Petrus everything, pausing only to slot one of the DVD's into the player in the sitting room. After, Petrus sat silent. And then.

'Okay. So, when are we going to kill this fucker?'

Garrett smiled. A humorless deaths head grimace.

'Soon, my friend. Soon.'

Garrett knew the doctor's name, he knew what he looked like and he knew where he worked. But now was the time for patience. Subtlety. This was not a man living on the fringes of society. On the edge of legality. No, this was a respected doctor. A surgeon. And, unlike the other hits that Garrett had instituted, this would attract much more attention from the law. Garrett was going to use that fact to his advantage.

The first thing that he and Petrus did was to visit the hospital where the doctor worked. A middle-sized private hospital. Very different from the National Health piles that Garrett was used to. Wall to wall carpeting, pastel colors and tasteful paintings as opposed to ragged vinyl, institutional phlegm-green and dirty handprints. He went to the reception area and asked if doctor Jakobs was in. One of the receptionists checked her computer.

'I'm sorry, sir but mister Jakobs is in surgery at the moment. Actually, he'll be in theatre all day. Scheduled to finish this afternoon. Two thirty.'

Garrett cocked an eyebrow. 'Mister?'

'Yes, sir. Surgeons are misters. GP's are doctors. Would you like to leave him a message?'

'No thanks. I'll try again later.'

Garrett walked back to the car where Petrus was waiting.

'He's here. If we come back at two and wait, we can follow him, see where he lives.'

'Okay, *Isosha*. Why don't we get something to eat?'

'Cool. Also, I need a hardware store.'

'You drive, I'll direct.'

Garrett turned right out of the hospital and then almost immediately left. They meandered through a myriad of walled townhouse complexes. Mostly Mediterranean style knockoffs in colors that architects refer to as Salmon or Savannah and normal people refer to as pink or yellow. Every now and then, in an effort to be different, someone had designed a neo-Georgian Bauhaus pastiche in blinding white. All angles and simple lines except for the front doors that were surrounded with elaborate porticos supported by decorative pilasters. A horrific blend of styles that made no sense apart from screaming out, look at me, I cost a fortune. Lifestyles of the rich and tasteless.

Small shopping centers consisting mainly of restaurants and bars, more townhouses and then a huge mall. Petrus directed Garrett into one of the massive parking areas. They locked the Jeep and hiked to the entrance.

Petrus went to buy some food and Garrett spent some time in the hardware store. They met back at the

Jeep. The two of them sat in the car with the doors open and ate the food that Petrus had purchased. Samoosas, filled with spicy lamb mince. Half a dozen bottles of lurid orange pop to wash it down. Afterwards they lit up and Garrett put the contents of his hardware bag into his pockets. A pack of nylon cable ties and a tube of superglue.

They had a couple of hours to kill before they went back to the hospital and they spent them in repose. Sitting idly in the car, smoking. Talking, but not much. The radio on in the background. Talk radio. Was breast-feeding in public acceptable? Bored housewives, receptionists sneaking a quick call at work, social workers, the odd student and of course the obligatory talk radio nut squad. Professional antagonists that kept the show alive and kicking. Garrett listened with amusement, Petrus with ill-concealed irritation.

Garrett started the Jeep and they drove back to the hospital, parking on the road outside where they had a good view of the exit. It wasn't long before the doctor drove out, BMW M5, Ray-bans, hair slicked back exposing ears like wing nuts. He drove fast. Confidently. Garrett struggled to keep up. Fortunately, he did not go far, pulling into one of the ubiquitous walled complexes. Armed guards at the gate. He showed his pass and drove in. Garrett waited outside.

'Shit. What now.'

Petrus laughed. 'No problem. How much cash you got on you?'

'Lots. Thousands.'

'Give me five hundred.' Garrett shifted in his seat, unzipped the top of his money belt and stripped out some notes. Handed them to Petrus.

'Cool. Now drive up.'

Garrett approached the gate. The guard held up a hand. Petrus hit the button and his window slid down. He beckoned. They spoke. Zulu. Voices low and urgent. Petrus turned towards Garrett.

'Another two hundred.'

The soldier complied. Petrus and the guard shook hands.

Petrus wound his window up. 'Drive through. Then go left. He's at number twenty-six on the right-hand side. He lives alone, no family. Uses a maid service so no one else at home.'

'The guard was helpful.'

Petrus nodded. 'Money well spent. There, pull in.'

Garrett turned the Jeep into the driveway at number twenty-six. Behind the BMW.

'So', continued Petrus. 'What's the plan?'

'No plan. We go in. We explain things nicely to him. We leave. He never touches a child again for the rest of his life.'

'Nice. Simple.'

The two men climbed out of the 4x4 and walked up to the door. The steel blade of the machete lay against Garrett's back. Cold against the furnace of his anger.

He rang the bell. After a short while the doctor came to the door.

'Hello. Can I help?' Expression concerned. A correct bedside manner. Lips almost smiling. Helpful.

Garrett punched him in the mouth snapping his two front teeth off at the roots and smashing him back into the house. Both he and Petrus hurried in, closing the door behind them. Garrett bent over the prostate doctor.

'Right, listen. You make a noise, any noise and I will break your neck. Understand?'

The man nodded. Garrett pulled him up by his shirtfront and dragged him down the corridor. The house was a large double volume open plan affair. Sitting area, dining area, freestanding bar. White tiles on the floor. Pastel curtains.

Garrett pulled out one of the dining chairs and slammed him down onto it.

The doctor whimpered. 'What do you want?'

Garrett ignored him, looking around for the phone. Found it. A table in the corner. Portable. He picked it up and put it on the dining room table. And then he stared at the doctor. The doctor that had raped the children. The doctor that had murdered the children. The doctor that had filmed himself doing it.

'Please,' the doctor begged. 'I have credit cards. I'll give you the pin numbers. You can draw money from the ATM.'

'We're not here for money.'

'What then?' Genuinely puzzled.

'We are here because of the children.'

'I don't know what you mean.'

Garrett pulled one of the DVDs from his pocket and placed it on the dining room table.

The murderer went white as the color drained from his face.

'Oh Jesus. I…it wasn't. I…they made me do it. Yes, they made me do it. Please, I'm as much a victim as the children.'

Garrett pulled the machete from his belt.

'Oh God, please. I'm sick. You can't, I'm sick. That's why I did it. It's a disease; I'll go for therapy. Oh God. Please don't kill me.'

Garrett shook his head. 'We aren't going to kill you.'

The doctor stared at him, a flicker of hope in his eyes. 'Not?'

'No, but we need to talk.'

'Yes, yes. Talk. Of course.'

'How long does it take an ambulance to get here?'

The man stared at Garrett as if he were an alien. 'What?'

'It's a simple question. If you phone your hospital for an ambulance, how long will it take to get here?'

He shook his head. Little drops of crimson detached from his pulped lips and scattered across the white tiles. 'I don't know.'

'Guess.'

Twenty minutes. Maybe twenty five.'

Garrett looked at his watch. 'Okay. So, who made you do it?'

'Men. Bad men.'

'Specifics, doctor. Specifics will keep you alive.'

'There was an Englishman. Ex-soldier of some sort. We did it at his place. In Hillbrow.'

'And?'

'A Nigerian. He always dressed in traditional clothes. A sort of kaftan thing.'

'An agbada.'

'Whatever. But we hardly spoke. Neither of them watched. The Brit would clear up afterwards. Keep prying eyes away. The Nigerian would take away the DVD. That's all.'

'Who paid you?'

'No one. I did it for free.'

'I need some names, Jakobs.'

'I swear, I don't know. The Nigerian lived in Hillbrow, I think. I think I heard him say that. Wait, his name was…not sure. A girl's name. Val…Valerie?'

'Doctor, you want to live, don't you?'

'Yes.'

'Well, we need more than that.'

'Please. I don't know.'

'What about others like you?'

The doctor shook his head. Garrett punched him again. Hard. His nose broke with an audible crack and blood spurted onto the pristine white tiles. He flipped over backwards onto the floor. Garrett dragged him up. Placed him back on the seat.

'Talk to me.'

'We contact each other over the net. Through unrelated websites. We use code. No one knows who the other person is. Not even what country they're in.'

Garrett stared at the doctor for a while and then he pulled the cable ties from his pocket and threw them at him. He made no effort to catch them. They fell to the floor. 'Pick them up.'

The doctor did so. Clumsily. Fear fumbling fingers.

'Are you left or right-handed?'

'What?'

'Fuck it. It doesn't matter. Put one around each wrist. Pull them as tight as you can.'

Again, the baffled look. 'What?'

Garrett stepped forward and slapped him. Hard, knocking him onto the floor. 'Get up and do it.'

The doctor crawled up onto the chair and tore the packet open. Black cable ties spilled out. He put one around each wrist. Pulled tight.

'Tighter,' commanded Garrett.

He pulled tighter. Puffing as did so. Blood dripping steadily from his ruined mouth, his pulped nose.

'Please, I've told you all I know. You said that you wouldn't kill me. Please.'

Garrett picked up the phone.

'What's the telephone number for the hospital?'

The doctor told him. Garrett dialed.

'Hello, yes actually you can help. It's an emergency. I'm phoning from doctor Jakobs' house. Yes. Please could you send an ambulance as soon as. There's been a horrific accident. The doctor has been very badly hurt. Oh, and could you send the police as well. It's seems as though there has been some foul play. Thank you.'

Garrett cancelled the call and put the phone down.

The door crashed open and the beast burst from its cage. Howling as it ran free. He swiveled and struck. The machete swept down in a glittering arc, slicing through the killer's right hand and bedding into arm of the dining chair. An animal howl tore from the doctor's throat. And the blade struck again.

The cable tie tourniquets stopped a lot of the blood flow but the tiles were soon still slick with red. The pedophile thrashed around on the floor. Keening wordlessly. Garrett put a boot on his chest to stop him moving. Then he bent down and, using the tube of superglue, glued the DVD to the murderer's forehead. He turned to Petrus.

'That's so everybody knows. Come on. Let's go.'

***

They did not speak. The enormity of what they had just done. The brutality of their deed had robbed them of their own essential humanity. Garrett drove automatically. Back to the orphanage. His exterior calm. Almost serene. But inside him the beast ran free, howling its joy, reveling in its very existence. Its animal stink filling his soul. And part of him ran with it. Liberated by an act of retribution. But the other side of his essence shrank back in horror. Not from what he had done but from the way that he had done it.

They pulled into the orphanage parking, got out of the car and went to Petrus' room. Garrett couldn't face seeing Manon. He needed time. To think. Readjust. He had no idea how he was going to tell her of the fate that her wards had suffered. Garrett sat on the small stool; Petrus opened a case in the corner of the room and took out a bottle. He cracked the top and offered it to the soldier. Garrett shook his head.

'Drink some, *Isosha*.'

'I don't drink. Well, I try not to.'

'Why? Because you think that it will lead to unhappy thoughts? Violence? Too late for that, my friend.'

Garrett smiled. 'True,' he accepted the bottle. Tilted, drank. The clear spirit was harsh on his tongue, burning his throat as it went down. Tears sprang to his eyes. 'Jesus, what is that?'

Petrus laughed. 'The finest cane spirits. Triple distilled. It's like rum. Rum for grown-ups.'

The guard offered Garrett a cigarette. Texan plain, as rough and uncompromising as the cane spirit.

Garrett accepted with a nod of thanks. Lit up off the proffered match.

'Tell me, *Isosha*, have you heard of *ubuntu*?'

Garrett shrugged. 'Vaguely. Some sort of African philosophy.'

'Not really. It is hard to explain, hard to translate. The complete Zulu proverb goes; "*Umuntu ngumuntu ngamantu*," which means: "I am a person through other people." In other words, if you treat others as less than human then you will lose your own humanity.'

Garrett pulled hard on his cigarette and then stared at the glowing tip. Rolling the white tube between his fingers causing tiny sparks to pepper down. A miniature firestorm.

'He deserved it.'

'Hey, I saw the videos. He was worse than an animal. Whatever we did he deserved.'

'So, what are you saying?'

'Nothing. Everything. *Ubuntu* is very difficult to achieve. But I think that it is an admirable thing to strive for. And you, *Isosha*? Do you have any creed?'

Garrett nodded.

'What is it?'

The soldier raised the bottle and took a swig. 'Fuck them all.'

Petrus laughed. 'I see that you are a philosopher.'

'Yep, deep thinker, that's me.'

Garrett lent back against the wall. His mind wandered. The smell of cordite. Green jungle. White tiles.

Red blood. On the edge of his hearing, he could hear the children playing in their dormitories. And in another time and place he could hear them screaming. Shaking with terror. On the bare earth. Strapped to a bed, a camera rolling. The cane numbed his feelings. He drank more.

'We haven't stopped anything,' he said.

'We have stopped a monster.'

'So? They'll find another monster. Monsters are easy to find. There's one under every child's bed at night. They're everywhere.' He passed the bottle to Petrus.

'So, what next?'

Garrett shrugged. 'No idea. We've got nothing. Some random Nigerian called Val-something, lives in Hillbrow. And some sort of long-range sniper dude that may, or may not be, helping us.'

'He's definitely helping us.'

'You're right. I've seen a lot of shooters in my life but nothing that comes close to what that guy can do. If he wanted us dead, we would be out of commission by now. But who is he? And another thing, what am I going to tell Manon about the missing children?'

'The truth.'

'Shit, Petrus. It's heavy. Can she take it?'

'She's stronger than she looks. You, of all people, should know that. In fact, she's probably stronger than us. She has her faith. What do we have? An old Zulu proverb and a belief that everyone should go and fuck themselves. I'm telling you, we can take it, and if we can take it then she can take it.'

Garrett sucked on his cigarette. Petrus was right. Manon could take it. Her faith was her pillar. But Garrett wasn't sure if he could. He had no faith. His engine was driven by anger and anger is a fragile emotion; its strength transitory, burning bright and brief. And like any flame it needed to consume to live. In Garrett's case it was consuming his soul.

'He stood up. 'I'm going to tell Manon.'

CHAPTER NINETEEN

For the first time in his life Valentine was afraid. Truly, viscerally afraid. He had found Brian's body in the Hillbrow studio. His head spread across the wall and ceiling. The air full of the rank metallic stink of death.

And then the next day he had seen the newspapers. Every one of them carrying the same story. Someone had broken into doctor Jakob's residence and mutilated him after, bizarrely, calling an ambulance and applying the necessary tourniquets needed to keep him alive after his appalling injuries. The reasons for the mutilation were obvious when the contents of a DVD that had been superglued to his forehead were viewed. The DVD showed the prominent surgeon to be a pedophile and a murderer and, from what the authorities were saying, it was easy to see that the police were not going to go out of their way to find the vigilante who had perpetrated the act.

In fact, there was already a rash of graffiti going up around the city, in six-foot high crimson letters; Matthew 18:8.

Valentine, who had attended a church school in England, knew the verse well. "If your hand or your foot causes you to sin, cut it off and throw it away." Already the newspapers were calling the vigilante, 18:8.

Valentine wasn't sure if the maiming's were religiously driven, but he was sure of one thing. He was sure that the doctor would have told 18:8 everything he knew. And that meant that he would be coming for him. Soon.

He grabbed his cell phone and scrolled through the numbers. Hit dial. Waited.

'Texas, it's Valentine. Have you seen the papers? …Front page, the 18:8 killing … Well, that's not all. I went to the Hillbrow studio. Brian's dead. He's been shot in the head … Well, what should I do? … Okay. I'll sit tight. I won't leave the building until you give me the all clear … Thanks Texas.' He disconnected and wiped the sweat from his brow with the back of his hand.

Texas put his cell back into his pocket, his face a picture of scorn.

'Fucking coward,' he said to himself. And then, 'Dubula!'

***

Manon had taken the news about the missing children as well as she could. And she had sympathized with Garrett when he told her that he knew not what to do next. He also told her how baffled he was about the phantom shooter.

The nun sat on the edge of her bed. Hands crossed on her lap. Face pale as death. Her eyes blank. And Garrett remembered back to Sierra Leone when she had told him that she no longer had any tears left to cry. But as he studied her face it came to him that something else was wrong. It was difficult for him to judge because she covered her emotions well. And, although Garrett had known Manon for a long time, he also hardly knew her at all. Eventually she looked up at the soldier. Her expression contrite but unashamed.

'I know who the shooter is.'

Garrett was careful to keep his face neutral, his voice calm.

'Okay, talk to me.'

'A few days back, just before you started going to question all of those gangsters about the children, His Most Reverend Eminence contacted me. He asked me all about you, everything that I knew.'

'Why didn't you tell me?'

'He asked me…commanded me not to. Of course, I obeyed.'

'You're telling me now.'

'I know. The next day he got back to me. He told me that he had assigned someone to watch over you. To protect you. Bishop Mandoluto.'

There was a low whistle from the doorway and Garrett turned to see Petrus. The guard raised an eyebrow. 'Mandoluto, hey?'

'I've met him,' admitted Garrett. 'Can't say that I saw anything special about him.'

Petrus laughed. 'Yeah well, some might say that you look pretty normal as well. At first impression. But this Mandoluto character. Mozambican. Portuguese, colored. Some call him The Long Gun, others, mister *Shabalala*, mister Death. Can kill a man at one thousand yards with a rubber band, or so they say. But seriously, he's probably the only guy around here that could shoot like what we've seen. Good man to have on your side. Very bad man to have running against you.'

'How come you know so much about him?'

'*Eish*, anyone who fought a war around here knows about The Long Gun. He's a legend. He fought for RENAMO. Killed over one hundred government troops before he was out of his teens. Even today, you meet an ex-FRELIMO grunt and mention The Long Gun; guy will shit himself like an incontinent pensioner.'

Manon frowned. 'Petrus.'

'Sorry, sister.'

'So why does the big boss want me protected?'

'He said that the church looks after its own. He said that you were sent by God to help the children. Not only now, but before. He called you the left hand of the lord.'

Petrus clapped Garrett on the shoulder.

'Well done, *Isosha*, you've been promoted. And to think, I met you when you were still a normal mortal.'

'Fuck off, Petrus.'

Garrett was embarrassed. But he was also relieved. He was not a religious man but the way that he saw it; a blessing from the Almighty wouldn't go amiss. That said, it was time to speak to the bishop. He took his cell out of his pocket, scrolled through the numbers and pressed call. It was answered on the third ring.

'Hello. Is that Bishop Mandoluto?'

'Yes.'

'Garrett here. Remember me?'

'Of course. How can I help?'

'We need to talk. Soon.'

'Why?'

'You know why, Mister Long Gun.'

'I see. Where are you?'

'Honeydew. The home.'

'I'll be there. Half an hour.'

Garrett hung up.

***

The soldier and the guard sat outside the front of the orphanage on plastic chairs, waiting for the bishop. The sun was on its way down. A massive red orb that dominated the darkling sky. As it often did in the Highveld, rain had poured down for the last twenty minutes and then stopped. Open, shut. It cleansed the dust from the air and filled the nostrils with the smell of ozone. The wet roofs and roads reflected the red of the sun and the dripping leaves on the trees shimmered in the same color. Christmas decorations. Or perhaps blood.

Far away a dog barked incessantly. Obsessed with guarding its territory, its entire existence the eight hundred square foot of garden it lived in, and the family that fed him. And in return for their munificence, he barked out his warning. Stay away. Mine. Mine. Mine.

Petrus sharpened his assegai. Running a small whetstone along the steel until it looked like it was edged with a sliver of blue ice. Garrett simply sat. Waited.

A black Audi A4 pulled into the parking area and Mandoluto stepped out. He wore a light gray linen suit, no tie, yellow shirt, black Chelsea boots. No shoulder holster. Garrett stood up to greet him. They shook hands and the soldier gestured towards a chair. Mandoluto sat, nodded to Petrus, took a slim leather cigarette case from an inside pocket. Flipped the lid. Offered. Dark hand rolled cheroots. Both Garrett and Petrus accepted and lit up. The area around them was quickly filled with deep blue fragrant smoke.

Petrus spoke first. 'Nice smoke.'

The bishop nodded. Remained silent.

'So,' said Garrett. 'Talk to me, Your Excellency.'

'Are you a religious man?' the bishop asked Garrett.

'Not really. I mean, I went to a church school. I believe in a God but I don't go to church. Weddings, funerals, that sort of thing, but otherwise not.'

'You see, Garrett. In many ways the life of a truly religious man is very simple. When one puts one's life in the hands of the Almighty one relinquishes certain responsibilities. I no longer have to decide for myself what is wrong and what is right, my church and my God have already decided that for me. In your case, His Most Reverend Eminence decided that you were the answer to certain prayers and thus he commanded me to do all that I could to protect you. This I have done and I will continue to do even though it causes me more pain than you will ever be able to conceive.'

'So that's it? Your boss says kill, and you do it?'

'Yes.'

'Without question.'

'Yes, without question or hesitation. For to go against the church is to go against God.'

'And what now?'

'Now? Whatever you decide. His Most Reverend Eminence told me to see you and tell you that I am yours to command. The children must be protected. Whatever is happening to them must stop.'

'I see. And just how much do you know about what has been happening to the children?'

Mandoluto shrugged. 'Not much. His Most Reverend Eminence is convinced that they are being kidnapped, we have asked around, investigated, but so far, nothing.'

So, Garrett told the bishop exactly what had been happening. The kidnappings, the filming, the murders and the retribution. As he spoke to the holy man, he could see the horror of the truth stripping away his veneer of civilization, eating through his armor of polite society. And by the end of the telling the man who sat opposite him was once again The Long Gun, mister *Shabalala*. The vestiges of his priesthood torn aside by the need to avenge the dreadful wrongs that Garrett had exposed him to.

'Our next step is to find the Nigerian. I will talk to our people. There are over two million Catholics in the greater Gauteng area. We will find him. It won't take long.'

The bishop shook hands, got back into his car and left.

***

The Long Gun was true to his word. Garrett had once again slept in Petrus' room and, shortly after breakfast, his cell rang.

'His name is Valentine Tsogo. He lives in a penthouse in Hillbrow. An apartment block called Glory Towers, Kotze Street. I'll forward a picture of him to your phone.'

It was still early morning and the roads were clogged with work-going traffic. Oil smoke filled the air and the taxis hooted at each other like flocks of huge migratory birds. Parp, parp. Touting for business.

Garrett parked the car a block away from the given address and they walked in on foot, stopping at a street vendor to buy some more cigarettes and a pack of *koeksusters*, a mega-sweet fried pastry product that made Garrett's jaw cramp when he chewed it. Petrus ate the rest of the packet with great relish. Licking the syrup from his fingers afterwards. They took up position diagonally opposite the building in a crumbling doorway of an old dry-cleaning shop. The place had been long boarded up and there were piles of old furniture, fridges and ragged car tires piled up around the entrance. A perfect urban hide. They sat comfortably in the hide all day, watching people going in and out of the building but no sign of Valentine Tsogo. Late afternoon Petrus went into the building and scouted around but with no luck. He reported to Garrett when he got back.

'There are two entrances to the penthouse; one is the fire escape. Protected by a thick steel door, so it's a no go. The other is via a private elevator from the parking garage. Also, behind locked steel doors, CCTV and armed guards. He has his own generator in case the electricity goes out and, according to a young girl that I talked to, he hasn't come out for a couple of days. He's even getting his food delivered. I'd say that he's gone into lockdown. A rat in his hole.'

'Shit. What now?'

'Not sure. If I were him and the left hand of the lord was looking for me, then I'd be in no hurry to come out.'

'Petrus.'

'Yes, *Isosha.*'

'Fuck off.'

Both of the men laughed.

'But seriously,' the Zulu continued. 'He could stay there forever. What do we do? Sit on our asses waiting?'

Garrett lit a cigarette. Smoked thoughtfully. 'Do you reckon that the Nigerian is the head honcho?'

'What? In charge of the whole snuff movie thing?'

'Yep. What think you?'

'Could be. I mean. I don't know him but a lot of those Nigerians have proved to be pretty ruthless. Well organized. *Yebo,* it could be him.'

'Okay, then this is the way that I see things. Let's have a chat to the bishop. See what he can do. If we can take out Valentine at distance and he is the main man…then, job done. If he isn't, well, we've still taken out one of the uglies and we're no worse off.'

'Sounds fair.'

Garrett took out his cell phone.

CHAPTER TWENTY

Valentine stood next to his rooftop Jacuzzi, gin in hand. The sun was setting over the city, his city, and the golden rays picked out the windows in the high-rise buildings creating a natural light display. He was at peace up here. An eagle in its eyrie. Aloof. Above the petty squabbles of the lesser peoples. He shrugged off his gown and let it fall to the floor leaving him in a pair of black swimming trunks. Then he climbed into the spa bath and lay back. The fragrant water effervesced soothingly around him and he drew a deep satisfied breath. In the next few days Texas would hunt down 18:8 and rid the world of him. And then, very soon, Valentine would be free again. Free from worry and doubt and fear. He raised the glass to his lips.

There was a sharp cracking sound. Like a tree branch breaking. And the glass in Valentine's hand disintegrated. The Nigerian slid slowly under the sparkling water. The bubbles turned pink and then red. And Valentine was truly free from all earthly worries and fears.

And two city blocks away a man wrapped a rifle in a bath-towel, slid it into an Adidas tog bag and took the elevator back down to the street.

***

Garrett had decided on a day out. After the children had taken breakfast and been sent to school, he asked Manon if she could take off. She had agreed.

They started by driving to Hartebeestport dam, normally an hour or so away but they took their time. Stopping at viewing points and roadside traders. Oohing and aahing over rock formations and wild flowers. Pointing out multicolored birds whose names they didn't know. Walking. Holding hands.

For an early lunch they chose a waterside restaurant where each individual table had its own BBQ and you purchased your meat and salad from a counter along with cheap, ice-cold wine or beer. Garrett chose a T-bone the size of a dinner plate and a jacket potato. Manon a couple of lamb chops and a bowl of green salad. They also selected a bottle of crisp white wine. Manon raised an eyebrow at Garrett's allowance of alcohol but said nothing. They talked of inconsequential things; favorite foods, memorable occasions, past pets, lucky numbers. Small snippets of nothingness that let them forget about murder and rape and evil.

Dragonflies dipped at the brown water, their over-large iridescent heads reflecting for brief moments as they kissed the surface. The swirl of fish and the ripple of wind. The smell of fire and charcoal cooked meat. The susurration of insects and the low croak of bull-frogs. The Highveld sun, high overhead, bleaching all primary colors from the vista as it washed over it. Garrett knew that this was one of those perfect moments that make a human life so precious. And he sat back and sipped his wine and let the feeling embrace him.

On the way back they stopped at a small dairy that specialized in making artisan cheeses. They were served by a large, bluff Afrikaner who showed great pride in his wares. Aggressive in his love of the art. Blessed are the cheesmakers. Garrett stocked up on belligerent blues and runny goat's cheeses, choosing more by depth of smell than by taste. Each cheese an open challenge to the next.

On the final leg, Manon leant against him in the car, her eyes closed. Not asleep, merely at rest. Her breath warm against his shoulder. The fragrance of her hair filling the car. And Garrett concentrated on the black ribbon unreeling in front of him, dragging him back to reality. Back to the orphanage, and later, to bed.

***

Garrett couldn't breathe. A dark figure loomed above him, hand over his nose and mouth. Powerful. But before he could react. '*Isosha*,' barely a whisper. 'There are men outside.'

Garrett nodded. He was once again sleeping in Petrus' room. He felt next to his sleeping mat. Picked up the machete. Stood up. There was enough light to see. But not well. Mere black on deep gray. The secret was to clear the mind. Let the other senses do the work. He cocked his head to one side. Listened. He could hear feet shuffling outside. The tiniest sound of a whisper. Sibilant. And then the unmistakable metallic snick of a safety catch being flicked off. Petrus held a hand in front Garrett's face. Four fingers. Garrett gave a thumb up in agreement. Put his mouth up against Petrus' ear.

'I'll go through the door. Keep low. Count to two and then you come. Dive, don't run.'

Petrus nodded.

Garrett took a deep, silent breath, went down on one knee and then sprung forward. He struck the door hard, tearing it from its hinges. As he hit the ground he rolled and then swept hard with the machete. The blade swung in an arc a mere six inches high. Struck. A man screamed. Fell. A dark shape next to him. Garrett swung again, slashing into the shape. Once, twice.

And then Petrus came out. Flying through the air. Landing, cat-like on his feet. The assegai already moving, cutting, slicing. Gunshots. Obscenely loud. Bright muzzle flashes. The wet sound of a blade being withdrawn from reluctant flesh. Running feet. Garrett sprang up and gave chase. Overhauling the running man. The blade lifted high. Down. Over. Deep breathes. So deep that the chest hurts. Euphoria.

'Petrus. You alright?'

'*Yebo, Isosha*. And you?'

'Hundred percent.'

Upstairs lights were being switched on. Children's voices rose loud. Garrett shouted out to Manon.

'No worries, sister. Get the children back to bed. I'll come talk to you soon.'

Garrett heard her walking down the steps to the dormitories. And then her voice, soft and reassuring. But this was Africa and midnight gunshots were not an uncommon occurrence so Garrett knew that, within minutes, the children would all be back asleep.

'Petrus.'

'Yep.'

'What now? Do we call the police?'

Petrus walked up to Garrett, offered a cigarette. They lit up before the Zulu answered.

'No way. Unnecessary trouble. Let's just load the bodies into the Jeep, drive down towards the Letamo Township. Dump them in the veld. Give us a hand. Let's do it.'

It took less than ten minutes to load the bodies. Petrus spread black bin liners over the seats first to stop the blood soaking them. Then he searched the bodies.

'What you looking for?' Asked Garrett.

'Car keys. They must have driven here. Their car will be down the road somewhere. We got to get rid of that as well. Ah, here.' He pulled out a set of keys. A BMW key chain. 'Right. You drive the Jeep. Wait for me to find the car first then follow me. I'll ditch it a few miles down the road. Leave it on the side with the keys in the ignition. Won't last twenty minutes.'

Petrus set off down the road at a fast lope. Within minutes Garrett saw car lights. Petrus pulled up in a five series BMW. Red. The window purred down.

'Let's go.'

Garrett fired up the Jeep and followed.

They left the car in a few miles down the road. Door slightly ajar and continued towards a more rural area to dispose of the dead.

Petrus whistled tunelessly while they drove. Three or four disconnected notes repeated in sequence. Like Morse code.

'This reminds me of the bad old days.'

'When was that,' asked Garrett.

'Back in the days of the apartheid regime. Late eighties, early nineties. Lots of fighting back then. Every day it seems.'

'Who? White security forces?'

'Sometimes. But mainly ANC.'

'I thought that they were on your side.'

'Fuck that. Why? Just because we're both black?'

'There are Zulus in the ANC.'

'Yes. But not real ones. Anyway, I wasn't that much into politics. I was younger and angry and I liked to fight. So, I fought. Good times.'

Garrett knew exactly what Petrus was talking about. The heady thrill of combat was a drug that was very hard to kick. The false rush that extreme sports gave one was like a non-alcoholic equivalent. Thrill-lite. Jumping off a building with a giant elastic band tied to your feet could never give one the same rush as being involved in a fire fight, where half the people involved died or were horribly maimed and disfigured. The higher the odds, the higher the rush. The relief that you had survived and the atavistic joy at seeing your enemy slain. It was a primal thing. But unlike Petrus who looked at it all through the misty glasses of nostalgia, Garrett feared what it had made him into. Because he had been caught in that whirlwind of destruction so many times it had scoured away parts of his humanity and left behind the black scorched soul of the beast.

Good times were walking the Highlands after a snow. The view of a hill covered in purple heather. A warm fire. A faithful dog. Not the mortal terror of combat. He noticed that Petrus was watching him as he drove. His expression one of slight amusement.

'You think too much, *Isosha*. Life is not so serious.'

'What do you mean?'

The Zulu merely laughed. 'Pull in here,' he pointed at a barely visible track veering off the main road. Garrett followed it. After less than a mile Petrus waved to stop. They pulled the bodies from the Jeep and simply left them there. Twisted and broken.

'Well,' said Garrett. 'We know one thing for sure. Valentine Tsogo wasn't the chief honcho. Someone else put that hit out on us tonight so it's obvious that there's some living dude out there who still wants us dead.'

Petrus grunted his agreement. 'No need to sound so happy about it.'

'Why not? Gives you more people to fight.'

'That was when I was younger. Now I'll settle for a few gallons of beer and a nice fat woman. Leave the fighting for the twenty-year-olds.'

'By the way, what did you do with the guns?'

'Left them with the bodies. We've already got weapons.'

Garrett had neither the strength nor the inclination to argue. And anyway, Petrus was more deadly with his stabbing assegai than most men are with an arsenal of weapons.

Speaking for himself he would prefer a 45. The machete was too personal. There was no way of remaining detached when you could feel the person dying at the end of your arm, jerking like a live fish on a rod. Better bang and drop. Extermination as opposed to killing. Better neither but he was too far down the road to go back. Unless they found the kingpin and put him down, then these atrocities against the children would continue. To go forward was only way that you could end up somewhere else.

And the halogen lights cut through the night. Blue-white beams creating a tunnel in the dark that they traveled down. Going someplace else.

***

Breakfast was a solemn affair. Both Garrett and Petrus shoveled down porridge like automatons. Replacing the massive amount of calories expended through the nights nervous energy. But their minds wandered. Thoughtful. After they had eaten, they went up to Manon's room. Garrett sat on her bed next to her. Petrus on the wicker chair. They all smoked. Garrett spoke first.

'We're stuck. I have no idea what to do next. But I can tell you one thing for sure; more uglies are going crawl out of the night to stop our clocks. And they are going to keep coming until they get us. People, we are in big shit here. Suggestions, anyone?'

'I can ask the bishop for help.' Said Manon.

'I suppose so, but I reckon that if he knew anything else he would have told us. They're as blind as we are at the moment,'

Garrett stood up, bubbling with frustrated random energy.

'I hate waiting for other people to react. You lose control in a situation like this and bad things happen.'

He lit one cigarette off the final glow of the last. Stubbed out. Walked over to the window and gazed through. Opened the pane and sucked in some fresh air. He tried to clear his mind. Empty it of preconceived ideas and thoughts. Let it drift. Like a fishing line on a lake. Baited and waiting. He watched the children playing, their high-pitched voices chirping together.

Mister Sweets had arrived and was receiving his normal joyous reception. He had finished handing out his jellybeans and fruit sparkles and was now pointing his cell phone at Vusi and Thandi. The kids all clamored to get his attention but he pushed them gently to one side so that he had a clear view of the brother and sister. Vusi stood facing the camera, arms folded, face stolid and unsmiling. Next to him his little sister was holding out her skirt, arms straight. Showing off the pretty yellow color. Gap toothed grin. Happy.

Garrett smiled to himself. 'Now he's taking photos.'

'What's that?' asked Petrus.

'Sweets. The kids love him.'

The Zulu glanced out of the window. 'Oh that. He always takes a photo of any new kids. That phone has a photo of just about every kid in the Sunshine Orphans group. The children love him to take photos. They're always bugging him. Take me, take me.'

Garrett had very few photos of his life. Somewhere, maybe, some school ones. Rows of boys in identical uniforms. Perhaps a school portrait. Short hair, ears and spots. As impersonal as a prison mugshot. A mere record of how he looked at that moment in time. Later, army identification photos, passport, driver's license. All variations of the same theme. Staring awkwardly at the camera. Unsmiling. Like Vusi. Photos to show other people who you were. No joy. He looked at the group again. Sweets had put his cell away. Thandi was still posing, as were some of the other girls. But photo time was over. The record had been struck.

'Only once.'

'What's that, *Isosha*?'

'Sweets. He took one photo. Only one. If you like taking photos of kids you take them. Lots of them. He only took one. One photo is a record. Like a mugshot or something. He's not photographing the kids; he's making a record of them.'

Garrett pinched the bridge of his nose. Thinking.

'Come on, I reckon we need a chat with the Sweetie man.'

***

The Sweetie man sat on the small stool in Petrus' room. Sweat ran down his face soaking his collar. Vinegary. An acrid odor. His face fixed in a nervous grin.

'I have done nothing wrong,' he said.

Garrett patted him on the shoulder. Reassuring. 'Don't worry, Sweets. I'm not accusing you of anything. I'm your friend. I was just wondering why you take a photo of every child. Do you keep them for yourself?'

'Yes. They are for me.'

'Why, Sweets?'

'Just to have them.'

'And sometimes to show other people?'

'No.'

'Sweets, come on now. I thought that we were friends. Friends don't lie to each other, do they?'

Mister Sweets looked down. Garrett had shamed him. 'No. Friends don't lie, mister Garrett.'

'So, sometimes to show other people?'

'Sometimes.'

Garrett pulled out his pack of cigarettes, offered Sweets one. He declined. Garrett lit two, passed one to Petrus.

'Okay, sometimes you show the pictures to…?'

Seconds passed. Smoke dribbled from Garrett's mouth, swirling lazily in the stillness of the room.

'There is a man. He asks to see them.'

'Okay, carry on.'

'He says to me, Sweets, he says, when any new children come to the homes you take a photo and show me, okay. I do this for the man. There is nothing wrong with this.'

'Who is this man, Sweets?'

'I meet him at the Elephant Drinking Hall in Alex. He name is mister Dubula.'

There was a sharp intake of breath from Petrus. Shock.

'No, mister Petrus. Dubula is not a bad man. He just wants to see the children.'

Garrett massaged his temples with the knuckles of his left hand.

'Why? Why does he want to see the children?'

Sweets shrugged. 'I don't know.'

Petrus stepped forward. Grabbed the food vendor by his collar. 'Fuck this. Tell me why you fucking monkey or I'll smash your face in.'

Sweets gibbered in terror. Froth formed at the corners of his mouth and he shook uncontrollably. Petrus slapped him. Hard. 'Tell me. Tell me or die.'

Garrett jumped between the two men. Pushing Petrus back. 'Slow down, Petrus. He can't take it.'

Petrus let go and Sweets sank to the ground. Boneless. Shivering in fear. Garrett knelt next to him. Put his arm around his shoulders.

'Are you alright?'

Sweets sniffed. Tears streamed down his face and he flinched when Petrus moved.

'Please, mister Garrett. Don't let the Zulu kill me.'

'It's all right, Sweets. We're friends. Petrus got a little excited, that's all. He's sorry,' Garrett looked at

Petrus. 'You're sorry, aren't you, Petrus. Tell Sweets that you're sorry.'

'Fuck that,' retorted Petrus. 'Fucking animal's lucky I don't gut him right now.'

Sweets went into another paroxysm of fear, blubbering like a child.

'Come on Petrus, apologize.'

'Fine then. I'm sorry, Sweets. Okay. I won't kill you yet.'

'Petrus!'

'Alright, I won't kill you. We're friends. Now speak to mister Garrett so that we can all remain friends.'

'That mister Dubula. He says to Sweets, show me the photos and tell me where they are. I show him. And then he downloads some from my phone, not all.'

Sweets wiped his nose with the palm of his hand and sniffed wetly.

'Carry on, Sweets.' Said Garrett.

'Then he shows the photos to other people.'

'What other people?'

'I don't know. Rich people. Not bad people. Just people who want children. And then, if they like the photo then mister Dubula he takes the child. Then he sells the child to the rich people. If they are happy then he gives me some money, one thousand Rands. You see? I have done nothing wrong. The children all go to rich families. Families that cannot have their own children. Mister Sweets loves the children. He would never hurt them. Please, sir. Please.' He looked sideways at Petrus. 'Don't let him kill Sweets.'

Garrett held his head in his hands. He could hear the blood pumping through his veins. A deep, dull thudding that seemed to shake his whole body.

'How many?'

'I don't know.'

This time Garrett grabbed the small man, his hand easily circling his throat. 'Think, how many times have they paid you?'

Sweets' eyes bulged from their sockets. A rope of thick spit hung from his open mouth.

'I think, about fifteen times,' he croaked. 'Maybe twenty.'

Garrett let him go. Patted his shoulder. 'Go, Sweets,' his voice was barely above a whisper. 'Go now. Quickly before Petrus kills you.'

The Sweetie man lunged for the door and ran, fumbling for his truck keys as he did so.

CHAPTER TWENTY-ONE

The old man woke even earlier than usual. He lay in the near-dark and analyzed what he was feeling. It had been so long that he had almost forgotten it. The tightness in the chest. The roiling stomach. Quickness of breath. Muck sweat. Yes, for the first time in many, many years he was feeling fear.

He rolled onto his side and then pushed himself up onto one knee. And then he stood. Ancient joints popped as he came fully upright. The old man was not sure how old he actually was, he definitely remembered the last world war. He claimed to remember the Great One as well. But, in all honesty, he was not sure if he could. There were memories, but when one got as old as he was one could never be sure whose memories they were. His? His fathers? Maybe even his ancestors.

Working more by touch than sight, so familiar were his surroundings, he packed and lit a pipe. The mix was slightly damp and he had to pull hard to get a good glow going. Using a calloused thumb to tamp down the burning plug. The pungent smell of marijuana filled the air.

Outside the pyramid shape of the false dawn arrived fooling the local cockerels into a premature vocalization of territorial defense. Crying out to all rivals. Warning them to keep their distance.

The old man sat at a rough wooden table. On a western style dining chair. When he was younger, he would never have done such a thing. He would have scorned any who did. But now his joints and ligaments were as old rusted iron. Pitted and scarred with age. So, he could no longer squat in the traditional way and had succumbed to the soft pleasure of western seating.

With the night-fear still on him the old man knew that he would have to take a deeper look at what was happening. He would have to call on his ancestors for help. He would have to confront the fear.

First, he took a pot of soured milk that was resting on the table and drank down a large gulp, smacking his lips at the tart taste. Then he spilt a bit on the floor as an offering. He followed this with a good pinch of tobacco, grinding it into the clay floor with his heel. After this he opened a small leather pouch that contained his throwing bones and he emptied it onto the table. The various items danced and skittered across the worn wood. Hyena bones, shells, a small red matchbox car, a single domino, double six. They spread and rolled to the edges of the table. And left together in the middle of the circle, a piece of the rib bone of the Aardvark or African Anteater and the knucklebone of the Hyena. The old man felt a chill wind blow over him. This was a sign that even the most callow of diviners could read. In all his years as a *Sangoma* he had seldom seen such obvious sign. The aardvark signified death and the fact that it was the rib bone meant that it was to be from a familiar source. And it stood next to the Hyena, the beast of the night, all else scattered away from it.

The old man rose slowly to his feet. He pulled on a faded pair of jeans, a pair of sandals made from old car tires and a red shirt. On his head he placed the beaded headwear of the witchdoctor, the *Sangoma*. He would have to warn the tribal chief. Death was coming. And he knew who would bring the chaos. The rib told him. It was the son. The son was coming home. And with him came the Beast that walks among us.

And the cock crowed for the third time as the *Sangoma* left his hut.

***

Texas was displeased. His organization made money in a myriad of different ways but most all of them led back to some form of tribute being paid to him. This payment was enforced through a network of guns under the immediate control of Dubula who then reported directly to Texas. Essentially this flow was subsistent on two major points; firstly, people paid because they were fearful of the consequences if they refused and, secondly; the payees were actually alive to do said paying.

Texas cracked his knuckles as he thought. Now, ever since this white foreigner had arrived with his obsession with the orphans, business had been suffering. Two of his biggest revenue streams, the Taxi man and mister Big were dead. Not only that, their guns were dead as well. So, to all intents and purposes their syndicates had ceased to exist. Wiped out by the foreigner and that mad Zulu. As well as this, for the first time in a long while, some other payments had been either late or a little light. The people all had seemingly valid excuses but Texas knew the real reasons. Two major crime families had been wiped out. Two major crime families that were meant to be under Texas' protection. And so, the people were testing the boundaries. Pushing back to see how far they could push. Well, Texas had made sure that the message was clear to all. You could not push back. Not even an infinitesimal push. You paid. On time. The full amount. Or bad things happened. In the last two days Dubula had caused very bad things to happen to three people. Two shop owners and a taxi operator who ran a fleet of six taxis. Dubula had brought back the past. His punishment had taken place in the form of necklacing. The victims were tied up and an old car tire placed around their necks. Then the tire was lit. They all burnt to death. Eventually.

However, the rot did not stop there. He had just been told that Valentine was dead. Killed in his

Jacuzzi. Shot. And then there was the British merce-nary, Brian. Whether he had killed himself or not was immaterial. He was dead, it was the foreigner's fault and it was causing Texas even more trouble. Add all of this to the nine guns of his own that the foreigner and the Zulu had either killed or disabled and it was fast becoming apparent that these two men were well and truly fucking up his business.

There was nothing that he could do about the loss of revenue from the two defunct families. So, he was going to muster his guns, all of them, and he was going to take these two men and cut the flesh from their bones with a small knife. And then he was going to throw the corpses into the middle of the main road in SOWETO so that the people knew, beyond all doubt; don't fuck with Texas Zangwa!

***

Petrus sat in the plastic chair outside the orphanage. Shirt off. Wearing only jeans and combat boots. His torso was finely muscled. Totally devoid of fat. But the skin was puckered and ridged with scars. Literally hun-dreds of scars. Long slash-scars from blades, tracks of rough stitching holes running next to them like little footprints. Short stab-scars, light triangular indents. And three or four bullet wounds. Dark craters, the skin around them rough and puckered like miniature dormant volcanoes. He was working on Garrett's machete, running a whetstone along the edge.

'There's a nick in the blade. You must have hit bone last time. I'll soon get it out though. Not a problem.'

Garrett said nothing. A cigarette smoldered untouched in his hand. Finally, Petrus stopped. Satisfied. He rubbed the blade with a lightly oiled cloth and put the weapon back in its sheath.

Garrett passed him a lit Gauloise. 'So, talk to me, my friend. Since Sweets buggered off you've been as quiet as a corpse.'

'I've been thinking. We need to talk. Now listen, *Isosha*, I don't want this to come out the wrong way. So, hear me out.'

'Okay, my friend, go for it.'

'*Isosha*, we have been drawn into a war that we now have little chance of winning. This Dubula character. I know him well. He is the running dog of a man called Texas Zangwa. Now, by himself Dubula is an almost unstoppable force. And I say this with no sense of exaggeration. I have seen you fight and you have seen me and, in my humble experience, I would say that few men could stand against either one of us. But this Dubula. We are as children to him. I can tell you with no shame; this man scares the shit out of me.'

Garrett shook his head. 'We can stop him. Together we can, no matter how bad he is.'

Petrus shrugged. 'Maybe, maybe not. He'll be coming for us so I am sure that we will get the chance to try. However, that's only one small part of the problem. The only reason we're still alive is that Texas hasn't taken us seriously enough yet. We know this because all that he has done is send a few of his boys around to sort us out. By now he will know that we pose a bigger threat than he first thought. Now, my friend, this Texas Zangwa is not a man known for subtlety of thought or action, the next time that they come for us they will come with overwhelming force. Forty, fifty, maybe sixty men. Maybe more.'

'So what? I've fought armies before.'

'As have I. But think on this, never before have we fought an army whose sole purpose is to destroy us.'

'That's true,' agreed Garrett with reluctance.

'You see, *Isosha*, you and I, we cannot win this war. We can try and I am sure that we will sorely harm the forces of evil, but we will not win.'

'What about Mandoluto? He can help.'

'Three against sixty? They will be armed with assault rifles, squad support weapons, grenades. Even the Long Gun cannot tilt the scales.'

Garrett sat for a while. Tight lipped. Logic told him that Petrus was right. And surely, only a fool continues to support a lost cause. Particularly one that will cost him his life. Garrett damned himself as a fool.

'I will not run. I will fight.'

'You cannot win without an army, *Isosha*.'

'I never said that I would win; I said that I would fight. There is no other road to travel, I do not have access to an army.'

And Petrus smiled. 'Ah, but you see, *Isosha*. I do!'

***

The Crowned Eagle flew high above the hills and valleys. Far below the Mngeni river sparkled in the sunlight as it roiled down the valley cutting ever deeper into the frangible earth. The valley of a thousand hills. He caught a series of hot air thermals that carried him higher still, above an *umuzi* or village. The *umuzi* was walled by a wooden stockade with a gated entrance. Directly opposite the entrance were two large mud walled *rondavels* or circular huts. The eagle did not know but these two huts would traditionally belong to the mother of the *Nkosi* or chief and to the chief himself. In times gone by there would have been a hut to the left of the entrance for unmarried girls and one to the right for unmarried boys. This custom had, of late, fallen away and now there were simply another dozen or so huts scattered around the walled *umuzi*. These were occupied by other members of the family group. There was also a smattering of much smaller huts used for food storage, beer brewing and workshops.

In the center of the village was another wooden fenced area called the *izibaya* or cattle kraal. This small enclosure was used to house the calves and was considered the most important part of the village. The entire village was built on a gentle hill with the entrance at the bottom so that, during a rainstorm, the water would flow through the village and naturally clean the *izibaya*.

There were many other smaller *umuzi* scattered around the area but none contained a house as large as this one, for none other was the *umuzi* of the chief. Each other smaller village was ruled over by an *inDuna*, who were, in turn, ruled over by the *inkhosi*. The chief was then directly responsible to the king.

At the moment almost all of the *inDuna*, seventeen in total, were squatting in the main room of the *inkhosi*. Between them these men had direct control of over two hundred well trained battle-hardened warriors. The *inDuna* faced the chief who, alone amongst them, sat on a small stool. To the right of the chief stood the *Sangoma*, smoking his pipe.

The *Sangoma* had already talked to the gathering, telling of the coming return of the son and now the *inkhosi* allowed them to talk freely amongst themselves before he called the *indaba*, the meeting, to order.

Whilst the *inDuna* talked the chief thought to himself. There was no question of whether the *Sangoma* was correct. He had not made a mistake in the last thirty years that he had been the chief's advisor. But why would the son return? Was he looking to reclaim the rights that were his? How could his sense of shame allow him to return? And who was the beast that walks among us? Chief Dlamini knew that all would be answered on the arrival of Petrus, however, a good leader plans ahead. But how do you plan for something that should not happen?

He thought back to those days when both the country and the Zulu nation were in turmoil. Civil war wracked the country and the white regime ruled with a steel fist. But death could come not only from the dreaded security forces but also from rival tribes and factions. The bloodiest of the internal conflicts being that between the ANC and the Zulu aligned Inkatha freedom party. This battle was a constant grinding low-level war of attrition that escalated sharply when white rule finally came to an end. The ANC had conscripted and trained a private army under the auspices of being SDU's or self-defense units. Inkatha had retaliated by forming SPU's or self-protection units. In a remarkably short time Petrus had risen to very high rank in the units. He did this by virtue of both his leadership and his awesome combat capabilities. But his rise to power ended with his self-enforced exile. With neither explanation nor warning he had simply left his family, his tribe and his people along with the trappings of power and wealth that came with it. As the only son in a family of daughters his leaving had brought great shame on his father and his family and, thus, he was never referred to by name, only as, the son.

But now he was returning and from the expression on the *Sangoma's* face, chief Dlamini knew that it bode no good.

***

The Sweetie man stared at the lump of black metal that lay on the seat next to him and shuddered with revulsion. A Star 30M nine-millimeter semi-automatic. Fully loaded with one round in the chamber and sixteen rounds in the magazine. He had rented the weapon off the owner of a gambling den who specialized in such things. He had rented it after the men had come to his house and spoken to him. And showed him the DVD. He wished from the bottom of his heart that the *Isosha* and the Zulu had not come to see him. He wished that they had let him remain ignorant to the facts. But they had insisted.

After they had left he had fallen to the floor and wept. He had been responsible for delivering the children into evil. With a few simple photos he had condemned them to the most horrific of deaths imaginable. For them there would be no loving family. There were no childless couples looking for someone to love. They had lied to Sweets. They had caused him to bring harm to the people that he loved. The people that had loved him. So, he had phoned Dubula on his cell phone and set up a meeting in the Alex beer hall.

And when he got there the Sweetie man was going to kill him.

Sweets pulled his delivery truck into the beer hall parking area, slipped the semi-automatic into his coat pocket and got out. He felt as though he were walking through water. His movements slow and sluggish. Terror had robbed him of his usual autonomic senses and every step that he took was achieved through conscious thought. Step, breathe, step, breathe. He walked into the dim building, momentarily blinded as his fear-dulled eyes adjusted from the African glare.

There were perhaps seven or eight other patrons scattered around the room. Dubula sat in his usual place, back to the wall, hands on the table in front of him. A tall glass of iced water. His eyes hooded. Expressionless. Lifeless. Like two black orbs of polished stone. For a moment Sweets was convinced that the big man was already dead and relief washed over him. And then Dubula spoke and reality returned.

'So, Sweetie man what do you have for me? More photos?'

Sweets said nothing. He could not. His tongue had cleaved to the roof of his mouth. His eyes were too dry to blink. His heart hammered against his chest like a child kicking off its blankets. He reached into his coat pocket and drew out the pistol. Pointed it at Dubula's face. The big man did not even flinch.

'For the children,' said the Sweetie man. And he pulled the trigger.

Nothing happened. He pulled the trigger again. As hard as he could. Still nothing.

Dubula stood up. 'You have left the safety on.'

Sweets scrabbled frantically at the weapon. But to no use. He had no idea where the safety was.

'There,' Dubula pointed. 'The small lever on the left-hand side. Push it up so that you can see the red dot.'

Sweets pushed up the lever and then dropped the pistol. It clattered onto the table.

'Pick it up,' commanded Dubula.

Sweets did so and pointed it once again at the big man. The weapon waved from side to side. They stood facing each other for several seconds. A lifetime. A block of obsidian and a Sweetie man. And Sweets pulled the trigger again.

The gun bucked in his hand. The report was obscenely loud in the closed room. Sweets felt it in his chest, his stomach. A vast compression. The nine-millimeter slug left the barrel at 1300 feet per second and struck Dubula at an oblique angle approximately two inches above his left elbow. The high velocity full metal jacket scored along the outside of his bicep and embedded itself into the wall behind him.

Using his right-hand Dubula drew his Desert Eagle action express, pointed at the Sweetie man's central mass and pulled the trigger. The massive half-inch round lifted the little man off his feet and threw him across the room in a fountain of flesh and bone. The broken body crashed into a table and eventually came to rest, sprawled on the floor, even tinier in death, his withered arm twisted awkwardly behind his shattered back. One of his jacket pockets had split open as he had been thrown back and scattered across the floor were a multitude of fruit sparkles. Yellow and purple and green. Sugar jewels.

Dubula looked down at the small broken Sweetie man and shook his head. He had given him every chance. But some men were simply not able to kill, no matter what the circumstances. He turned to face the other patrons in the hall. They sat still. Faces wary. Some fearful. He pointed at a group of four of them.

'You four will take care of the body. I want him buried with respect. I will cover the costs. He was a good man. A gentle man. He deserved more than this.'

He holstered his weapon and strode from the room. And if you had been close to him, you would have heard him whisper to himself.

'We all deserve more than this.'

The Jeep droned down the highway on its way from Gauteng to KwaZulu. Garrett had the cruise control on and the eight speakers pumped out Glazunov's 8th symphony. The sweeping, typically Russian music swept and flowed around the interior in rolling waves of sound. Neither him nor Petrus spoke. They were comfortable in their own silences, as was the third passenger who sat in the back next to his long Adidas tote bag.

Before they had left, they had done two things; firstly, Garrett and Petrus had visited Sweets and told him the whole story. They had decided that it was fair for the man to know what he had done, not to punish him but to prevent him from doing anything similar in the future.

Secondly, they had approached his Eminence and spoken to him about ensuring sister Manon's safety. He had dispatched eight guards to protect the orphanage around the clock. The church would protect its own. The holy man had also insisted that Bishop Mandoluto go with them to KwaZulu. It was not a request and neither Petrus nor Garrett were inclined to resist at any rate. As well as this they had explained their plan to his Eminence and he had assured them that he would put out the word to his people. He would ensure that Texas Zangwa knew exactly where they were heading. Because they were not running, they were attempting to lure evil from its lair and confront it in a situation more to their advantage. They needed the gangster to follow them. To hunt them down.

And here they were, three men heading west. Each for their own reason and each for the same reasons. Retribution, duty and redemption. Three men who had learned to abhor violence reacting against it in the only way that they knew. The only way that they were capable of. And in doing so they had become the personification of their own loathing.

Petrus closed his eyes and thought back to before times…

…the men stood in ranks before him. Three lines of five. Members of the SPU that he was in command of. They were dressed in a blend of traditional war dress and western style clothing. Cow tails around their calves and biceps, calfskin kilts, tee shirts, leather sandals or running shoes. Nikes. The married men with headbands. All carried five-foot cowhide shields, a stabbing assegai and a hardwood knobkerrie. There were no firearms.

The lack of firearms was not through choice, it was primarily due to the fact that the Inkatha freedom party found it very difficult to obtain assault rifles and semi auto pistols. The ANC, on the other hand, were well supplied with communist issue AKs and a mixture of other sundry weapons. Tokarevs, RPGs and even the odd type-67 machine gun. However, today's raid was hopefully going to change this fact. They had obtained intel that led them to believe that an ANC arms cache was situated in the General Smuts hostel in Howick. The plan was relatively simple. Attack the hostel, find the arms and take them. When they came up against any armed opposition and were unable to get close enough for a killing blow then the warriors were told to wait until the shooter had expended a full magazine and then attack fast while they were reloading. A tactic that required both speed and an unprecedented amount of courage. Petrus' men had both.

The Zulus had bussed in the night before and had hidden in a copse of trees close to the hostel and now they stood in silent ranks. Waiting. False dawn started to bleach the color from the night and Petrus gave the go. The band slipped out of the cover of the trees, running with swift feet towards the U-shaped red brick hostel building. Four stories high, it loomed black against the grayness of the coming day. A huge block of rooms. An ANC stronghold containing over sixty armed men. Being attacked by sixteen men wearing animal skins and carrying weapons of iron and wood. Petrus' heart swelled with pride at such courage.

The group hit the entrance lobby at a dead run, the only sound; running feet and heavy breathing. There were two armed guards sitting in the lobby, holstered pistols at their sides. Both were asleep. Petrus' assegai swung. Blood fountained high from slashed throats and pattered gently to the floor. The devil's rain.

Petrus pointed left and right. The group split and ran down their respective corridors. Seven men on one side, eight on the other. Petrus and his group ran to the top, as they passed each floor a man would peel off to start a room-to-room search. By the time he got to the fourth floor the battle had been fully joined. From a couple of floors below he heard the sound of gunfire. AKs on full auto combined with the flat crack of sidearms. People boiled out of the rooms on each side of the corridor that he ran down. The warriors next to Petrus barrelled straight into the armed opposition, using their shields to knock them off their feet, their assegais to finish. A man came out of the room at the end of the corridor. Small weapon. Skorpion submachine gun. He pointed it and fired. Twenty rounds burnt off in a fraction over a second. The man next to Petrus went down. Alive. Dead. Petrus lunged forward. His assegai struck the scorpion wielder full in the chest, plunging through his breastbone and into his heart. The flesh sucked obscenely as he withdrew the blade.

End of the corridor. Steps. Top floor. Another man. Close. Muzzle flash. Loud. Strike with the blade. Resistance. Leap frog over the dead body. Men on either side of him kicking open doors. Killing. Dying.

End of the corridor again. Last door. Petrus kicked it open. A black shape moved towards him, something in his hand. He struck. Another shape loomed to the side. Shield. Assegai. Warm blood.

Over. From the floors below a shrill keening. The wail of the defeated. No more gunfire. The sound of his men shouting. Zulu. Victorious. They had won. His ears rang with the sound of his own blood. His limbs light with the power of the conqueror. He turned and flicked on the light switch.

The dark shapes became human. Became real. Petrus looked down. One held a toothbrush. Another a small rag doll. The wounds from the eighteen-inch blade had exposed their bones. Small and white. Pick up sticks. Their intestines had spilled out, coiled on the floor like some obscene gelatinous worm. Blood already congealing around them. A pool of red to play in. Pat-a-cake, pat-a-cake.

The world shifted. Tilted. Petrus fell against the wall. Bile burnt its way up his throat, spewing out of his mouth like molten acid.

So he left the next day. He traveled to Johannesburg, far from his home. His people. For a while he did nothing, living from hand to mouth. And then he became a guard at the orphanage. To protect the children. But still his wards had come to harm. And now he traveled back home for the final battle. It was time to bring an end to the evil. Time for redemption…

…Garrett had turned off the music and they drove in silence. As they dropped in altitude the air became noticeably thicker. More humid. The landscape changed from shades of khaki and mustard to greens and purples. Flat to undulating hills.

They stopped once to fill up with gas and take a bathroom break. Lounged against the Jeep for a while smoking Mandoluto's rough-rolled cheroots. All of them were pictures of relaxation. Self-control. Hidden feelings locked down tight with hasps and staples of self-control.

Petrus had briefly explained his past to Garrett, telling him of his lineage and thus his possible access to an army of Zulu warriors. He did not tell him about the children although he had hinted at the fact that things may not run that smoothly.

On the surface the plan was simple. Go to Petrus' home. Speak to his father, the chief. Gather together an army of well-trained ex-SPU members. Wait for Texas and his cohorts to follow. Ambush them and kill them. Job done. Go home. But Garrett had fought short wars all over Africa. Short wars that had lasted a lifetime. Wars that were still being fought. Interminable. Every soldier dreams of being home for Christmas but most veterans know the dream for what it is. Fantasy. And Garrett was under no illusions. This had become a war. He flicked the stub of the cheroot into a trashcan and they all got back into the Jeep.

Two more hours brought them to the beginnings of a dirt road that meandered down into the valley. Loosely bound lengths of rusty barbed wire fencing that had strung between untreated fence poles lined the side of the road. Beyond, herds of indigenous Nguni cattle. Massive horns and dappled coats. Many with ribs showing. Slightly undernourished. Quantity of cattle being far more important than quality. Numbers equating directly to wealth. Garrett stopped the Jeep at the top of the road, before he began the descent, to take in the view. It was magnificent.

The river glittered at them from the bottom of the valley. Gently folding hills ruched up the landscape, every hill topped with a palisaded village. Mud huts washed in a variety of pastel colors. Women walking from the river with water buckets balanced on their heads, dressed in a colorful mix of traditional and western clothing. Bright colors. Swirling skirts. Young herd boys steering massive heads of cattle around using a small stick and a whistle. Almost naked, their black sun burnt skin glossy with health. Smiles white and wide and open. Dogs barking for the simple joy of noise-making. The smell of wood smoke and sun warmed green grass. And Garrett wondered how Petrus could ever have left.

He put the Jeep into gear and headed down the road, the large tires sliding and spitting out loose pebbles as they moved forward. Petrus guided him silently. Hand movements indicating left or right. Eventually the road gave way to a track, bumpy and rutted. Petrus gave the clenched fist sign to stop.

They had arrived at the gates to the largest village in the vicinity. Two men stood outside the gate, dressed in jeans, boots and tee shirts. Both carried an assegai and a hardwood knobkerrie. They walked towards the Jeep, stopping when Petrus climbed out and approached them. The men took one look at Petrus and immediately fell to their knees. '*Inkosana*, we see you.'

Petrus touched each on the head, like a priestly blessing. 'I see you too, my friends. Stand, please.'

The men stood and then, one after the other hugged Petrus and clapped him on the back with much smiling and delighted laughter. Garrett was impressed; no one had ever knelt in supplication before him. Mandoluto's lips twisted slightly. Sardonic.

And then another man walked out of the gate. His resemblance to Petrus was uncanny. But for the speckles of gray in his hair and the slight thickening of his waist he was identical. Petrus fell to the floor and prostrated himself.

'*Baba*, father.'

The man stopped before the prostrate guard.

'I see you, my son. Rise, it is time to talk.'

***

The view from Texas Zangwa's window did not bring him the pleasure that it usually did. Behind him stood Dubula and his five lieutenants. Five very nervous men and a block of stone.

The Sweetie man had tried to kill Dubula. The enormity of the act had stunned Texas. What had become of the respect that he had built up over the years? Hard years. Years of fighting, dragging himself up from the streets. Instilling terror. And now a small, crippled food seller had made an attempt on his muscle. But it was now time to strike back. All was in place.

He had put feelers out to see exactly who his opposition was and the info that came back to him had been surprising. The mad Zulu was none other than Petrus Dlamini, son of chief Dlamini. Texas had actually come up against him before, back in the day. When Texas was a leader of a SDU and Petrus, his opposite number in Inkatha. He was a man who commanded great respect, particularly from Texas, for only a fool does not show some deference to a powerful enemy.

The second man involved was the greatest surprise to the gang lord, namely, bishop Mandoluto. Everyone who had been involved in the struggle knew of this man. In fact, he was more myth than man. His rumored supernatural capabilities such as invisibility and night-sight plus his elevation to the priesthood gave him a mystical aura that was bound to give even the bravest man a shiver of awe. And it left Texas with no questions as to who had exterminated Valentine.

But the final man, the white foreigner who went by the name of Garrett, was Texas' source of greatest concern. It had taken a lot of digging and eventually he had gained his information from a white ex-SADF soldier turned mercenary who had once actually fought for the foreigner. When asked for Garrett's surname the mercenary had shrugged. He could not remember. But he could remember what the people called him. *Popobawa*. The beast.

He had also given Texas some advice. Leave it, he had said. Whatever this man has done to you, simply walk away.

Texas had laughed in the man's face and told him that he would be taking almost one hundred men to destroy this so-called beast. Then he had offered to take the mercenary onto his payroll. The man had refused. He had told Texas that he had become too used to living, and then he had left.

This may have caused concern in a lesser man but with Texas it simply served to galvanize him. Because he believed that a man's prowess is dictated by the strength of his enemies and, if all that was said about these men was true, then he was most definitely a man of great prowess.

However, the three men had fled from the Gauteng area. Word on the street was that they had returned to Petrus' village in KwaZulu. If so then this could create a new set of problems. But then, if Texas' memory served him correctly, the Zulu had left his home under an inauspicious cloud and, as a result, was close to being *persona non grata* in his own home.

In fact, if Texas was a gambling man, and he was, then he would bet the house that Petrus would find short shrift with the chief. Especially when the gang lord pitched up with almost one hundred armed men to exact his retribution. Yes, he was confident that he could convince chief Dlamini and his *izinDuna* to stay out of the conflict. As long as they knew that he would not be staying in their domain longer than necessary. And that would be fine with Texas; he had no ambitions to take on the Zulus. In and out. Bring the bodies back, display them for all to see, get his business back on track, and days would be happy once again. He allowed a touch of a smile to play on his lips before he wiped all expression from his face and turned to face his men.

***

Things had not gone well. Petrus had put forward his request to the *izinDuna* and they had paid him the courtesy of listening. But they had turned him down flat. While they appreciated that Texas was in the wrong, they insisted that it was not their war. Tell the police, they had said. Or just walk away. After all, they were only orphans. It was not the job of the Zulu *impis* to protect a bunch of unknown children.

And now the three stood together and wondered what to do next. Garrett and Petrus smoked. Mandoluto simply stood. Impassive.

Garrett spoke first. 'So, bishop. Any ideas?'

'We run away.'

'Sorry, no can do.'

'I thought as much. Okay, we wait. They come. We fight. We kill some. We die.'

Garrett shook his head. 'Can't say that I like that plan much either.'

'There is no plan, Garrett,' continued the bishop. 'We are three. They are legion. I have been commanded to protect you to the best of my ability. This I will do. I need no plan to achieve this. You do, I follow. As long as I do my best then I have done my duty. Win, lose, live, die. It is immaterial.'

Garrett drew on his cigarette. 'Fuck me, bishop. That's heavy.'

Mandoluto nodded. 'Yes.'

While Garrett and Mandoluto were talking, four other men had approached. Garrett recognized two as being the gatekeepers that had first greeted Petrus. The four knelt before the guard.

Petrus acknowledged them. 'Stand, my friends.'

'*Inkosi*,' said the one as they stood up. 'We have asked a boon of the chief and he has been generous. We have asked permission to join you in your fight and it has been given. We stand with you.'

Petrus turned to face the soldier and the bishop, his face all agrin. He pointed at the four newcomers.

'You see, bishop. And now we are legion. For the first time we are close to outnumbering the evil ones.'

For the first time since they had all met, Mandoluto smiled. He looked younger. Much younger. As if the simple gesture had broken through his thick layer of fatalism and allowed hope to shine through.

Petrus introduced the newcomers, all of whom were ten years or so younger than him. He pointed as he called out their names.

'Winston, Bongani, Cowboy, Jabu. They all fought alongside me back in the old days. They were much younger then, as were we all. But these four were younger than most. They are the very best.'

The four smiled at the compliment.

'Right then,' said Garrett. 'If this is our army then there's really only one way to play it. Gather round, gentlemen, I've got a plan.'

CHAPTER TWENTY-THREE

Seven Toyota High Ace people carriers and one Range Rover. Seventy-four people. Sixty AK47 assault rifles. Thirteen Skorpion sub machine guns. Twenty-seven TT30 Tokarev pistols. One hundred and twenty Chinese stick grenades and over eight thousand rounds of ammunition.

When Texas decided to make a statement there was no such thing as overkill. He was going in with such a ridiculous show of force not because he needed it but because it was his version of the Red Army march past. And, for the intent of this particular exercise, he was the obligatory Russian dictator. A symbol of overwhelming power. Comrade Texas Zangwa.

The cavalcade cruised down the highway. The Range Rover led. It did not exceed the speed limit. They arrived at the boundaries of Drummond in the midafternoon. The Range Rover turned onto the dirt road that led to Chief Dlamini's tribal area. After a mile or so they came up against a roadblock consisting of a row of forty-four-gallon drums and a loosely coiled roll of razor wire. On either side of the road stood waist high green grass.

In the middle of the road on a plastic chair sat an old man dressed in jeans, sandals and a faded red tee shirt. Arms folded; he had an unlit pipe in his mouth and a faraway expression on his face.

The cavalcade ground to a halt. Texas leaned out of the passenger window of the Range Rover.

'Hey! Move this shit, old man.'

The old man in the plastic chair did not move. Did not acknowledge the presence of the armed men in any way whatsoever. Texas pushed on the horn.

'Move, or we will move it for you.'

Finally, the old man looked at Texas. His face was crinkled and weather-lined, his hair frosted with white but his eyes were those of a youth. And they sparkled with wit.

'Go away,' he said and then he removed the pipe from his mouth, took a tobacco pouch from his pocket and started working on a fill.

Texas leaned out again. 'Fuck you, old man. Move or face my wrath.'

The old man had packed his pipe and was now lighting it with a match. When he was satisfied with the burn he stood up and walked slowly over to the Range Rover. Smoke billowed from his mouth like a stream engine of children's literature. I think I can, I think I can. He stopped at Texas' window.

'Go home, boy.' Puff, puff.

Texas literally started to vibrate with rage. His neck swelled up and his eyes became bloodshot. Such was his anger at being treated like this that he struggled to get his words out and when he did it sounded as though he were chewing on them and spitting them out as individual little packets of malice.

'If you do not start moving this shit in the next ten seconds then I will get out of the car and I will cut your withered old cock off and choke you with it. Do I make myself clear?'

The old man stared at the ganglord for a few seconds and then burst into laughter.

'*Hau*, boy,' he pointed at his crotch. 'To cut this monster off you will need a very big knife. And a boy like you won't have the strength to wield such a weapon. That is a man's job. Now go away. Okay?'

Texas grabbed the door handle, ready to jump out and teach the old idiot a lesson in respect. But he could not move. Dubula had grabbed hold of him and had pulled him back into his seat with a grip of iron.

'Boss, look.'

The urgency of his bodyguard's tone cut through his anger and he stopped.

'Take a look around, boss.'

Texas scoped out the surrounding area. On both sides of the road stood ranks of Zulus. Hundreds of them. They were dressed in a variety of clothes but had one thing in common. All carried a five-foot shield and at least one assegai. And as Texas looked, they started to rattle their spears against their shields. Softly at first and then with increasing volume. The sound of thunder rippled across the land, building until the hair on Texas' neck stood up. The drumming louder than he could believe. The windows of the car shook. The doors shook. The very ground itself shook in sympathy. And then as one the *impi* raised their right foot and slammed it back onto the bare earth. A single crashing detonation of sound followed by a long drawn-out expulsion of air.

'*Jeeeeeeeee.*'

And for the first time in a long while Texas was afraid. He could clearly hear the sound of his men in the cavalcade cocking their weapons. The metallic sound small and pathetic when compared with the primeval sound of the warriors that surrounded them. He held his hands up in supplication.

'I am sorry for my rudeness, ancient one.'

The old man nodded, accepting the change of address. The respect that it conveyed.

Texas continued. 'We do not come here to war with the people of the sky. We come on a personal mission.'

'Yes, mister Zangwa,' spoke the old man. 'We know. You seek Petrus Dlamini.'

Texas nodded his agreement.

'He is not here.' The old man noted the disbelief in the gang lord's eyes. 'He was here. He came to ask a boon of the chief. He wanted…' The old man gestured at the *impi* that surrounded them. 'This.' He puffed again on his pipe and stared at Texas. 'The boon was refused. He has left chief Dlamini's lands.'

'Where has he gone?' asked Texas.

The old man pointed at a mountain range in the far distance. Blue and gray and green. 'He has gone there. To hide.'

'And why do you tell us?'

The old man shrugged. 'It is not our battle. It is something that he has brought on himself.'

'Thank you, ancient one. Tell me, how do we get there?'

Again, the old man shrugged. 'The mountains are called, Qiniselani Manyuswa. Get there any way that you want but do not cross into Dlamini's land or you will never leave it. Do I make myself clear, boy?'

Texas swallowed his anger.

'Yes, old man.'

The old man chuckled and puffed his way back to his plastic seat.

When Texas looked around him there was no longer any trace of the *impi* that had ranged before him and, when he turned back to the roadblock the old man had also disappeared. Texas shivered with superstitious dread.

'Come on,' he said to Dubula. 'Let's get the fuck out of this place, we've got some people to kill.'

***

Garrett parked the Jeep at the foothills of the mountain range. They had driven it in amongst a copse of thorn trees and then covered it with grass and cut branches to hide it. Afterwards the seven men took to foot. The four new Zulus carried a shield, an assegai and a burlap sack with a rope tied to it so it could be slung over a shoulder. Garrett, Petrus and Mandoluto also carried a sack each. Each sack contained a plastic two-liter water bottle, a bag of maize meal, salt, and sugar, cooking utensils, a canvas ground sheet and a few pounds of *biltong* or dried beef. Garrett had a few extra items in his sack as well as his machete in a sheath on his belt. Petrus had his assegai and the bishop his long gun.

Taking lead from Petrus they formed a single file and jogged along a narrow track that headed into the hills. The track zigzagged upwards in an effort to keep the ascent from becoming too steep. But to anyone who was not in the peak of fitness it would still be a very hard race to run. After a few miles they came to the peak of the first of the foothills and stopped.

Garrett looked back. 'So, Petrus. You reckon this is the only way up here?'

His friend nodded. 'It's the only safe way. There are other tracks but they peter out into dead ends. If you want to get into the heart of the mountains then this is your only choice.'

Garrett nodded approval. 'Perfect. Let's keep going then.'

The group loped on. Soldier's strides eating up the miles. They ran into the early evening, stopping only once for a drink of water. Before it got too dark to see Garrett suggested they make camp. They broke from the trail, moving to the right for a few hundred yards and settled down in the lee of a large oblong rock. A granite loaf of bread. The Zulus started a small fire and cooked up some *phutu pap,* maize meal boiled up with salt until it achieved a stiff dough-like consistency.

Garrett organized the watch, taking the first hour for himself. They weren't yet worried that Texas would be close to them but Garrett considered them to be at war, and when at war you set watches. The rest of the crew wrapped themselves in their canvas groundsheets and lay down on the earth.

After almost an hour Garrett felt the presence of someone close and he whipped his head around to see Mandoluto approaching. The bishop moved silently, not through design but merely because that was how he moved. Rolling on the edges of his feet. Each step taken with innate care. A natural predator. He raised an eyebrow in greeting and sat next to Garrett. Neither of them smoked. Not on watch.

'And then we were seven,' he said as he sat.

Garrett smiled. 'Better than three.'

'Yes. But not as good as three hundred.'

'Three hundred would have been nice. In fact, it would have been the only time that I would have been able to fight on the side of overwhelming strength.'

Mandoluto laughed. A small sound. An expulsion of air rather than a true vocalization of mirth. 'Me too.'

'I wonder why those four chose to join us. Friendship? Duty?'

Mandoluto stretched his arms above his head. Reached hard until his spine realigned with a series of tiny pops.

'You know, Garrett, the British Empire has only been defeated three times. Once in the American war of independence and then two more times right here. In this very land that we sit. Firstly, at *Isandlwana*, by a bunch of men with spears, and the second time in the Boer war by a group of farmers on horseback. The people that live in this land are the fightingest bunch of people that you will ever meet. I suppose what I'm trying to say is; who knows why they joined us, probably they simply like a good fight. Don't question it. Have faith, my friend. It moves mountains.'

Garrett smiled his acceptance. 'So, you good here?'

The bishop nodded.

Garrett stood up. 'Right. I'll get some shut-eye. Tomorrow it starts.'

He walked off into the darkness leaving the bishop to watch over them.

They woke early that morning, before the sun. Breakfast was similar to dinner except that the pap was not as stiff and sugar was added. By the time the sun had awoken they had been on the move for over an hour, moving ever up and into the craggy heart of the range. Into the broken ground where nature had formed hundreds of natural traps. Loose rocks. Grass covered pitfalls. Trails of scree and mud.

Around mid-morning the trail cut around the crown of yet another peak. The air had grown colder and a fine rain misted the atmosphere. Soaking and chilling. Garrett called a stop.

'Here,' he said and pointed up at the peak above them. 'That's the place. Come.'

He headed off the track directly up the treacherous slope to the top. When they reached the top, the surrounding vista was incredible. The savage folded, broken land stretched for miles around. Harsh and uncompromising. It reminded Garrett of the Scottish Highlands. He felt at home. This was a good place to start the fight. Here in this brutal landscape, he would begin to bring Texas Zangwa to justice. This is where it would commence.

He called the others in close and explained what was to happen. There were a few arguments and then they turned as one and jogged off, carrying Garrett's sack and leaving him alone on the mountaintop. And when they were gone the soldier sank to the ground and became invisible.

***

Texas had left three men with the cars. The rest, another sixty-four men, had been issued with their weapons. Each man carried either an AK with one hundred rounds of ammunition or a Skorpion with the same. Those that Texas considered as officers or long servers received a handgun as well. Everyone carried two Chinese stick grenades thrust into their belts. They had gotten directions from the locals to the bottom of the trail that headed into the mountains and had left the cars at the beginning of the track. And now they climbed, strung out like a baggage train of colonial proportions. The men carried full rucksacks, hurriedly purchased from a trading store in Drummond, containing tinned food, water, tea, coffee, tents, sleeping bags, torches, batteries, gas stoves and changes of clothing. The train stretched for almost two hundred yards with Texas and Dubula in the middle. The weather had turned and the air was frigid and heavy with moisture. Rain as fine as waterfall spray saturated all to the skin. Insidious and subtle. Whenever you stopped walking the cold crept into your bones and joints like symptoms of premature old age.

But the men's morale was high. There was much laughing and joking. After all, it was little more than a sporting excursion. One of the locals had told them that the three men they were searching for had been joined by four others. But still these were the sort of odds that appealed to the men in the train. Ten to one advantage. After all, no one hunts down seventy foxes with a single dog. No, the odds always work the other way. To the rulers go the advantages. This was not a war, this was an example. Texas was proud of his men. He felt like a marauding conqueror of old. Crossing the mountains with his army of warriors, ready to do battle. Ready to teach the foreigner and his friends a lesson. Hannibal must have felt the same when he set out with his elephants.

And ahead of him, lying still in the grass, lay a single soldier. Waiting.

CHAPTER TWENTY-FOUR

Petrus, Mandoluto and the four new Zulus had clambered around the back of the mountain, a torturous and dangerous route that brought them out behind Texas and his unwieldy train of gangsters. Then they had watched them from afar and waited.

When the train was well past them Petrus spent some time selecting the perfect spot on the trail. Eventually he decided. It was where it reached its narrowest point, cutting along a particularly steep ridge, an almost sheer drop below and a climb as steep above. Then they spent the next four hours finding and rolling over as many large boulders as they could. By late afternoon they had collected over thirty of them. Then they had climbed down to the trail and, using sharpened sticks, dug out a trench underneath the trial. The trench ran for about twenty feet. Finally, their bodies aching from the physical strain that they had been subjected to, they rolled the boulders down onto the weakened trail. The first ten boulders made no seeming impact at all but by the fifteenth the trail had collapsed. When they rolled the last boulder down the hill there was no visible sign of any trail at all, merely a treacherous landslide of rocks and mud and loose scree. The way home had effectively been cut off.

***

The sun was going down and Texas had called to make camp. They had found a flattish area slightly off the beaten track but they would be unable to form a circle or square of any sort, the bulk of the tents would be strung out along the trail. But this did not bother anyone unduly as there was no possibility of them being attacked. The small handful of men that they were seeking would be attempting to get as far away as possible. In fact, Texas' biggest concern was that they were not traveling fast enough to catch up with the offenders that they wanted to punish. He made a note to himself to push harder to the next day.

The men formed groups of five or six and used their gas stoves to heat up some dinner. The tents were pitched, watches allocated and rest taken. The fine rain continued and the men standing watch pulled their coats over their heads to take refuge.

At two hours and seventeen minutes past the witching hour Garrett began to creep forward. He had noted that Texas had made the usual amateurs mistake of changing watch on the hour. Garrett had learned of old that watches should be changed at irregular times. Thirteen past or seven minutes to. Never on the hour or half hour. Because who knew, perhaps someone just like him was lurking in the long grass.

Texas and Dubula shared a tent in the middle of the flat area, surrounded by four other tents and seven watchmen who rotated around the clock. It would be impossible, or at least very costly, to get to either of them.

They had also placed another four watchmen along the trail, one at each end and one half way down towards the middle. The watchers were all stationary. Sitting huddled up against the rain. Focusing in on their own discomfort rather than out at what was happening around them. Rule number two, keep your watchmen mobile and get their patrol routes to intersect so that they had regular interaction. Keep them awake and on their toes.

The gangsters were sleeping in a variety of tents; they had taken all that the trading store had in stock so there was no choice. They ranged from small two-man to double height four-man affairs in a mélange of colors from green to Day-Glo orange.

Garrett chose a daffodil-yellow two-man about a third of the way along the stretched-out encampment. With infinite care he leopard crawled towards the tent, not taking a direct route but rather sliding from shadow to shadow. He had tied a dark cloth over his mouth to stop any condensate forming in the low nighttime temperatures and he had blackened his face with mud. His machete was in its sheath but that was not to be his weapon of choice. In his right hand he held a small, razor –sharp skinning knife, its blade smeared with mud. In his left an eight-inch sharpened hardwood stick, about the thickness of his thumb. And as the night wore on the soldier edged towards the tent. As slow and insidious as cancer.

When Garrett finally reached the back of the tent undetected, he used the skinning knife to cut an opening in the nylon. The blade whispered through the fabric and Garrett eased it open. Lying there were two men. One lay on his back, the other on his side. They lay with their heads at the door, their feet towards Garrett. Both were breathing the rhythmic breath of deep sleep. Garrett chose the one sleeping on his back. Throat exposed. Slowly, he moved into the tent, supporting himself on his arms so that he was above the man. A selfish lover readying himself to enter a woman. And then with one smooth movement he let himself fall onto the sleeping form. His right hand clamped over the man's mouth and nose and the left hand plunged towards his throat. The sharpened stake shredded the man's voice box, preventing sound, and then continued its upward journey, penetrating the roof of his mouth and entering his brain. The body twitched slightly but Garrett was lying full length on top so the other sleeper remained unaware of the violent scene that was taking place a mere foot away from him.

The soldier waited a complete minute before he moved, and when he did it was with the same death-like stealth as before. He slid backwards off the body and then, inch-by-inch, he pulled the corpse out of the tent after him.

The return trip took even longer than Garrett expected and it was literally minutes before false dawn when he had finally moved far away enough to stand. He picked the body up, threw it over his shoulder and jogged off. After twenty minutes or so he came across a concealed pit fall, covered with grass. Treacherous. He dumped the body into it and ran on towards his pre-planned rendezvous point with his Petrus.

***

Texas was apoplectic. The gangster who had shared the tent with the missing man lay sprawled on the ground in front of him. Blood seeped from a cut on his lip and his right eye was swollen shut. Texas kicked him again, eliciting a grunt of pain.

'How can someone cut a hole in your tent and simply take your partner without you knowing?'

The prone man mumbled an answer.

'What?' Screamed Texas.

'I don't know, boss. Maybe Daniel went by himself. Maybe he ran away.

'Don't be fucking stupid. He would have gone out of the front of the tent, not through a hole in the back.' He swung another kick at the man but missed, lost his footing and fell to the ground. The men around him kept their faces carefully expressionless. No hint of a smile. To laugh was to die. The gang lord sprang to his feet and started around him belligerently. Satisfied that he had not made a fool of himself he turned on Dubula.

'Why didn't your watchmen see something? Am I surrounded by idiots and blind people?' He shook his head. 'Strike camp. Double time. We catch these people today. Move it.'

Around him everyone burst into frantic effort, each man keen to show his dedication to the master.

Dubula went to the missing man's tent and spent a while studying it and its surroundings in minute detail, going down on one knee to check for spoor. By the time that the men were ready to go he had pieced together what had happened and the sheer effrontery of the deed brought a smile of respect from him. Whoever had done this had balls of steel and a mind as cold as ice. The scary thing, he thought to himself, was that any one of the three men that they were seeking was capable of doing such a deed. The foreigner, the mad Zulu or the bishop. Dubula's smile broadened. It was good to have such powerful enemies. It showed that you were a man of note. With a spring in his step, he joined the train.

They did not catch up with anybody that day. In fact, by the time that they formed camp again that night, they had found no discernable trace of any human life, let alone that of their intended quarry. And, although he did not say anything, Dubula was starting to question the wisdom of his master's plan. To himself he thought that it would be best to pick a smaller team of the very best men, led by him, to seek out the enemy. But the boss wanted a show of strength and so they blundered along like a huge unwieldy multi-limbed animal. All strength and no subtlety.

The next morning when the camp awoke there was another man missing. This one from a tent only two away from the master's. And this time there was no shouting and screaming. No pointing of fingers. Texas appointed a group of three men to retrace their steps of the last two days and see if they could find either of the bodies. In the back of his mind he was hoping that they would find evidence that the men had simply run away, although it seemed unlikely. They jogged off without packs, traveling light and making good time.

***

The six men lay still in the long grass as they had been for the last four hours since sun up. Petrus was not convinced but Garrett was running the show at the moment and he had promised them that this was the correct time and place to set an ambush. Personally, Petrus wondered why any men would be coming this way, in the opposite direction to the rest of the gangsters. But when he had questioned Garrett, the soldier had simply smiled and told him to have faith. And after what he had done over the last two nights, killing and abducting two men from under the very noses of the enemy, Petrus was more than happy to take the soldier's word. At least for a while.

Slowly, without disturbing any of the surrounding knee-high grass, he crawled over to Garrett. He placed his mouth right next to his ear before he talked in the faintest of whispers.

'Hey, *Isosha*. I'm bored. This is not how a Zulu makes war, hiding in the grass like a frightened herd boy. How much longer?'

Garrett simply raised a finger to his lips and then pointed. Petrus saw them, coming around the crown of the hill. Three men running in single file. All carried AKs. Every now and then they would stop and take a cursory look at their surroundings before the jogging continued.

Petrus felt adrenalin surge through his system. The plan was simple. They had laid an ambush on each side of the track as it ran into a steep dip. The loose scree and mud would force the assailants to slow down and, most likely, bunch up. It was imperative that they killed them all before they got off a shot. Garrett was very explicit about that. No noise. Although he had posted Mandoluto on a nearby hillock to provide sniper cover if anything went wrong.

It worked perfectly. The runners slowed to a walk as they crested the rise and started down the hill, slipping and sliding up against each other. Leaning on one another for support. Garrett and the five Zulus rose up as one, their blades stabbing, withdrawing and stabbing again. Fast balanced movements. Silent but for grunts of exertion and the wet tearing sounds of blades rending flesh. Within seconds the three men lay dead. And now Garrett and his friends had three AKs, six Chinese stick grenades, a Tokarev pistol and over three hundred rounds of ammunition.

Petrus looked up at Garrett with a grin.

'Well-done, *Isosha*. With these weapons I think that the enemy will now find themselves outnumbered.'

The other Zulus laughed their appreciation.

***

Texas had no idea what to do next. The three men that he had sent on a recce had not returned. Had they fallen to some misfortune? Had they simply gone AWOL? Or had the foreigner and his friends waylaid them? Whatever, he could not show any vacillation in front of the men. In a position such as his, implied strength was everything. So, he struck camp and pushed on, keeping the pace high enough to keep the men concentrating on going forward. Keeping their minds off their slowly dwindling numbers and their boss' seeming inability to do anything about it.

That evening the camp looked more like a festival than a military post. Half the men had declined to pitch their tents, preferring to sit back-to-back in order to stay safe. Every man had his torch switched on and they all swept the darkness like children playing at hide and seek. A carnival of lights. Texas did nothing to stop them knowing that a nervous man is usually an alert man.

And the night passed with infinite slowness as the men watched and waited and wondered who would be next.

As it happened Garrett found that the surfeit of light actually worked to his advantage. Instead of using quiet stealth he simply blacked his face with mud, walked calmly into the camp, trusting that his attitude would convince people that he belonged. He approached one of the men sitting alone near the outskirts of the camp and, with one swift stroke of the skinning knife, slit his throat. He left the body where it lay and walked away from the camp into the darkness.

CHAPTER TWENTY-FIVE

Thousands of people had lined the streets for the entire three-miles from the church to the cemetery. In fact, such were the crowds that the funeral cortège traveled at a slower than walking pace.

And all along the route people threw, not flowers, but sweets. Fruit sparkles, jelly bears, ice mints and wine gums. The sun caught the translucent confectionaries and refracted through them like a sunrise through a million miniature, stained glass windows. And all along the way the children called out his name.

Sweets. Sweets. He is gone, they cried. The Sweetie man is gone.

The men growled amongst each other. He was a man, they said. He took a stand for what he believed in. And he paid the ultimate price.

Sweets. Sweets. The Sweetie man is gone.

And the hearse's tires crunched slowly over the strewn sugar jewels. Crushing them into mere white powder. The crowd picked up the chant. Building. Gaining a life of its own.

Sweets. Sweets. The Sweetie man is gone.

The cortège reached the end of Louis Botha Avenue and turned towards Alexandra, passing by a large drinking hall that was owned by Texas Zangwa and associates. The crowd surged into the building, smashing the windows, destroying furniture. The manager was hauled out into the street and beaten by the chanting crowd.

Sweets. Sweets. The Sweetie man is gone.

Someone put a match to the curtains and the flames licked hungrily upwards. Within minutes the building was fully ablaze. The crowd surged forth, seeking out other premises that belonged to Texas Zangwa.

Sweets. Sweets. The Sweetie man is gone.

CHAPTER TWENTY-SIX

Garrett told them the plan. It was relatively simple. Cut off any means of escape, put the enemy into a position where they were nervous to rest at night, obtain some weapons from them and then, place Mandoluto on a hill a half a mile or so away and tell him to start killing. When they came to look for the bishop, ambush them.

But this morning had brought with it a new enemy. An enemy that Garrett had not even known the existence of before now. Impenetrable and gray. A mist as thick as a Swiss duvet had settled over the mountains.

'Shit. How long is this going to last?' Garrett asked Petrus.

The Zulu shrugged. 'Not sure. This time of year, maybe a week. Ten days. Not longer.'

'Maybe shorter?'

Petrus shook his head. 'A week.'

Mandoluto lit up a cheroot.

'I don't think that we should smoke,' said Garrett.

'Don't worry;' answered the bishop. 'The mist will kill the smoke. It won't travel. Even if it does, they know that we're out here. Anyway, I'd rather get shot than spend another day without a smoke.'

'Well then offer.'

The bishop laughed. 'Smoke your own. These things don't come cheap and I've only got five left.'

'Fair enough,' conceded Garrett who pulled out his pack of Gauloise and offered them around. All of the Zulus accepted. The men all stood quietly in a circle for a while. The reverential silence of the true smoker who has abstained for a few days.

Petrus was the first to speak. 'Well, *Isosha*, this mist has fucked your plan up good and proper.'

Garrett nodded agreement.

'So,' continued Petrus. 'What now?'

Garrett looked at the guard. 'Now, my friend, we become the monsters in the mist. But first, let's eat.'

Petrus delegated the breakfast to Cowboy who boiled up another pot of the ubiquitous *pap* with sugar and the men sat and ate with their fingers.

'Bishop, what're your close combat skills like?' asked Garrett.

'They call me the long gun, not close-combat-man. Does that answer your question?'

'Yep, as good as. Do you know how to use those Chinese stick grenades?'

'I'm familiar with them.'

'Good. This is what we'll do. Three groups. Bishop, group one, you guys, group two, and Petrus and I group three. Now give all six grenades to Mandoluto.'

***

Texas peered into the gray but couldn't make out anything. Men standing more than ten feet away became simple dark blobs. Beyond that they weren't visible at all. The mist brought a spectral quality to the surroundings that did not sit well with the men's current state of mind. The fact that one of the enemy had simply walked into their camp the night before and slaughtered one of them like a beast for table had unsettled even the most hardy of them. All except for Dubula who seemed to look on all that was happening with a sort of wry humor.

Against Dubula's advice the gang lord had sent another detachment of five men back down the trail to see if they could find any hint of what had happened to the first lot. Texas was sure that the cover of the mist would give them the protection that they needed. Fear had given the men wings and they had covered the two days march in a little less than four hours. And they had returned with disturbing news.

'What do you mean, the trail has been destroyed?' Shouted Texas.

'I'm sorry, boss. But the trail, it's gone. There's just a big area of rocks and mud and shit. No trail.'

'So how the hell do we get home when all this is finished?'

The gangster shrugged. 'Don't know, boss. You could probably climb around it. Maybe. Would be dangerous though.'

Texas took a deep breath. 'You're a moron.'

'Yes, boss.'

'A useless fucking moron.'

'Yes, boss. Sorry, boss.'

'Fuck off.'

The man scurried away, thankful that he had gotten off so lightly.

Texas turned to Dubula. 'Well, what do you make of that?'

'I'd say that they collapsed the trail.'

'Why?'

'To trap us here.'

Texas laughed. A short bark that lacked the confidence of true amusement. 'How can they trap us, that's the job of the hunter? And the fact is that we are the ones doing the hunting, not them.'

'Maybe,' said Dubula. 'But has anyone actually bothered to explain the fact to them?'

Before Texas could reply the world was rent apart with a series of explosions. Shrapnel buzzed through the air like a swarm of wasps and the pillow of mist was ripped aside by three massive concussions. Dubula jumped forward and threw himself onto Texas, covering his body with his own. A human flack jacket. But there were no more explosions. Instead, they heard the crackle of automatic gunfire coming from the rear of the camp.

Dubula jumped to his feet and ran in the direction of the gunfire, rallying the men as he ran.

'Come on, face the rear. Return fire. Move, move.'

Metal-jacketed slugs whipped and cracked through the air around him as he ran, one bullet coming close enough to pluck at his coat. A desperate street vendor trying to attract attention. He couldn't see his assailants for the mist but he could see the muzzle flashes from the rifles. He drew his Desert Eagle and started to fire back.

'Fire at the muzzle flash,' he shouted.

The gangsters had finally got their act together and were returning fire in withering sheets. Skorpions burning off twenty round magazines in sharp jagged bites of sound, AKs hammering away like an insane blacksmith at an anvil underplayed by the light pock of handguns and the massive boom of Dubula's hand-cannon. Every now and then someone would throw a grenade, the explosion a torso compressing crump of sound followed by a wave of hot air.

And at the other end of the camp two figures ghosted through the mist. Silent. And where they went, men died. Sharp metal slashing through reluctant flesh. Assegai and machete. The Zulu and the beast in tandem. And then exactly two minutes after the first attack another three explosions ripped through the camp. At the same time the attacking rifle fire stopped and the assailants retreated behind the mist. As did the machete and assegai wielders.

The gangsters continued firing for a while until, under Dubula's shouted instructions, the battle hiccupped to an end.

'Stop firing. Check around you for the wounded and take them to the front of the camp.'

Texas came staggering out of the mist. 'There are more bodies over here.'

'What?'

'Here, at the front of the camp. While you were all busy shooting the shit out of something out there, something else was in the camp killing people.'

Dubula strode past his master to see what he was talking about. As he walked the charnel sights loomed out of the mist. A badly written horror movie. Too much gore. Too much blood. Dismembered limbs. Intestines. No one wounded. Only dead. Five bodies. Three more at the other end of the camp. Two more felled by the grenades. Four wounded. In the last three days they had lost sixteen men.

They had yet to even see the enemy.

***

Garrett pushed down hard on Winston's chest in an attempt to stanch the flow of blood but he knew that it would be to no avail. One of Dubula's .50 cal rounds had hit him high up on the left-hand side and barreled through leaving a massive wound channel.

'*Eish*, that was a good fight,' Winston whispered.

Petrus took his hand and squeezed. 'Yes,' he agreed. 'A good fight.'

'You know, we don't get to fight as much as we used to. Times are not as good anymore; it's all politics and talk. I miss the old days.'

Petrus smiled. 'Yes, those days were good. Much fighting.'

Winston coughed weakly. 'Man, I'm tired. Must be this mountain air. It's too thin. I think I must rest a while. Wake me before the next fight, okay?'

Petrus nodded.

Winston closed his eyes.

And died.

Garrett stood up and took a couple of steps into the mist. A gray curtain to hide emotion.

Petrus stayed next to the body, stroking his head. '*Hamba gashle*, go in peace, my friend.'

The other Zulus filed past, touching him once on the face and saying their farewells.

'We will sacrifice an ox for you, Winston. When this is done you will be buried with honor.' Petrus said to his dead friend.

Finally, the long gun knelt down next to the fallen warrior. From his pocket he took out a small glass vial of olive oil with which he anointed Winston. The Zulus looked on with approval. Although they did not believe they still had great respect for the power of the church and figured that it could do no harm.

'Through this holy anointing may the Lord in his love and mercy help you with the grace of the Holy Spirit. May the Lord who frees you from sin save you and raise you up.'

There was a chorus of Amen. Petrus covered him with his canvas ground sheet and weighed the ends down with small rocks.

Then they all squatted in a circle and lit up cigarettes. The Zulus talked of Winston for a while. Little stories that spoke of the man. They meant nothing to Garrett or Mandoluto who did not know him, but they were the type of stories that would encapsulate any young man's life bar differences for culture and time. When he had come close to burning down his grandmother's hut as a little boy. His first girlfriend. When his father had beaten him for letting the cow with the crooked horn stray into the road. His initiation ceremony. His first kill. But after a while they stopped, for a man's life contains both too much to talk about in one sitting as well as too little. He was different. He was the same. He is dead. Silence.

Petrus spoke first '*Isosha*, what now?'

'We don't actually have many options but my granny did once say to me, "If it ain't broke don't fix it."'

'So,' said Petrus. 'More of the same?'

Garrett nodded. 'More of the same. But let's wait until just before nightfall.'

***

Dubula was now *ipso facto* in charge of the operation and would thus be held responsible for anything more that went wrong. For, although Texas was a remarkably good tactician in the tight confines of the urban jungle, he was very uncomfortable with the actual outdoors. Dubula had also spent his life surrounded by concrete and steel but his mind worked in a military fashion whatever the situation. He had come up with a plan. Firstly, he needed to find an area of the trail that he could build a proper camp, as opposed to a rambling row of tents clinging to the side of a steep incline. So as soon as they had taken care of the wounded, he struck camp and pushed the men on, leaving the bodies.

As it happened, luck smiled on him and, within an hour, they came to a small, flat area where the trail broadened out for a short while. He got the men to pitch enough tents for half of the people, figuring that half would always be on watch. Then he split his men into five groups of roughly ten men each. These groups were then split in half and allocated one shift each. Then he divided the surrounds into five equal portions and gave each group a specific area to cover. This

concentrated their attention and ensured better cover-
age of the surrounds. If they saw anything at all, or
even thought that they saw something, then they were
to open fire at once. He placed Texas in the center of
the camp and then he prowled around keeping everyone on their toes. They would wait. For he knew that
the enemy would come to them. They were so few that
attack was their only reasonable option.

***

As the sun set over the mountains the low-level rays lit
up the mist, turning the gray to white. It was like being
inside a ping-pong ball. Garrett had done a recce and
measured out where the new camp was placed. He had
explained its setting in detail even down to how many
paces it stretched from one end to the other.

Once again, the bishop was to take the high ground,
this time using his rifle to fire into the middle of the
camp, or as close to the middle as he could estimate
through the mist.

Bongani, Cowboy and Jabu would circle around the
camp and attack from the rear, getting in as close as
possible in order to be able to see their targets. This
was the part of the plan that worried Garrett. The mist
had now gotten so thick that the Zulus would have to
be within ten to twelve feet of their adversaries. Almost
hand to hand combat. He and Petrus would then strike

from the front. Quick in and out. After two minutes they would all pull back.

As Mandoluto's first shot echoed around the hills the three Zulus started forward. Using the mist as cover they ran crouched over, heading towards the camp. But as it came into view they were surprised by a sudden accurate fusillade of sustained fire. They immediately went to ground.

'Hey,' shouted Bongani. 'What the fuck? Are these the same idiots we attacked yesterday, how come they can shoot now?'

'They've been taking lessons,' replied Jabu. 'Cowboy? Hey, Cowboy.' Bongani crawled over to their friend. He lay flat on his face in as pool of blood. One of the AK rounds had hit him in the throat, tearing out his jugular. Bongani swore, then he took Cowboy's magazine off his rifle and slid it into his own pocket. All around him the air was alive with the spiteful buzz of hypersonic rounds. A hundred bullwhips cleaving the air. He raised himself up onto one elbow, sighted carefully at the muzzle flashes in the mist and started firing. On his left, Jabu joined in.

Mandoluto crouched behind a small rock while all around him the air crackled with fire. Someone had organized the gangsters. The moment that he had started firing he had drawn return fire directed at his muzzle flash. After his fourth shot he had been forced to take cover. He sank to the ground and, carrying his long gun in the crooks of his arms, he leopard crawled away from the rock for around twenty feet. Then he got up onto one knee, brought the rifle to his shoulder and started to fire again, moving after every two shots.

Garrett leant in close to Petrus. 'I don't like the sound of that.'

'What? Gunfire?'

'Gunfire is fine. It's their volleys of controlled gunfire that I don't like. These guys aren't just firing blindly like before; they seem to be picking their targets. I've underestimated the situation. Someone has organized this rabble into a cohesive force.'

'So, who cares? They'll die just the same.'

'True, let's go.'

The two men continued forward. Unlike the three Zulus they did not attract any fire as they ghosted unseen through the mist. Garrett went left, Petrus right. Wraiths. Moving undetected until they were within touching distance of the foe. And to the defenders it was as if the mist had suddenly become solid and attacked them. Garrett moved fast, downing the first man with his swinging machete. Cleaving his neck and clavicle. He snatched the Skorpion from the man as he fell and fired one handed at the next visible defenders. Three quick bursts took out two men and then the weapon ran dry. As Garrett moved on to connect with the fourth gangster, he felt the strikes. High up on his left-hand side. Like someone had taken a run up and hit him in the shoulder with a baseball bat. Twice. He turned fast. Right behind him a man holding a Tokarev.

The pistol had jammed, the offending round sticking up out of the breach like a smoke stack. Garrett leapt forward swinging upwards as he did so. The shooter staggered back clutching at his stomach as his intestines seemed to boil out of him. Blue and purple and gray.

More shots from behind him. Fire flicked at Garrett's hip, spinning him around and driving him to the ground. The pain from his multiple wounds crashed through him, momentarily blacking out his vision. When his sight cleared, he saw an AK lying on the grass next to him. He grabbed it, jammed the butt into the soil and used it as a crutch to pull himself upright. As soon as he was steady, he brought the rifle to his shoulder and started firing at two more shapes in the mist. Saw them go down. Someone reared up out of the gloom. He turned to fire.

'Hey, *Isosha*. It's me. Let's get the fuck out of here.'

The two of them loped out of the camp. Petrus slowed down once to pick up an AK and an extra magazine and two grenades from a dead body then they ran again. Fast disappearing into the mist.

Bongani had been hit three times. The first bullet had struck him in the arm, the next had taken out his left eye the final shot had shattered his hip. The pain was indescribable. But still he continued firing back, killing and killing again.

Jabu crawled over. 'Hey, Bongani. Let's go, man.'

Bongani didn't answer. He simply drew another careful bead and squeezed the trigger. The target dropped to the ground. He looked up at Vusi. 'Hey, brother. My hip's fucked. No more dancing for Bongani.' He grinned, face a mask of blood, the side a gory mess. 'Eyesight's a bit screwed up as well.'

'Come one. I'll help you. We can fix you up.'

'No way. I'm having too much fun. You go. I'll just stay here. Shoot a few more of these fuckers. Seriously, I'm fine.'

Jabu grabbed his hand. '*Shlala gashle*, my friend. Stay in peace.'

'*Hamba gashle*, go in peace.'

Jabu crawled away. Behind him Bongani continued to fire. His shots aimed and unhurried.

Mandoluto crouched down and ran. Things were getting far too hot and it was time to bug out. Anyhow, he figured, a sniper firing blindly into the mist wasn't the best usage of firepower. In fact, all that he seemed to be doing was giving a bunch of gangsters something to shoot at. Every time he took a shot, they were onto his muzzle flash like moths to a flame. Even as he ran, he could feel the nudge and buffet of shot as it cracked close past him.

And then he stumbled and fell. He hit the ground hard and rolled, cursing his clumsiness. But when he tried to get up, he couldn't. His legs were numb. He glanced down and saw that his pants were soaked in blood. He took out his knife and cut a slice down his pants leg. Saw the wound. Laughed out loud.

The slug had entered the back of his thigh and exited at the front completely severing the femoral arteries. Blood was being pumped out at a rate of around five liters per minute. Mandoluto figured that he had about a minute left. Killed by a stray bullet fired blindly into the mist on the top of a mountain in Kwa-Zulu.

The bishop pulled his cheroots from his shirt pocket, opened the case and lit up. His hand did not shake. In fact, he felt quite good. Warm. Relaxed. He was not unhappy. He had done his best. He laughed again. It was a good feeling; it had been a long time since he last laughed. Felt good. He tried to take another drag of his cheroot but couldn't lift his arm. Strange that, he never knew that a little tube of tobacco could become so heavy. Then he saw a bright light come towards him. Envelope him.

He smiled.

The light smiled back.

CHAPTER TWENTY-SEVEN

The children were lined up at the feet of their beds. On their knees. It was a nightly pre-sleep ritual that Vusi was still getting used to. He had never prayed before. It was not that he was a non-believer, he had simply never been told about the Christian God. When his mother was still alive, she had told him stories of the Creator, *Unkulunkulu*, but she had told him that He was above interacting with people on a day-to-day basis. Common requests were to be directed to the *Amadhlozi,* or Ancestor spirits. But they were capricious and should really only be approached through a *Sangoma* or witchdoctor.

This Christian God was different. Sister Manon had told Vusi that he could be approached at any time. And you could ask him for anything. Obviously, as with all things in life, there did seem to be rules, although they were implied rather than explicit. One shouldn't be selfish and one should always give thanks for all. Simple rules that Vusi had not found at all onerous.

And so, he knelt at the end of his bed and prayed.

'Dear God. Hello. It's Vusi here. I used to live in Alex but now I live here. But it's the same Vusi. My sister Thandi is also here. Thanks for us being here. It is very warm and safe and there is lots of food. I don't need my yellow screwdriver any more. That is nice. Thank you for Thandi's new dress. And for the colored crayons that we draw with. Especially the green one. I like it a lot.'

Vusi paused for a while, thinking. After a short time, he figured that he had got the thanking done so he could now get down to the meat of his actual request.

'Dear God. It's still me, Vusi here. Please, God. Take care of *Isosha*. Watch over him and make sure that the bad ones don't kill him. Thanks. Oh yes, can you also make us peas for dinner tomorrow. I like peas. Thank you, God. This is Vusi saying goodbye.'

***

Garrett grunted as Petrus pulled the stitching tight on the wound in his hip. They had cleaned the two gunshot wounds on his shoulder and then packed them with mud and bound them. Both Petrus and Jabu were unharmed. Jabu had just returned from a recce at Garrett's request and squatted down next to the soldier.

'*Isosha*. The bishop is dead.'

'Shit. How?'

'Through the top of the leg, where it bleeds. He was smiling.'

'Yeah, well. He had somewhere nice to go. Did you bring his rifle?'

Jabu shook his head. 'No.'

'Why?'

Jabu shrugged. 'He was holding it. It was part of him. It should stay.'

Garrett nodded in agreement and then pulled himself upright, using the AK. 'Listen, guys. I'm sorry but I've fucked this up. We're in a no-win situation here. We did what we could. I want you to go.'

The two Zulus stared at Garrett like he had spat on them. Eventually Petrus spoke.

'I will forgive you for what you have just said. Obviously, your wounds have affected your brain. Rest, and when your senses return, we will speak again.'

Jabu offered cigarettes. They accepted. He lit. 'About thirty.'

'What?' asked Petrus.

'We've killed about thirty of them. Give or take. Wounded a few more. That's almost half. We've got three AKs. About twenty-five rounds, two grenades and our real weapons.' He looked at Garrett. 'Rest tonight, *Isosha*. Tomorrow you can tell us of your plan to kill the rest of these animals.'

Garrett pulled his canvas groundsheet around him and closed his eyes, wishing he had the confidence in himself that Jabu had.

***

Texas had come within half an inch of death. During last night's attack one of the shots coming from above the camp had taken off the top half of his left ear. Dubula had bandaged it with a turban style dressing that even now was soaked with blood. Also, it stung like all buggery.

And with first light when they had taken a reliable body count, he now saw that he had lost thirty-two men. Another three were too wounded to be of any use. And somewhere out there lurked the foreigner and the mad Zulu. Texas was less than happy. But the truth of the matter was, he had no idea what to do next. However, by the time the sun had fully risen it looked as if things may be turning in his favor. The mist had retreated, leaving behind only a few tattered remnants. Now it would be impossible to hide from his men. It was payback time for Texas and his boys.

Dubula formed the men into five equal groups and strung them out on each side of the trail. They moved ahead slowly, two of the men in each group looking for tracks, the others keeping a watch. They were under instructions to give a shout as soon as they came across any tracks that might lead to the enemy.

The first thing that they found, almost directly above the camp was the body of the bishop. He was sitting propped up against a rock, a burnt-out cheroot in one hand and his precious rifle in the other. The men attempted to remove the rifle but it was as if the bishop's hands had been permanently molded to it. Save breaking his fingers or perhaps even sawing his hand off, they could not remove the weapon. As well as this, the bishop was smiling. Not a deaths head grin or some unpleasant ricture. No, this was a genuine, gentle smile. A smile of joy. They left him where he lay and continued their search for spoor.

Soon after they had left the bishop's body Texas called Dubula over.

'Dubula, we need to talk.'

The bodyguard stood close to his master and listened.

***

The three men sat in a sheltered rocky overhang. Almost, but not quite a cave. It was protected on three sides and had a small naturally formed wall of rock in the front, perhaps two feet high. Garrett stared across the valley at the searching men. It was only a matter of time before they cut spoor and started to track the soldier and his friends down.

'Hey, Petrus. I thought that you said that the mist was here for a week at least.'

'Yep, that's what I said.'

'Well, where's it gone?'

Petrus shrugged. 'Not my fault. I tell you what; someone's got a sense of humor. When we had a long gun we couldn't see, now our long gun is gone we get thousand-yard visibility.'

'Whatever,' replied Garrett. 'We need a plan. You see that *vlei* there,' he pointed out a boggy area of rushes and longer grass. Petrus nodded. 'As they come across the valley, they'll bunch up there. The only way through is to the right of the *vlei* and to the left of the cliff. You see?' The Zulu nodded again. 'Do you reckon that you could get down there without anyone seeing you?'

Petrus didn't deign to answer such an unnecessary question. He merely sniffed theatrically and said nothing.

Garrett grinned. 'Sorry. Anyway, get your butt down there, take the two grenades, prime them and stretch a tripwire across the trail. That'll take care of a few of them. As soon as they blow then we'll pick the rest off from a distance. The ones that survive will die by the blade.'

'Good plan,' agreed Petrus.

Jabu also nodded his agreement. None of them bothered to point out that the odds of the three of them killing over thirty well-armed men with only a couple of grenades and a handful of ammunition were slim to say the least.

Petrus took an AK with ten rounds of ammo, the grenades and a ball of fishing line and ran down into the valley, disappearing into the long grass as he did so.

Garrett and Jabu waited and watched. They could pick up no sign of Petrus as the gangsters drew ever nearer. As Garrett had predicted, the enemy started to bunch together as the marshy ground and the incline of the cliff herded them in. They had seen no sign of Petrus setting the tripwire and Garrett could only hope that he had done so.

And then the group walked through the most compacted section of the trail. Nothing happened. Garrett cursed. But in his concern, he had forgotten the four-second delay. The grenades exploded simultaneously, the sound at this distance a muted thud, felt rather than heard. And then Garrett saw Petrus rise up out of the grass at almost point-blank range and open fire. He held the rifle to his shoulder, snapped off ten aimed rounds in under three seconds, dropped the empty weapon and ran. A fusillade of shots followed him as the gangsters burnt off hundreds of rounds in his direction. Garrett could see him bobbing and weaving through the grass and felt like cheering him on but held himself back. Instead, he took a quick count of the fallen. Two had gone down to the grenades and a further four had been taken out by Petrus' rapid fire. Six less to worry about. Over twenty left. He brought the AK to his shoulder and fired three carefully aimed shots. One man went down. Next to him Jabu fired twice. No hits. But the enemy had pinpointed them.

The return fire was withering. Chips of rock buzzed around them like shrapnel and the whine and crack of passing shot filled the air. Garrett flattened himself against the ground. A sliver of stone hit him in the head slicing through to the bone. Warm blood caressed his face. He blinked hard to keep it out of his eyes.

Jabu popped up and snapped of another couple of shots to no avail. Garrett heard a rustle in the long grass and Petrus burst out and threw himself to the floor of the shelter. His breathing ragged. At first glance Garrett thought that he must have run through waist high water. His pants were soaked, the khaki a dark brown. And then he realized. It was blood.

Petrus lay down, flat on his back, chest heaving.

'Fuck me, *Isosha*. I'm broken.'

Garrett crawled over to inspect him. He pulled Petrus' shirt open. There were two wounds. Both had entered low down on his torso. Entry wounds in the back, exit wounds in the front. Hit while he was making his escape. Both wounds were bleeding copiously. Garrett tore up one of the ground sheets and used them to bind the wounds, pulling tight in order to staunch the bleeding.

Next to him Jabu pulled off another two shots. 'Ha, got one. Take that you fuckers.' He turned to Garrett. 'Got one.'

The bullet hit the rock wall and ricocheted up striking Jabu in the solar plexus. Blood frothed immediately from his mouth and he slid sideways onto the floor.

Garrett crawled over and applied pressure to the wound but there was no point. It wasn't bleeding. The blood was all internal. There was nothing that the soldier could do.

Jabu craned his head and looked down at the wound. 'Oh, shit,' he said. 'I'm dead.'

He closed his eyes. His legs twitched twice and then there was no more movement.

Garrett picked up his AK, sighted and squeezed off his last rounds. Two more down. They were out of ammunition. He lay down next to Petrus. Took out two cigarettes. Lit. Passed one. Dragged.

'Well,' he said. 'This sucks.'

'Marginally,' agreed Petrus.

'We got about forty of them.'

'Good, less to kill now. Just as well because I'm fucked. Can't actually feel my legs.'

'Doesn't matter. I reckon they'll finish us with grenades. That's what I'd do.'

'Yeah, me too.'

Garrett peered over the rocks. The gangsters were about four hundred meters away and advancing cautiously. Fanned out in a line. He lay back down. Lit another cigarette off the last one.

'*Isosha*, why don't you go. Run for it, maybe you get away.'

'I might. Think I'll stay though. See what happens.'

Petrus grinned. 'Thanks. Never wanted to die alone. Don't know why. Dead is dead.' He held out his hand. Garrett grasped it. They lay in stillness for a while.

In the distance Garrett could hear rain coming. Hissing as it swept across the long grass. And with it a faraway rumble of thunder, long and drawn out.

'Great, now we're going to die in the rain. How fucking Hemmingway can you get?'

Petrus burst out laughing. Then coughing. Then laughing again.

Garrett was puzzled. 'Hey, it's not that funny.'

Petrus laughed again. 'It's fucking hilarious, *Isosha*. That's not rain.'

'Of course it is, I can tell a storm when I hear one.'

'Yes, *Isosha*. There is a storm coming. But not the one you thought.'

Again, Garrett peeked over the rocks. And he saw, sweeping across the valley, their shields brushing through the grass and making a sound like rain, their feet thundering over the ground, at least two hundred Zulus in full battle array. And as he watched they took up their battle cry.

'*Jeee*!'

The sound echoed around the hills and set the hair on Garrett's arms upright. It was an atavistic sound that went straight to your soul, a wolf's howl. A lion's roar. If fear had a sound, that was it.

'*Jeee*!'

The gangsters did not even try to fight, they simply turned and fled. But it was to no avail. Within seconds the *impi* was upon them. Assegais rose and fell, turning from polished steel to dull red flames of metal.

Garrett could hear the cries of the Zulus as they struck.

'*Ngadla!* I have eaten.'

And then he too was laughing alongside his friend.

CHAPTER TWENTY-EIGHT

The Sangoma put eight stitches into Garrett's scalp. He also tightened his dressings and proclaimed him fit for service, albeit a little shop-soiled.

He spent a while longer with Petrus, boiling up a poultice and cleansing his wounds. After swathing his torso in bandages, he declared that he would live but would need at least a months bed rest.

Garrett wandered the battlefield with chief Dlamini who explained to him that the *Sangoma* had come to him in the middle of the night and told him that he needed to ready his *impi* for battle. The *Amadhlozi* had come to him in a dream and told him that it was his duty to protect his son and the foreigner. And the words of the ancestors are as steel. He had gathered his warriors, they had appropriated two buses and a couple of cars and driven around the back of the mountain reserve, a mere two hours run away.

It became obvious after twenty minutes of searching that neither Dubula nor Texas was amongst the fallen. Garrett grabbed the first living gangster that he came across, pulled him to his feet.

'Where is Texas?'

The gangster, who was bleeding from multiple stab wounds, felt under no obligation to resist questioning.

'They went this morning, sir. Mister Zangwa called Dubula to him, they talked, they issued us instructions to continue on, then they left.'

'Why?'

'When we got to the top of the one mountain this morning mister Zangwa got some cell phone signal. He had some messages. The messages said that his business was in trouble. The people in Joburg were burning mister Zangwa's places down. He took Dubula to put a stop to it. He told us to phone him after we killed you.'

'Where is his place? What's the address?'

The gangster blurted it out. Garrett made him repeat it twice more, and then he pushed him back to the ground. A wave of exhaustion washed over him causing him to stagger slightly. Chief Dlamini steadied him with a hand on his shoulder.

'Are you alright?'

Garrett nodded. 'I thought that it was over. But it's not. Not even close. Until Texas and his dog are no more then we have achieved nothing.'

'Look around you, *Isosha*. You have achieved a great victory.'

'Yes,' Garrett agreed. 'And I thank you for it. But this is simply one battle. We have yet to win the war.'

'Can I help?'

'I have to go back to Joburg.'

Chief Dlamini shook his head. 'I will not send any of my men there. But I can give you weapons and a car. I am sorry, but that is all.'

Garrett clasped the chief's shoulder. 'Thank you, chief Dlamini. That is more than generous.'

The chief beckoned to one of his warriors who ran to his side. 'What weapons do you want?' He asked Garrett.

'Skorpions. Two of them. Lots of ammo.'

Dlamini flicked his fingers and the warrior ran off, searching amongst the bodies for Garrett's request. He returned shortly. Two fully loaded Skorpion submachine guns and two more full magazines of extra ammo. He handed them to the soldier.

Garrett shook the chief's hand, the African way, reversing grip as he did so.

'This man will show you the way back to the cars,' said the chief. 'Two, maybe three hours run. Be careful, Isosha. When Zangwa does not receive the call telling of your death he will know that you are coming for him. He will be ready and waiting.'

Garrett nodded. 'I'll be careful.' Then he walked over to Petrus who lay on a litter, waiting for the warriors to take him back to his father's village.

They shook hands.

'Sorry I can't go with you, *Isosha*. It appears that I am out of order.'

Garrett smiled. 'No worries, my friend. Anyway, there are only a few of them. Wouldn't want to share at any rate.'

'That's the problem with you foreigners, selfish to the extreme.'

'Take care, my friend.'

Petrus nodded. 'You too, *Isosha*. You too.'

Garrett turned and ran after the warrior who was leading him. He felt stiff and slow. He hoped that he would loosen up or the next three hours would be very uncomfortable.

***

It had taken Garrett a little over two hours to run to the car. Although he had loosened up en route he had pulled the stitches on his hip and the wound was seeping blood into his khakis. However, he now had at least four hours of driving ahead of him and he trusted that it would staunch itself over that time.

The car that the chief had instructed his warrior to give Garrett was an old three-liter Ford Capri. The engine smoked and rattled unhealthily but when he put his foot down it responded in a game fashion. An old horse still keen to run. The warrior had also given Garrett a denim jacket to cover his blood-soaked shirt. The car had a full tank of gas but from its current consumption Garrett knew that he would have to make a pit stop before he got to his final destination.

The soldier pulled into a service station just outside Joburg, filled up and then went to restrooms to wash the blood from his face before he paid. Making sure that the jacket covered his shirt and hip he purchased half as dozen cans of Red Bull, a bar of chocolate, a meat pie and paid for the gas. He ate as he drove, forcing himself to finish it all. He needed energy and energy needed fuel. His scalp stung, his shoulder throbbed and his hip hurt like hell. On a scale of one to ten, ten being the strongest, he was running on around three. And he was about to come up against Dubula, a man that seemed to have a default strength setting of around twenty. Garrett downed the last can of energy drink and tossed the empty onto the back seat.

'Fuck it,' he said to himself. 'I've been in worse situations than this.' But when he tried to, he couldn't actually think of one.

The old Capri did not boast a satnav so Garrett got lost twice looking for Texas Zangwa's mansion. Eventually he found the address that he had been given. A pair of ten-foot-high iron gates attached to a similar height wall protected the entrance. The ubiquitous electric fencing that all Joburg houses consider to be *de rigueur* surrounded the entire property. The driveway curved to the left from the gate so the house was not visible from the road.

After a moment's thought Garrett decided on the direct route. He pulled the Capri up onto the opposite side of the road. Pointed it at the gates. Gunned the engine and dropped the clutch. The tires spun frantically, screaming and pouring out pungent gray smoke. The old car leapt forward, keen to impress. It was doing twenty and increasing as it hit the gates. The squealing tires blended with the tortured sound of grating metal as the two thousand pounds of car smashed through. The windscreen exploded into a million shards of glass and the bonnet tore off, hanging to the side on one crippled hinge. Steam shrieked from the mortally wounded engine but the old car kept accelerating. Garrett powered on up the driveway. Swept around the curve and slammed into a solid Rococo style stone water fountain that graced the middle of the circle at the end of the driveway.

The three-liter engine revved freely for a few seconds and then died with an abrupt bang. Water poured over the front of the car cooling the overheated engine to the sound of gentle pinging.

Garrett had to kick the door a couple of times to open it. He grabbed his two Skorpions and left, running up the stairs to the double height entrance door. He tried the door. Locked. Aimed a sub machine gun at the hinges. Pulled off two quick bursts. Ran at the door. Slammed his shoulder into it. The door fell inwards. Garrett felt something go in his shoulder wound. Warm blood flowed down his back. Then the air around him seemed to explode. He threw himself down and rolled. Bullets struck the floor all around him. Buzzing spitefully, close enough to pick at his clothes. He kept rolling until he came up against another door. He scuttled through. Poked one of the Skorpions around the doorjamb and squirted off a couple of rounds. Waited. Listened.

No sound. He appeared to be in some sort of sitting room. Plush overstuffed sofas and ottomans. Dried flower arrangements. The odd coffee table. He scuttled over to the window, opened it and slid out into the garden.

He was just in time. As he hit the ground the room behind him exploded. Grenade, he thought. No, two grenades. Texas obviously didn't mind fucking his house up.

Garrett replaced his one magazine with a fresh one and waited. Still. Twenty seconds. Thirty. He popped his head up and glanced through the window. Two men were sneaking into the room. Bent over in an attempt to conceal. Garrett stood up, Skorpion in each hand, pulled the triggers, firing through the window. One and a half seconds. Forty rounds. Most of them hit their intended targets, the little .32 mm rounds shredding flesh and clothing alike. The two dead bodies slumped to the floor. Garrett climbed back into the room, changed magazines. Crawled to the door. Head around to see. No one. He went back out into the corridor.

The corridor ended in a set of oversized double doors. White with ornate brass trim, maybe gold plate. The doors were slightly ajar. On each side of the corridor were three more sets of single doors of the same design. Recessed lights in the double height ceiling. Like a home built for a giant. Fee Fi Fo Fum.

Garrett glided down the corridor. Walking on the outsides of his boots. Rolling each step. Before each movement he would stop and listen. Endeavoring to feel someone's presence. Using his battle honed sixth sense in an attempt to give himself that hundredth of a second advantage that was the difference between living and dying.

He dropped to the floor as the door to his right burst open and someone started firing at him. AK on full auto. Steel jacketed rounds ricocheted around the enclosed space. Something burnt into his torso. No pain just the sensation of heat. He fired back. Both machine guns yammering insanely, bucking in his hands. His assailant spun in a full circle and dropped to the floor. The Skorpion sub machine gun is a truly magnificent weapon for close quarter combat, with only one major flaw. It uses up ammunitions at a prodigious rate. Garrett was out. He dropped the guns to the floor and stood up. Checked his assailant's weapon. Also empty. The burn in his side had become a painful throb and when he looked down, he could see that he had been hit. A ricochet had torn through the flesh on the left side of his torso, the wound ragged and untidy. Bits of fabric and flesh dangled from the gash and blood flowed freely. Garrett decided that there was nothing that he could do so he simply ignored it. Continued towards the twin doors at the end of the corridor. Limping. Unsteady.

Just before he got to the end of the corridor the doors swung open. Dubula. One hand by his side, the other pointing his Desert Eagle at Garrett. Behind him stood Texas, his head swathed in a bandage, a full glass of whisky in his hand.

'Please, foreigner, come in,' he raised his glass. 'Royal Salute. Fifty-year-old. An affectation really, personally I can't taste the difference between the twenty and the fifty. I only buy it because it costs over twenty-five thousand dollars a bottle and I can. Would you like some?'

Garrett nodded.

'Dubula, if you could.'

The bodyguard holstered his cannon, strode over to the liquor table and poured Garrett a stiff three-thousand-dollar dram. He walked back to the soldier and handed it over. Garrett took a sip. It was fantastic. Earth and peat and apples and raisins.

'So, what do you think?'

Garrett raised an eyebrow. 'I think that it's the best whisky that I have ever tasted.'

Texas looked genuinely pleased. 'Good, good. Please, savor it. Don't rush it as it's the last thing that you will ever drink.' He raised his glass in a salute.

'Dubula, when he finishes, kill him.' Dubula drew his pistol. 'No, no,' said Texas. 'The knife. That firearm of your is so inelegant.'

Dubula replaced his pistol and drew a nine-inch-long Bowie knife from a shoulder holster.

Garrett dropped his glass and pulled his machete out from his belt.

Texas shook his head. 'What a waste of good whisky.'

Garrett and Dubula stood facing each other. Neither moved.

In the movies, knife fights are fast moving affairs. The two antagonists circle each other, dancing and weaving, slashing away with gay abandon. Steel on steel. Flashy and well-choreographed. In reality nothing is further from the truth. When two experienced combatants with blades in their hands face each other, the fight will usually last for one or two strokes. As a result, there is very little movement.

A real knife fight is more like chess than dancing.

Garrett kept his breathing level. Calm. His shoulder wound was tight, his hip and torso both bled. He was exhausted. He knew Dubula was too strong for him. Microseconds became seconds. Seconds stretched out into infinity.

And Garrett threw his machete up towards the ceiling. Dubula's eyes followed the blade for perhaps a fraction of a second. No more. But that was enough time for Garrett to draw Vusi's screwdriver from his boot and plunge it full length into Dubula's chest. The big man dropped his knife as his arms went slack. He looked down at the bright yellow handle sticking out of his chest. It throbbed in time with his heartbeat. He looked back up at Garrett and a small smile flickered on his lips. Respect.

Slowly, like a falling tree, the big man fell sideways and lay on the ground. The yellow handle stopped moving as his heart stilled.

Garrett bent down and picked up his machete. Turned to face Texas Zangwa.

The gang lord held his hands up. 'Wait. This is the part where I offer you money. Women. Anything you want.'

'Yes,' said Garrett. 'And this is the part where I refuse.'

Texas laughed. 'No, foreigner. This time you've got it wrong. This is actually the part where I shoot you dead and piss on your corpse.'

Texas brought his right hand down, at the same time flicking a small two shot .25 acp, sleeve-holstered derringer pistol into his hand. He pointed and fired. Both shots hit Garrett in the chest, the small rounds shattering ribs and driving him to his knees.

Zangwa took a step forward and kicked Garrett in the face, flicking his head back and knocking him to the floor. Garrett heard his nose break. A sound like a footstep on gravel. Before he could drag himself to his feet Texas kicked him again. And again. Garrett rolled across the floor, bumping into Dubula's dead body. Texas was screaming as he laid into the soldier. The same phrase over and over.

'Fuck. You. Fuck. You.'

Each syllable punctuated by another boot.

Garrett's body was fast shutting down. He could no longer feel the kicks and his eyesight was reduced to a small dark tunnel. Somewhere far away he thought that he could hear children singing. He tried to move but couldn't. He was stuck. Pushing up against Dubula's corpse like a puppy suckling its mother. Darkness descended. He gave it one last try but to no avail. His head bumped up against something hard. Metal. The kicking continued. Somewhere the children's singing got louder. Slowly he moved his hand towards the metal object. Like a crushed insect it crawled over Dubula's chest. A life of its own. And his fingers closed around it. He drew it out of its holster and rolled onto his back. The look of surprise on Texas' face was almost comical.

'No more fuck me, you animal. Fuck you!'

Garrett pulled the trigger. The massive round hit Texas in the crotch, lifted him into the air and threw him against the wall in a fountain of blood and gore.

The soldier pulled himself to his feet. Texas lay in a broken heap, his life's blood pumping out of the place where his genitals used to be. He was screaming. An inhuman sound. Steam escaping from a pressure cooker. High pitched and formless.

Garrett dropped the gun and headed for the door that led to the garden. It seemed so far away. He staggered and fell, facing the glass door. Outside it was getting light. The sun broke the horizon in a flaming golden ball. Garrett smiled. It was beautiful. But bright. So bright. He wished that he could close his eyes. But he couldn't.

The sound of the children singing got louder still. And Garrett was happy. They were safe. They were singing. The children were singing.

His eyes closed.

EPILOGUE

A slight mist hung in the air. An hour after sun up. The world was awake but not yet up to normal speed. A slight wind. Not enough to clear the mist, merely enough to shift it around, shepherding the gray into the folds and depressions of the landscape. Enough to shiver the leaves on the trees. There were still beads of dew on the grass. Polished spheres of liquid silver. Nature's costume jewelry. Waiting to be stolen by the sun.

The armed men stood twenty abreast, lining the whole of the valley. Waiting. Ahead, a flurry of movement. The sound of gunshots rippled down the line. A shape tumbled to the ground. At once made small and insignificant by death. The smell of cordite drifted on the wind. Acrid. Fourth of July without the beauty.

It was August, the glorious twelfth, the Laird had invited his guests over and there they stood. The men in tweed, guns in hand, shooting grouse. Ritual slaughter followed by Sloe gin and breakfast. Soon the dead would be piled high, bright eyes turning dull. Feathers of burnished gold becoming leaves of unpolished copper.

Close by, on a small hill, Garrett stood and watched, his muscles still tight from his recovering wounds. His dark hair tumbled to his shoulders. His deep green eyes took in the sight and sounds of the land around him.

And somewhere, ever so far away, a beast howled.

Hi and thanks for reading…

There are also more Garrett & Petrus books –

Choice of Weapon
Another way Home
Blood of Lions
Savage Justice

This is a novel. I made it up. However, there are parts that are true. I won't bore you with sources, texts and libraries. I will direct you to the World Wide Web. The things that happened to Garrett in Sierra Leone did actually happen. Search; *"Sierra Leone Amputees"*. You will be saddened and disgusted at man's ability to sink lower than the most rabid animal. You will understand why Garrett did what he did. Someone had to protect the children.

Regarding the belief that raping a virgin child can cure you of AIDS is also a well-documented phenomenon. Search; *"Infant Rape to Cure AIDS"*. Once again, who is protecting the children?

Also, people may ask; does the traditional Zulu warrior still exist? And, if so, does he still fight with assegai and shield? The answer is – Yes. I have seen many such battles first hand. It happened many years ago, it happened in the eighties and nineties and it happens still. People armed only with courage and bladed weapons successfully engaging people with modern assault rifles. *For they are men of men and their fathers were men before them.*

And finally, some of the people in this story are real. They know who they are. Some of these people are not real…and I sincerely hope that someone remembers to tell them so.

Thanks – Craig.